A.S. FENICHEL

DESPERATE BRIDE

FOREVER BRIDES

Desperate Bride

An unexpected promise... an everlasting passion.

An accomplished musician, Dorothea Flammel has refused more proposals than any London debutante; her only true love is her music. Dory's shimmering talent and beauty have long been adored from afar by Thomas Wheel, an untitled gentleman who can only dream of asking for the hand of a nobleman's daughter. But when her father, the insolvent Lord Flammel, arranges for Dory to marry a lecherous Earl in order to pay off a debt, she runs to Thomas—and proposes marriage to him.

Eloping to Scotland saves Dory from a disastrous fate, but what is for her a mere marriage of convenience proves more passionate—and more complex—than either imagined as rumors, scandal, and buried emotions come to light. And when a vengeful challenge from a drunken and embittered Lord Flammel puts Thomas's life on the line, will the fragile trust between husband and wife be enough to save them both?

Original Copyright © 2017 by A.S. Fenichel

All rights reserved. No part of this book may be reproduced in any form or by any means without the prior written consent of the publisher, A.S. Fenichel, excepting brief quotes used in reviews.

This book is a work of fiction and any resemblance to persons, living or dead, is purely coincidental. The characters are productions of the author's imagination. Locales are fictitious, and/or, are used fictitiously.

Edited by Penny Barber

Cover design by KaNaXa

For Dave, who always knows just what to say to make everything okay.
And for Llonda, my sister by love if not by blood. No one could ask for a better friend.

Acknowledgments

A book does not happen by accident. The author sits and toils over words and sentences. She tries to make every phrase have purpose and beauty. Without certain people in my writerly life, I would never finish a single book. Thanks to: Juliette Cross, Gemma Brocato and Kristi Rose for always cracking the whip when I needed. Without my dear friend Karla Doyle, I would likely have one published book. Her words of encouragement always push me to go on. Working with Penny Barber has been the best, most educational and fulfilling author/editor relationship of my career. I cannot thank her enough.

Chapter One

More than an hour reading the Westgrove Estate titles and entailments left Thomas Wheel with an aching neck. If he acquired the property, those two fields neighboring his two family estates would be perfect for the Dutch four-crop rotation method. Increased productivity could mean putting the local children in a schoolroom rather than laboring for pennies to help feed their families. The little barn on the property could be converted into a schoolhouse.

Crowly cleared his throat. The butler was tall and wide and occupied the entire doorway. "Yes, what is it, Crowly?"

"Sir, I know you said you didn't wish to be disturbed, but you have a visitor." Many visitors found the unseemly size of the man intimidating. Crowly was quiet and efficient and that was good enough for a bachelor of Thomas's standing.

Thomas pulled the watch from his pocket. Nearly midnight, no decent person called so late. "At this late hour? Send whoever it is away. It is too late for callers."

The butler shuffled his feet but did not leave.

"Is there a problem, Crowly?"

"Well, sir, you see, the visitor is a young woman of apparent good breeding. She arrived in a hack and I am reluctant to put her back out on the street."

Thomas stood. "She is alone?"

"It would seem so, sir."

"Who is it?"

"The lady refused to provide a card and wishes to speak to you rather urgently."

After pulling his jacket from the back of his chair, he dressed himself. "I suppose you had better let the mystery lady in."

"Yes. Thank you, sir." Crowly's shoulders relaxed.

Within seconds, a woman draped in a black cape with a hood hiding her face entered the study.

Thomas stood behind his desk and waited for her to speak, but she fussed with the edge of her cape and shifted her feet. He suspected that she was contemplating running away. "How may I help you?"

Her head snapped up and her hood fell away. There, standing in his study, was Lady Dorothea Flammel. The amber in her blond hair came to life in the firelight and Thomas had to grip the back of his chair for balance. He did not know what he had been expecting, but in his wildest dreams he never thought to see Dory in his home. Well, maybe in his dreams, but never in reality.

Compared to the burly Crowly she looked lost in the doorway. She was petite and her green eyes ringed red as if she'd been crying.

His initial excitement overshadowed by her distress, his concern mounted. He crossed the room, stopping only when he realized that she backed away from him. "Lady Flammel, what is wrong? Is it Markus?"

Markus Flammel, Dory's older brother and one of

Thomas's closest friends, lost his wife during childbirth a year before. The child had lived, but losing Emma had sent Markus into a desperate depression.

"No. It's not Markus. He is in the country as far as I know." She stared at her feet.

Thomas waited for her to say more, but she pressed her lips together while avoiding his gaze.

"Perhaps you would like to sit," he suggested.

When she looked up, he thought she might run, but then her expression softened and she nodded.

When he offered her the chair in front of his desk, she skirted away from him to reach the seat. Never had he seen her so out of sorts. He rounded the desk and sat in his office chair.

The silence in the room was palpable. Thomas cleared his throat and the sudden noise made her jump in her seat. Dory had always appeared so calm and in control, his interest piqued. "Lady Flammel?"

"Yes?" Snapping her head up, she revealed her wide eyes and pale skin.

He smiled. Most women found his smile engaging, but she looked at him with wide eyes and trembling lips, like he'd bared his teeth for the kill.

He leaned forward, resting his arms on the desk. "I can only assume that you have come to me for some reason. You risk quite a lot coming to a bachelor's home, in the middle of the night, in a hack and all alone. You must permit me my curiosity at such an unorthodox act. I have known you most of your life and this is the first time you have arrived on my doorstep. What can I do for you?"

She sighed. "Perhaps it was a mistake."

"Was it?" he asked.

She stared at him. He had watched her play the pianoforte dozens of times over the past few years. She was an artist of the highest order. Her emotion when she played was enthralling, but away from her instrument she always appeared so calm and controlled. Here in his study that seemed to have escaped her. She was near tears. He wanted to stand up and go to her but he did not wish to scare her. The last thing he wanted was to allow his height to intimidate her.

"I am in trouble," she said.

Anger seared through Thomas. "Who was it? I will cut out his innards." He pounded his fist on the desk.

She flinched then waved her hand in a dismissive motion. "Not that kind of trouble, Mr. Wheel."

His fury seeped away. Watching her from the shadows for years, her music had drawn him in but those full eyelashes and deep green eyes kept him mesmerized. For a long time, he had yearned to touch the soft skin of her cheek and kiss those delicate ears. It was impossible. She was the daughter of an earl. She would marry a man of her own station, not Mr. Wheel of Middlesex.

"Perhaps you should just tell me why you are here since you have made the trip. I will help you in any way I am able. I assure you that your presence here will remain our secret. My staff is very discreet."

She frowned. "I suppose as you are a bachelor, they would have to be." There was a bitter twist in her voice.

He did not comment, though her distaste rang through her statement and the twist of her lips.

She took a deep breath, making her full bosom rise.

Distracted for a moment, he then steeled himself and watched her eyes, which he found almost as intriguing.

She cleared her throat. "I am in need of a husband and I have decided that, if you would not mind, you and I would suit nicely."

It took a full count for her meaning to penetrate his mind.

4

"Perhaps earlier you didn't understand my anger." Anger rose again in his gut. He didn't want to frighten her. "It would seem that I must be blunt. Are you with child?"

She picked up her chin. "I understood you, Mr. Wheel. I am not with child nor have I been ruined. It is only that I need to marry immediately."

He sat back in his chair and scratched his chin where the late hour had left him with a shadow of a beard. No one intrigued him as Dorothea Flammel did, but she was the unattainable. Now, here she was in his home offering herself to him. Saying yes and rushing off to Gretna Green rumbled through his mind, but doubt reared its head and he asked, "Why?"

Those beautiful eyes drew together. "I suppose you have a right to know." Staring at her shoes, her hair fell in loose curls around her neck and shoulders. She shook her head. Some inner turmoil etched on her face. "My parents will sign a betrothal agreement for me in the next week."

His stomach clenched. "To whom, if I may ask?"

"Henry Casper, the Earl of Hartly," she said through clenched teeth.

Thomas jumped from his chair. "Henry Casper is old enough to be your grandfather. What are your parents thinking?"

She flinched but did not cower. "That I will be a countess."

"There are other earls in the realm."

"I am afraid that I have refused quite a few offers of marriage."

It was almost legend the number of offers that Lady Dorothea Flammel had turned down. A duke had even offered for her and reports indicated she had broken his heart. "There must be someone left other than a man who walks with a cane and can no longer hear a word spoken."

She stood and pulled her cloak back over her head. "I

completely understand. You do not wish to marry or the idea of marrying me is repellent. Forgive me for taking up your time, Mr. Wheel."

She headed for the door.

He rushed over and took her arm turning her around to face him. "I am honored by your offer, Lady Dorothea, and wish I could help you, but I am only Mr. Wheel. I have no right to marry so far from my station."

Her face reddened. "I did not realize you were such a bigot, Mr. Wheel."

"Thomas."

"I beg your pardon."

"My name is Thomas."

His face was close to hers. Her warm sweet scent filled his head with nonsense, a mixture of flowers and herbs.

"I..." she stuttered. "Forgive me for the late intrusion. I am sorry."

He did not release her. "Tell me one more thing, Lady Dorothea?"

"Dory, my name is Dory," she said in a smoky voice, while looking up at him.

It took every ounce of his control to keep him from sweeping her up in his arms and taking her to his bed. To hell with society and rules. "Why me?"

"I beg your pardon."

He leaned in closer. "I am curious why you chose me for this honor. You could have gone to any number of men who would jump at the chance to have you. I would like to know what made you come here."

She pulled away from him. "You seemed the safest choice."

He laughed so hard that she flinched as the noise of it filled the room.

"I do not mean to insult you."

"I am not insulted, Dory, just surprised that you would see me as a safe choice." He continued to laugh.

She was not laughing. Her eyes were again filling with tears.

The sight sobered him. "I am sorry to laugh but I see nothing safe about me being alone with you, my dear."

She dashed the tears away. "I only meant that you would not intentionally hurt me. You have a reputation for being kind to women and you like my music. I knew you would never stop me from playing or composing."

His gut twisted. "Why would you have to stop?"

"Mother has long told me that once I am married, my music must be put aside. I have resisted marriage for the last five seasons so I can continue to play."

"Dory, I will give you two insights into men of which you may not be aware. First is that we are not all tyrants and the second is that not all men are like your father."

Sorrow coursed through her eyes like the waves in the sea. "He lives to find ways to embarrass my mother in public. I will grant you she is no treat to be around, but I think she loved him once a long time ago. He is cruel beyond reason."

"Not all men are like that."

She shrugged. "I know. I do not think you are like that. For example, when you take a mistress you will be discreet. You would never cause me undue pain. That is why you would suit so well."

He crossed the room to where she stood with her arms wrapped around her middle. His hand moved of its own accord and reached out and touched the skin where her shoulder met her neck. It was like silk under his fingers. "What makes you think I would take a mistress?"

"All men do eventually. At least you would be kind about it." She pulled away from his touch.

"I must repeat myself, Dory. All men are not like your father."

She shrugged and waved off his comment. "Will you help me?"

How he wished he could. "What is your plan?"

Turning, she faced him. "I would like to leave for Gretna Green in the next day or two. It is best to not tell anyone. I have not even let on to Sophia and Elinor about my plans."

Sophia and Elinor had married two of his closest friends and were Dory's longtime confidants. It was incredible that she would not share something so monumental with her best friends.

"I know I can trust them, but I thought it best not to put them in an awkward position. It's not fair."

He sat on the chair near the fire. Too big for the delicate seat, he'd always hated it as it suited a lady better. He curled his long legs under, leaned his elbow on one knee and his chin on his fist. "Once we married how would we get along in this plan of yours?"

"What do you mean?"

"Would you share my bed?" He sat up and found her standing only a few feet away.

She flinched but did not run away. "It would seem the least I could do."

Laughing, he said, "Not exactly the romantic image I had hoped for."

She walked closer until she stood in front of him with only an inch separating them. "You may have me now if you wish." Her voice trembled.

His groin jumped in response to her offer, but he put his hands on her hips and leaned his head against her stomach.

She trembled, but stood her ground.

Incredible as it sounded, she would allow him to deflower her. "Oh, Dory, you do tempt me."

Tentatively, she touched his hair. "I think I heard a 'but' coming next."

He gazed at her perfect face. Her hand was still in his hair moving in tiny circles. It was an innocent touch but it felt erotic to him. Any touch from her would have had that effect he suspected.

Forcing a smile, he only wanted to ease her fear of him. "But it would be beneath both of us to make love here in my study without a marriage to make it legal."

"Are you saying you will marry me?" No joy bubbled in her voice at the notion. She sounded more like a death sentence had been averted and she would only suffer life in prison.

He took her hands out of his hair, kissed the back of one, and then the other, and stood. So she could sit in the chair he'd vacated, he pulled another from a few feet away. He sat so close, their knees almost touched.

"I hope you will forgive me, Dory, but my answer is no. I cannot believe I am saying it myself. If you truly wished to be my wife, it would make me unspeakably happy, but like this it is less than romantic. In fact, it borders on the morbid."

She frowned. "I could have come to you with lies and told you I was madly and rapturously in love with you and could not live without you another moment. Would that have altered your decision?"

"It might have."

A furrow appeared between her brows.

Thomas reached out and smoothed the wrinkle. "I am glad you did not attempt to mislead me, Dory. I wish I could help you. For the first time in my life I wish I was a lord or a knight so I would be worthy of your hand. However, my station is to be a gentleman and yours a countess. It would be selfish of me to lower your status in society."

She let out a long sigh. "I do not give a damn about titles. I am to be married to a lecherous old man who will keep me as a trophy and perhaps allow me to play pianoforte from time to time to entertain his friends. Everything I have ever wanted tossed aside. My mother will do as she has always threatened and burn all of my music." She leaned forward and touched his face. "Everything I am is about to be ripped from me. Can you understand, Thomas?"

He put his hand over hers and kissed her palm. "You are overwrought and have exaggerated the situation. I have never heard anything violent about Henry Casper. Though he is old for you he lives well and will provide for you in the fashion to which you have been raised."

"You are wealthy," she said.

He laughed. "I have ample funds, but I am not titled and I never shall be."

"You are a snob, Thomas. If I do not care about a title, then, why should you?"

"You should care, Dory. I will admit that my association with Marlton and now with Kerburghe has afforded me more invitations than most gentlemen of my station receive, but I fear you would find life as Mrs. Wheel very unappealing."

"Are you a man with a terrible temper?" she asked.

Surprised by the question, he sat up straighter. "I do not think so."

"Would you keep your wife from pursuing her own goals?"

"I don't believe so, as long as the goals did not put her in harm's way."

"So, if I wanted to join the fire brigade you would be opposed to that venture?" Her eyes narrowed but she did not smile.

He shook his head but answered. "The fire brigade would be quite a dangerous endeavor, and I would advise my wife against such foolishness."

"Yes," she said. "You do sound like a tyrant. I think it obvious we would not suit." Sarcasm dripped from her words. She squared her shoulders and stood.

"I do not believe you have thought this through." He stood with her.

She turned and raised her eyebrows. "You believe I am impulsive and rash?"

A small voice inside his head told him he should take care with his next statement, but he ignored it. "In this decision, you seem to have jumped before looking."

Pursing her lips, she nodded. "Do you know what it takes to play the pianoforte as I do?"

The question was so out of context, he fumbled for his answer. "I believe I do. I have tried to become more accomplished and my talent has limited me."

"Have you sat for hours at a piano to achieve perfection in one stanza?"

"I have," he admitted.

"I have not heard you play, Thomas, though I hear you are accomplished, and I have heard you say you are not. I suspect you play very well but are not gifted with that something which makes one musician stand out among the rest."

He hated that she was so accurate in her description of his skills.

"I do not mean to insult you. It is just fate that makes one person good and another great. A cruel joke, if you will. My curse is being a woman. If I were a man with the talent that God gave me, I would play to massive crowds and kings would sponsor me. Not that this is what I want really. I want to be allowed to play every day for the rest of my life. I am not the type who jumps in without looking and have been analyzing my options for weeks. I examined it as I would a new piece of music. You were not a whim of mine to get me out of trouble. I believe we could make a nice marriage."

"Nice," he repeated in the same monotone she gave her speech.

"There is nothing wrong with nice."

He closed the distance between them.

Her chest heaved.

"Nice is not good enough for me." His arm came around her waist and in spite of the twelve-inch difference in their heights his lips were on hers before she could protest. She was stiff in his arms, but she put her hands on his shoulders and did not push away. Patience kept him gentle while he wanted to thrust his tongue in her mouth and taste her sweetness. One sip at a time, he caressed her lips with his. He ran his hand up and down her side from her hip to the edge of her breast, longing to feel her flesh rather than the soft material of her gown. Not touching her anywhere too intimate strained his desires.

She softened in his arms.

A sigh escaped her lips and Thomas took the opportunity to sweep the inside of her lips with his tongue.

She gasped and he plunged inside. Her tongue was less forceful, but she joined him in the pleasure of the kiss.

Nipping at her lips, he watched her. "I will think about everything you have said tonight, My Lady. I am also cautious and like to give a large decision my full attention before jumping in."

He released her.

Dory straightened her dress. If he had wanted to put a name to the expression on her face, he would have said she appeared confused. He thought it was not a bad start.

"May I ask why you are so hesitant?"

"Shall I be completely honest?" he asked.

"I would prefer that you were always honest with me."

He nodded. "I am very fond of you, Dorothea, and have long thought you are one of the most beautiful and talented women in London. What you propose opens you up to a rather large scandal. Elopement is bad enough, but to run off with someone beneath you in station could be something you would not recover from."

"I am not concerned with my reputation," she protested.

"Well, I am. I think not being invited to the most fashionable homes in London would make you unhappy. I would not want my wife to be unhappy."

"That is very kind of you, but I am willing to risk censure to have a life that includes my music."

Wishing she would say something more heartfelt would not make it so. "I would like a wife who wanted me for something other than my love of music. I am also concerned by your apathy toward a romantic involvement."

"So idealistic, Thomas." She rolled her eyes.

His fingers itched to pull her back against him and take all she offered, but the damned voice of reason kept his hands at his sides. "I did not realize it myself, but I find the notion of a wife whose only interest in me is escaping a worse situation abhorrent." He held up his hand to stop her from further comment. "However, that kiss we shared was not apathetic nor were you uninterested. I wonder if helping you would not also suit my own desires."

Her eyes widened. "I already told you I would share your bed."

He touched her cheek. "Oh, Dory, I wish you could believe all men are not cut from the same cloth as your father."

She shrugged.

"Perhaps in time you will learn differently." He brushed a single tear away from her lashes.

Straightening, she stepped away from him. "My parents will announce my betrothal in less than a fortnight at mother's ball."

He dropped into a low bow. "You will have my answer before then."

Chapter Two

"You did what?" Sophia Fallon, the Countess of Marlton, screamed in her private parlor where no one else could hear her except for her dear friend.

Sophia's dark Italian features were stunning, but at the moment her eyes filled with concern and focused on Dorothea Flammel. As an American, she was not as steeped in the rules of London Society. Though, she had learned of the ton's wrath after marrying the Earl of Marlton two years earlier.

"You heard me," Dory said.

"Say it again just so I can assure myself that I have not gone mad." Her narrowed eyes made it clear arguing wasn't an option.

"I proposed to Mr. Wheel three nights ago, to avoid this ridiculous marriage Father has arranged."

"Do I even want to know how you accomplished this private moment with Tom?" Sophia asked.

"No, probably not."

"Oh, Dory, this is crazy."

"Do you think he would make a bad husband?" Her voice

trembled. She had thought Thomas Wheel a good choice for a husband. He loved music and seemed to like to hear her play. He was not violent and had never been the center of any scandal. She thought they could live a contented life together.

The nanny entered the room. "Pardon me, your ladyship, Charles is asking for you."

Sophia smiled. "Tell my son I will come and play with him in a little while. He can have a biscuit now if he wishes."

Susan curtsied. "Yes, Ma'am."

Once the nanny left, Dory said, "I will let you get back to your life, Sophia. I needed to talk to someone and Elinor is in the country with her brood and Markus has been so distraught over Emma's death he is not capable of counsel."

She had gotten up to leave and was nearing the door.

"Don't you want the answer to your question?" Sophia asked.

Sophia was plumper than when the two girls had met; she was happy with her husband and baby. They had become fast friends because Sophia had helped Elinor Burkenstock, now the Duchess of Kerburghe, out of a ruinous scandal. Since Dory and Elinor had been best friends since childhood, the mutual desire to help her friend had endeared the women to each other.

At the moment, Sophia sat in a large chair that framed her like a queen. Her hands folded in her lap, she wore a knowing smile on her red lips.

"You know I do."

"Then come and sit down and don't run away as if I am going to censure you."

"Aren't you?"

"Perhaps."

They both laughed and Dory walked back inside the room and sat across from where Sophia was enthroned.

"All right," Dory said, "Do you think he will make a good husband or not?"

Sophia took a deep breath and frowned. "Thomas Wheel is one of the kindest and best men I have ever met. Daniel thinks the world of him and consults with him on many things. He has seemed quite taken with you for some time now."

"And," Dory prompted.

"And I hate the way you have gone about this. I don't like the idea of Thomas being trapped into marriage any better than I like what your mother has done with this arrangement with an old man who is not even very nice."

"What would you have me do, Sophia? Should I go along with my parents' plans and marry a man whom I can never even like? At least I like Thomas. He is a gentleman. I have been honest with him and he says he will think about it."

"Oh, but I think he may be in love with you, and if you do not return his feelings then you'll hurt him, Dory."

"Nonsense," she said, throwing her blond hair off where it had settled on her shoulder. "He is no more in love with me than I am with him. He likes to hear me play the pianoforte and I believe he will allow me to continue in that endeavor. In return I will allow him his husbandly rights and I will give him a child if he wishes it. It will be a very amicable arrangement. No one will get hurt."

"I hope you are right." Sorrow filled her words.

"Of course I am. Besides, it may make no difference as Thomas may say no to my proposal and I will have to marry the codger and live a miserable, music-less life." While she tried for a light tone, anyone who knew her well could hear the terror in her voice. To live without music would be worse than death for someone like Dorothea, who lived to play and compose.

Wearing a sad smile, Sophia crossed the room to hug her friend. "I am sure this will all work out. If Daniel or I can be of some help you must let us know. We are your friends, you know."

Dory smiled and kissed her friend's cheek. "I know. Thank you."

❧

Dressed for the Bromely ball, Dory watched her reflection in the mirror for a long time. She stared at the woman in front of her for so long that her features blurred into a distorted monster before her.

"You look very well, Dorothea,"

Margaret Flammel stood in the doorway in a dark blue gown that was exquisite but too old a style for her age. She liked to give the impression of being in mourning despite the fact her husband was very much alive. The blue of the gown was so close to black and should have been reserved for a funeral gown. Much like Dorothea herself, her mother was petite and formidable. Her hair was darker and had no red in it. Her eyes were the same green as her daughter's.

"Thank you, Mother," Dory said, not turning away from her own reflection.

"I expect you to pay special attention to Lord Hartly tonight. I want him to know how thrilled you are to be marrying such a prominent and important man." Countess Flammel pulled her gloves on.

Dorothea turned in her chair and looked at her mother. "You really intend for me to go through with this ridiculous marriage to a man more than three times my age?"

The placid look on her mother's face changed in an instant. Her eyes narrowed and her lips thinned until they were invisible. "I intend for you to do your duty as the daughter of the Earl of Castlereagh. You had your chance to marry some eligible young men in the past four seasons. Now you have embarrassed me with the need to begin yet another season. You will soon be one and twenty and you have made it clear you will not choose a husband. You left me no choice, Dorothea, but to choose one for you. Lord Hartly is well respected and wealthy. He will be a suitable husband for you."

"What I want is of no consequence?"

This statement enraged her mother even more and her voice rose to near screaming. "You want only to play that damned pianoforte. I wish we had never brought that thing in the house. You might have been a normal child if you had never discovered that you were cursed with talent."

"You never seemed to think it a curse when I was entertaining your friends."

The countess waved off the comment. "You could have done as well by playing any ballad adequately. There was never any need for you to learn Mozart or write your own music. You take everything too far, Dorothea. You always have and now the consequence is that you will marry whom I have picked and you will do it with a smile on your face. I command it and that is that."

"What are you commanding now, Peggy?" Earl of Castlereagh said from just out of Dory's sight.

She could see her mother's back stiffen and her eyes narrowed to a pin's point. "Do not call me by that common name. You know I cannot bear it."

Geoffrey Flammel, Earl of Castlereagh, just laughed at his wife's discomfort. He poked his head in his daughter's door and smiled in the way most ladies found charming. Unfortunately, his wife and daughter only found him distasteful. He had engaged in so many public affairs over the years that the family had become a joke.

Markus had escaped early and had made a respectable

name on his own, but the death of his wife had sent the stoic man into a tailspin.

His smile dimmed. "Good evening, Dorothea."

"Hello, Father."

"You look lovely."

"Thank you, Father."

"I think Hartly will be pleased with his acquisition. You will make him a fine wife."

"How romantic," Dory said and turned back to her mirror.

Her father laughed. "Romance, bah, that is not the object of marriage, daughter. You may find that elsewhere. Marriage is a financial arrangement. Isn't that right, Peggy?" He gave his wife a sound slap on the bottom.

"Geoffrey, you are trying my patience this evening," Margaret warned.

Miraculously, the carefree earl was cowed by her warning and only smiled, nodding.

"I am afraid the financial benefit is lost to my sensibilities, father. I am the cattle being sold at auction. You are the farmer who gets the bounty and no longer must feed the cow."

"Very harshly put, Dorothea," he said. "Not incorrect, but harsh." He chuckled and strode down the hall.

Dory shared a knowing look with her mother, who did not waver. "Thank you, Mother," Dory said. "I am sure I will be as happy in my marriage as you have been in yours."

"Nonsense," Her mother said. "Hartly is old. He will be dead in a few years and you will still be a countess and it is arranged that you will inherit a large sum to live on for the rest of your life. You may think this is all cruel, but we are only thinking of your future, my dear. Your father will not live forever and everything will go to Markus. You will not get a penny."

"Markus would not let me starve."

Her mother shrugged. "Perhaps not, but we could not leave an extra burden on our son's shoulders. Now he will remarry and then he can have a son of his own. He should not be burdened with you."

"So thoughtful of you both."

Her mother ignored her sarcasm. "Be downstairs in fifteen minutes. I am calling for the carriage now."

Once her mother left, Dory stared back in the mirror and put her expression back to calm. She dabbed powder on her already perfect complexion and left her monsters in the glass while she went to face the monsters in the real world.

～

The Bromley townhouse was one of the largest in London. Towering ceilings were painted with the most exquisite frescos in the Old Italian style. The money spent to make the ballroom look like the Sistine Chapel was exorbitant and the result grotesque in Dory's opinion.

Looking up, she said, "I have not seen the original, but I imagine the subject is much more appropriate in a cathedral than it is here in the ballroom."

Sophia shrugged. "It is rather daunting, I agree."

The two ladies were so engrossed in the ceiling they did not notice the Earl of Hartly approach. "Admiring one of the great works of London, Ladies?"

Dory rolled her eyes.

"Lord Hartly," Sophia said, "You are good friends with Lord and Lady Bromley, are you not?"

"Yes, his lordship and I went to school together. I helped him find the artist who created that masterpiece," he added pointing to the ceiling.

"Of course you did," Dory said under her breath.

"Excuse me, my dear?"

She flinched at his use of an endearment in public. She looked over at Sophia who had also noted the familiarity and was staring wide-eyed. "Nothing, I was just noting the detail," she lied.

He nodded, took a step back, and fixed his stare on Lady Dorothea Flammel from the top of her head to her satin slippers as if she were a horse he was thinking of buying. He lingered for an extra second at her bosom where it swelled over the neckline of her gown.

She felt soiled, as if the deep green confection had become transparent under his gaze. Her eyes narrowed on the old man before her and a sharp set down was on her tongue. She opened her mouth to tell the lecherous old man what she thought of him.

"Lady Dorothea," a man said, with a deep, familiar voice. "May I claim the next dance?"

The sea-blue eyes of Thomas Wheel could almost make her forget the leering of the gray-haired lord next to her.

She had no chance to answer.

"Yes, go, go," Hartly said waving his cane. "I am in no condition to dance."

It took every ounce of her strength not to inform the earl she would rather have a tooth extracted than allow him to touch her. She managed a short curtsy and took Thomas's arm. One last glance at Sophia revealed the earl giving her figure a thorough perusal, but Daniel arrived in short order. One look from the Earl of Marlton and Hartly shuffled away cane in hand.

Once she was in Thomas's arms, she had a better look at those blue eyes that had been her salvation a moment before. Now she could see the anger in them. He looked dangerous to her for the first time.

When the first note of music began, a waltz echoed

throughout the room. Thomas offered his hand and Dory took it. She felt his arm curl around her waist and settle at the small of her back. She allowed herself to be led around the floor in silence.

In all the years she had known Thomas Wheel, she had never feared him. He had been one of her brother's closest friends and had summered at their country estate more than once. If anyone asked her to describe his demeanor, she'd have said he was a lighthearted, good-humored man. However, the look in his eyes as they made a loop around the ballroom was far from the happy fellow of her youth.

He was a stranger to her. His jaw tightened and twitched in a way that made her at once wish to run and put her hand on his cheek and soothe away his anger. For a fleeting moment, she thought she ought to be afraid of him. After all he, like her brother, had worked for the foreign office doing things that one must presume would make a lady cringe. Markus never spoke of his time overseas and she suspected Thomas would be just as closed-mouthed about the war.

The silence was thick, though she did not find it uncomfortable. Her parents often engaged in small talk to fill the silence, but she preferred quiet to mindless chatter. If she were honest, she would rather sit with her music than with a person, which is how she ended up about to be married to a lecherous old man.

Pushing unpleasant thoughts from her mind, she focused on the dance. Thomas moved with smooth assurance. His arms felt safe and sure around her. His warmth seeped through her gown and corset and she wondered if the warmth was normal or caused by whatever had made him angry.

She inhaled and his scent was also warm and spicy. Looking up, she found him staring down at her the anger gone from his eyes.

"I think I must apologize," he said.

Her eyebrows rose. "Whatever for?"

"I have wasted half of our dance fighting my temper. You must feel neglected."

She thought about how she felt. "Not neglected," she said. "I feel quite at ease, Mr. Wheel. You make me feel safe. Does that sound strange?"

His smile was so private, she blushed.

"You are safe with me, Dorothea, as long as you never call me Mr. Wheel ever again," he said pulling her closer.

"Thomas, then," she corrected smiling up at him.

His expression hardened. "You cannot marry that old lascivious pig," he commanded.

Hope filled her and she had to swallow twice to speak. "Do I have a choice?"

His eyes softened. "Are you certain I am what you want?"

Gulping air, she blurted the answer. "I am sure, Thomas."

He nodded. "I will find a way to send word to you of my intentions."

It was as if a large cloak had lifted off her and she could breathe again. "I appreciate your kindness more than I can say."

The music ended and he bowed deeply taking her hand. His gaze met hers and he spoke in a whisper meant for her ears only. "It is not kindness, but I will do my best to make you happy, Dorothea Flammel."

His eyes were so earnest that her eyes welled with tears. "I know you will." Face warm, she didn't know why she was blushing as he escorted her to the edge of the dance floor.

Hartly had moved off to speak to a man with a brown coat and whiskers. Dory was relieved he'd gotten distracted, but the man seemed out of place in the ballroom. Leaning in, she whispered, "Thomas, do you know who Lord Hartly is talking to?"

Her hand rested on his forearm and he placed his other

hand on top. It was intimate and protective. "His name is Sanford Wormfield. Hartly keeps him as a protector. I understand the man is quite dangerous. You should stay clear of him."

"Is he a soldier?" A long red scar ran from just below Sanford Wormfield's left temple to just under his jaw. He met her stare and a shiver ran up Dory's spine. She looked away.

"Of fortune, perhaps. He is an unsavory character." He slowed their pace, keeping them out of the crowds formed around the dance floor.

"Why would Lord Hartly need such a man in his employ?"

"That is an excellent question." Thomas led her back to her mother who spoke to Lady Dowder. "Thank you for the dance, Lady Dorothea."

Over Thomas's shoulder, Wormfield watched her. She whispered. "Should I be afraid?"

Thomas turned in the direction of her gaze. A crooked smile lifted his lips, but did not touch his eyes. Leaning in, his breath brushed her ear. "I will not let anything or anyone harm you."

"Hello, Mr. Wheel," Serena Dowder interrupted, her voice filled with enthusiasm.

Dory would have sworn she heard Thomas groan. "How do you do, Miss Dowder?"

"I am in perfect health, thank you. I have an opening in my dance card. I saved it just for you." She flipped her brown curls over one shoulder and fluttered her eyelashes.

Dory stifled a laugh. "It is nice to see you again, Miss Dowder."

"Oh, hello, Lady Dorothea. I did not see you there."

It was a ridiculous lie, but Dory smiled. "I understand your sister is recently engaged to Mr. Gautier. You must be delighted for Sylvia."

Something ugly flashed in Serena's hazel eyes before she masked it with the bubbly smile Dory associated with both Dowder twins. "We are all thrilled with the match. Hunter is a fine gentleman."

"If you ladies will excuse me?" Thomas stepped away.

"You won't forget our dance, Mr. Wheel?" Serena called far louder than was necessary.

Thomas bowed. "I would not miss it."

"He has been courting me," Serena said.

A knot clogged Dory's throat. "Has he?"

"Yes. I think I will have an offer from him soon. I know he has no title, but he is handsome and rich. My father will approve." Her hair bounced as she nodded her own agreement.

The idea that she might be stealing Thomas away from another woman didn't sit well with Dory. "How long has he been courting you?"

Serena was a wisp of a girl. Thin and tall, she cocked her head and put her finger on her chin. "It must be a year now. Maybe more."

Thomas and Sophia were great friends, and Sophia had never mentioned that he was courting anyone let alone close to making an offer. "Is he attentive?"

"Not as much as I would like." Serena sighed. The music started and she ran toward the other side of the room where Thomas spoke to Daniel.

With a bow, he offered Serena his arm and they found their place for the dance.

"Sometimes my sister is a bit too enthusiastic," Sylvia said.

They danced well together. Dory wanted to look away, but she couldn't. "Better that than to sit in the corner and wait."

"Perhaps." Sylvia smiled before turning back to the conversation with Mr. Gautier.

Chapter Three

His promise still haunted her thoughts the next day. *"I will do my best to make you happy, Dorothea Flammel."* Dory wondered if her father had said the same to her mother before they married. If he had, had he meant it at the time? What had happened between her parents that change his desires from love to torment? Had her mother refused him too many times or had his eyes wandered elsewhere and his promises wandered as well?

She shook off these thoughts. "It doesn't matter," she said to her empty room. "I am not in love with Thomas Wheel, so he can never hurt me that way."

"Did you say something, my dear?" Her mother asked from the doorway.

There was not a piece of lace in decorating her room. Frilly décor made her uncomfortable and too much like an average debutante. The green silk drapery around her bed shone in the late morning sun and her walls, stripped of pink, were covered with warm cream damask. Her desk was a sturdy little table and there was not a ribbon in sight. It held several pieces of music that had ink splatters and scratches all around. All frills were neatly tucked away and brought out only for adornment and fashion. She kept a small harp in the corner of the room and she played it each night to relax before bed.

Dory turned to find her mother standing just inside her room consulting a piece of foolscap and smiling. She had not overheard her daughter's mutterings or she would not be so happy. With a sigh of relief, she said, "Nothing, Mother. Can I help you with something?"

"I was just making a list of tasks that will need to be done for your engagement ball. You will need a new gown, of course, and I thought I might have one as well." She looked up from her list and smiled like a girl of sixteen. "I am the mother of the bride after all. Then we will need to have a new set of ear bobs for you. I adore you in emeralds. You like them, don't you?"

"It is all a bit premature since there has been no formal engagement yet, Mother. How well do you know Lord Hartly?"

Margaret frowned, once again distracted from her list. "Know him? He is an earl, he is rich beyond your needs, and he wants you for his wife. What more do I need to know?"

"I had hoped to marry for love," she lied.

Now her mother's frown turned fierce. "Don't be stupid, Dorothea. I raised you better than that. Love is for the poor and for fools like your friend Elinor."

"You forget, Mother, that Elinor is a Duchess now," Dory said.

Her mother huffed in disgust. "Raised to the rank. Not a family title and little money."

"She still outranks you, Mother, and Kerburghe has done quite nicely in spite of a father who left his family near poverty. I heard they have three carriages." Dory could have cared less about how many vehicles her friends owned, but she knew her mother would be impressed even though she'd never admit the fact.

Shrugging, Margaret said, "I will admit that His Grace has done better than I expected and that friend of yours snapped him up handily. She is more devious than I gave her credit for. However, this talk of love makes my skin crawl and I will have no more of it. We expect an offer from Lord Hartly before the week's end and you shall be married at the end of the season."

"He is a miserable little toad," she said, keeping her temper simmering just below the surface.

Her mother's eyes narrowed. "He is an Earl. You will be a Countess. You will do your duty to your family and marry where you are told and that will be that. Do you understand me, Dorothea?"

Anger filled her head with roaring but she kept her temper in check. She couldn't let on about her plans. "I hear you fine, Mother. You are clear in the fact that my happiness is of no concern to you, as long as I marry a wealthy lord of the realm. The fact that he is wretched and lecherous is of no concern to you either."

Margaret's face softened. "Once you are married you can do as you wish. Don't you see? Hartly is perfect. He will pay your father's debts and be in the ground before long. After that, you will inherit a comfortable settlement and a nice piece of land in the country. I have been very specific in how you are to be taken care of after your husband's death."

She imagined that her eyes were as big as teacups. Not only had her mother planned her wedding to this horrible creature, she had also planned his funeral. She should have known there would be money exchanged. Her father never could manage his lands and his bad habits.

Her mother took her silence as agreement and went back to her list. "I was thinking you should be married in a light green to bring out the color of your eyes. I know you don't like frills, but I think I shall have St. Georges sprayed with lilies."

"Lilies seem appropriate."

Margaret did not catch the sarcasm or did not care to connect the flower with funerals. She nodded and said, "I am planning our most fantastic ball this year in honor of your engagement, my dear. You will be the most celebrated debutante of the season."

"I am sure it will be an event to remember, Mother."

"Of course, it will and we have only a week to make all the preparations. Not much time at all." She left the room still consulting her list.

Dory sat at her desk and pushed her musical compositions aside. She pulled out a piece of foolscap and wrote a quick note.

Sir,

My parents will announce my engagement before the end of the week. I apologize for the need for expedience but once an agreement is signed the damage shall be irreparable.

D.

With shaking hands, she sealed the note and asked a footman to deliver it within the hour.

∾

"You are going to do what?" Daniel Fallon, the Earl of Marlton asked in a pitch that hurt Thomas's ears.

"I think you heard me well enough, Daniel." Thomas accepted a note from his butler's beefy hand. "Thank you, Crowly."

Crowly bowed and left the room.

Daniel ran his hand through his dark blond hair, causing some of it to escape from the queue at the back of his skull. He looked rather mad as he rose and paced. The pacing was a joke within his circle. When they were young, Daniel's title was imminent and they called this the "earl walk." "You plan to elope with Dorothea Flammel, the daughter of an earl? Have you lost your mind?"

Thomas laughed, in part because he could not help but laugh every time Daniel did the "earl walk," and also, he had to agree with his friend. "Maybe, but I cannot abide seeing her sold off to Hartly like a piece of chattel."

"What do you mean, sold off?"

"After the lady came to me for help, I made some discreet inquiries, and learned that Flammel is deep in debt to Hartly. He has already paid him quite a tidy sum and the final payment is his only daughter's hand in marriage."

"Does Dorothea know this?" Daniel asked.

"I do not think so. She would have mentioned it."

Daniel frowned. "I agree the business is distasteful, but marrying her seems extreme. This is a rather large gesture to make to a girl who is the sister of your friend. You will spend the rest of your life with the woman, Tom. Have you thought of that?"

He leaned back in his chair and steepled his fingers. "I have thought of everything. I must marry eventually. The lady is beautiful, talented, smart, and I like her more than most of the ninnies running around the London ton these days. She loves music as much as I do and I adore listening to her play. I don't think it is a bad match for my part. She is the one who is stepping down. I am a mere mister and she could have been a countess. The lady came to me and not the other way around."

"I know you find her intriguing, Tom. I am just concerned that your return to London will be less inconspicuous than you anticipate. This could ruin key relationships in your business dealings. Flammel may be an ass but he is an Earl and his word still holds sway in England. And Hartly..."

"Is a repugnant toad. Would you have me abandon Dory to that pig? You know his reputation. Even at his age he chases every skirt that crosses him. You saw the way he looked at your own wife at Bromley's last night. My servants tell me he has impregnated no less than five of the girls on his staff and one this year. Tosses them to the street once they're with child. I cannot allow her to be married to such an animal." He pounded his fist on the desk.

Shaking his head Daniel heaved a sigh. "Will you go to Gretna then?"

"I think not. I don't like the stink of gossip that comes along with marrying there." Thomas broke the seal on the note Crowly delivered. He read it and frowned before pushing the missive aside. "It seems my plans must be completed with more expediency than expected. Flammel will sign an agreement before the week's end."

"What will you do?"

Thomas smiled. "It so happens we know a duke living in Scotland."

Daniel smiled too but he was shaking his head.

"I know you think me mad."

The earl shrugged. "She's a good girl. No frills about her. She will not send you to the poor house over bits of ribbon and lace but she may bankrupt you with the purchase of musical this and that. I am worried that the way this marriage is to be carried out will open the two of you up to a world of censure."

"The ton shall have their gossip for a while and then they will forget and we will go on as any married couple does."

Daniel shook his head. "I hope you are right, Tom. I really hope that for your sake you are right."

~

D ory's voice was unsteady as she admitted, "I think Mr. Wheel has changed his mind."

Sophia rose and closed the door to her parlor against any ears that might be listening. Servants could sometimes carry gossip to the worst places. "I am sure that's not true, but what makes you think so?"

"I sent him a note two days ago, indicating my engagement is imminent and I have not heard a word from him. Perhaps he has come to his senses." She sighed, and all her dismay pressed out of her lungs in the tiny noise.

Sophia rang the bell for her maid. A few moments later a young woman with dark hair and eyes opened the door and said, "Yes, my lady?"

"Thank you, Anne. Is his lordship in the house?"

"I believe so, ma'am."

"Would you ask him to join me here, please?"

The girl curtsied and fled.

"Where is Marie?" Dory asked.

Sophia had brought a maid with her from Philadelphia when she arrived in London. Marie had continued as her maid when she married so her absence was surprising.

"We've promoted her to housekeeper. She's capably

33

running the entire house ever since Mrs. Wallace retired," Sophia said.

Dory's eyebrows rose. "An American housekeeper must have been quite a change for the staff."

"They are bearing up very well." Sophia smiled.

A firm knock sounded on the parlor door heralding Daniel's arrival. He strode in and kissed his wife's cheek and took her hand, before noticing her guest. "Dorothea, how delightful to see you." He bowed.

Dory stood and made a small curtsy. "How do you do, my lord."

Daniel smiled. "I have learned from my stunning and wise wife that in the privacy of one's home, when no one can hear, we should call our friends by their Christian names. I would be honored if you would count me as your friend."

She brightened, "Thank you, Daniel. It is an American custom I am quite fond of, just as I am fond of your wife."

"The two of you will make me blush," Sophia said.

Daniel kissed his wife's hand still clutched in his. "I assume I have been summoned for more than a salutation, my love."

"Yes. Has Thomas changed his mind about marrying Dory?" Sophia was as direct as ever.

Dory wished she could climb under the settee and disappear.

Daniel's eyes sparkled with mirth. "I do not believe so. I spoke to him yesterday and he was making plans for the happy day."

Dory breathed out in a huge sigh she hadn't realized she'd been holding.

Sophia frowned. "Why has he not answered Dory's note?"

"That I cannot say. He received the note when I was in his company and he set several of his plans into action. Perhaps he does not believe a response is necessary until he can relay those plans. Did you request an immediate response, Dory?"

"I did not," she admitted.

Daniel came and sat on the chair in front of Dory. "I have learned during my short marriage that men and women are different in their expectations. I am sure that Thomas will contact you as soon as he has something to impart but probably not before."

"Thank you, Daniel. You are very kind."

The earl's mouth turned down in a frown. His focus grew far away for a moment before his gaze returned to Dory. "Forgive me, Dory, but we are friends, and just as I did with Thomas I shall caution you in the same manner. This elopement will be infamous. You will find a great deal of censure when you return to London and will not have the benefit of a title to hide behind. I fear you will both lose a great deal by entering into this marriage."

Dorothea sat up straight in her seat and raised her chin. "I appreciate your concern, but I believe the risk is worth taking. I don't care about the titles as others might."

His lips tipped up in a half grin. "Please don't think me a snob, Dory. I have been friends with Thomas for many years. He is like a brother to me, just as your brother is. I would do anything for Thomas, Markus, or Michael. My life would not be half as rich without them as my closest friends. I only worry that once the gossip begins, you will both find life in society difficult, and that can put a strain on any marriage, especially when you will not have the support of your family."

A tear escaped Dory's eye. "Forgive me, Daniel. I am far too used to having to defend myself and I forget who my true friends are. I know you want to protect me. Thomas and I are lucky to have such wonderful support from you and Sophia. My brothers may support our marriage. Adam is still young, but

Markus has long been the only relative whom I trust. You are correct, my parents will likely disown me when the news reaches them."

He was nodding. "Except for Markus that is a probable outcome."

"If I did not believe Thomas and I could make an amicable marriage I would not go through with this. He is kind and we have much in common. I am determined to go ahead with our plan."

"You may be sure you will continue to have our support regardless of how the rest of the ton responds to your nuptials."

"Of course, we are on your side." Sophia rushed over, knelt in front of Dory, and took her hands. "We will do whatever you need in the days and months to come."

"Thank you." Tears managed an escape and Dory brushed them aside.

Chapter Four

On Wednesday morning, three days before the Flammel ball was to take place, a note arrived.

Tonight, at Southerton's. If you leave your trunk in the gazebo near the back of your garden I shall have it picked up. All arrangements have been made.

T.

Heart beating wildly, Dory called her maid. Was she really doing this? Could she, after years of playing at being disobedient, be such a woman? A lifetime with Thomas Wheel. The idea was heady, but not terrible. Mrs. Thomas Wheel did not sound bad at all.

She sat on the edge of the bed and smoothed the coverlet, tracing the stitching and letting her mind wander. This was madness, but the alternative was crazier still.

Her maid scratched at her bedroom door and entered.

"Emily, I need your help."

Emily crossed her arms over her chest. "What's wrong now? Has that father of yours done something we must cover up?"

"It's far worse than that. He plans to sell me to a man three times my age to get himself out of debt."

Emily's dark curls shook with temper and she stomped her foot. "I know he's my employer, but that man is no good."

Sighing, Dory patted the bed next to her. "Sit with me a moment, Emily. I have a plan, but I will need your help."

"What can I do?" Emily sat and took Dory's hands.

"Thomas Wheel has agreed to marry me. It's my only escape and I think maybe my only chance at happiness. Well, if not that, then at least I will have my music." A weight pressed against her chest. She might be making a terrible mistake, but a life with Hartly was certain doom.

Eyes wide and face pale, Emily shook her head. "You'll be ruined, miss."

"I will be safe with a man who is good and kind rather than one who is an even worse version of my father. At least father doesn't chase the servants. I have heard rumors about Hartly." She shivered.

Emily squeezed her hands. "What do you need?"

"I need a small trunk packed and put in the gazebo."

A tear rolled down Emily's cheek. "I will take care of it."

"What is wrong?"

She shook her head and dashed the tear away. "I will be sacked, is all."

Dory hugged her, her heart full. "You do not think I would let mother put you out on the street do you, Emily? Pack your own trunk too and see that you are ready when the carriage comes for it."

"What will your husband say?"

It was a good question. "I do not know, but we will see what Mr. Wheel is made of."

Leaving Emily to do the packing, Dory went in search of her mother. She found the countess in her private parlor writing letters. "Oh, Dorothea, I am so glad you're here. Do you think it impertinent to invite Prince George to your wedding?"

Her gut twisted. "It is high handed, Mother. We are not close personal friends with the prince. I had hoped for a small wedding with as little fuss as possible."

A crease formed between Margaret Flammel's eyes. "You have obligations as do we all, Dorothea. You will marry as befits a countess."

"Of course, Mother." Dory waited for her mother to return to her letter writing. "I would like to go to Southerton's tonight."

Margaret put aside her writing. "I had the distinct impression you dislike large fancy balls like Southerton's."

"I do, but I know you enjoy them and as I am soon to leave this house, I thought it might be nice to go together."

Cocking her head, Margaret examined Dory. "I think it is a wonderful idea. We have not attended one of Lady Southerton's balls in some time. It will be a good opportunity to be seen in public before your marriage."

Dory wished for a relationship with her mother filled with more than lies and posturing, but it had always been this way. Her mother used her to get back at her father and for social status and Dory used her mother's vanity and social climbing to get what she wanted. They had been playing the same games since Dory was a child and she didn't know how to stop. "I had better prepare if we are to get there early enough to make an impression."

Margaret looked at the clock. "I have a few letters to write.

Half the day gone. We shall manage to be ready before eleven, Dorothea."

"Of course we will, Mother."

～

The ball at Southerton's was a crush of people all vying for the attention of this one or that. As soon as they arrived, Margaret found a passel of women with whom she was acquainted. "Go dance with the Earl of Ridgley, Dorothea. Do not waste the evening. We can make a few advantageous connections before you take your vows."

It sounded as if she were joining a convent rather than marrying. Dory left her mother and wove her way through the crowded ballroom. The heat swamped her, and between that and her nerves, a wave of dizziness swept over her. Gripping a column, she steadied herself before making for the garden doors.

She was steps away from fresh air. A hand closed around her wrists.

Sanford Wormfield gripped her hard enough to leave a bruise. "Lady Dorothea, where are you going in such a hurry?"

Her head rang with Thomas's warning to stay away from this man. "I do not believe we have been introduced, sir. There-fore, you have no right to accost me in such a way."

When he smiled the scar on his face deepened to purple. "Oh, but you know who I am and I certainly know you. My employer has an interest in you and so I am at your service."

"Are you trying to scare me, sir?"

"Why would I want to do that?"

The syrup in his voice nauseated her. "I have no idea, but you are holding me hostage and I do not know you. Unhand me before I scream for help." Dory prayed he did not wish to be discovered. She knew she didn't, but her choices were limited.

He leaned in until his face was an inch from hers. He smelled of day-old tobacco and cheap whisky. "If you dance with me I will leave you in peace."

"I do not dance with strange men."

Letting go of her, he bowed low. "I am Sanford Wormfield. I am the assistant to the Earl of Hartly. Certainly, you can spare one dance for a man who is practically family."

"Where is his lordship?" She searched the room.

"Playing cards with your father in the parlor. You see, we are already closer than you think."

There was something evil about Sanford Wormfield. His stink turned her stomach while his stare sent chills down her spine. "I will not dance with you. It would cause a scandal and I have no use for being the center of gossip. Now, walk away, Mr. Wormfield, or I will scream and bring the entirety of this ballroom down upon you."

Danger flashed in his pitch eyes. He bowed. "Until we meet again, Lady Dorothea. I'm sure once you are under Hartly's roof, you will form a different opinion of me."

He was not a full step away from her before she bolted for the garden. She ran down the verandah steps. Looking back, she tripped and had to catch herself. There was no sign of Wormfield, so she slowed her pace to look for Thomas.

Inside the ballroom, the ladies and gentlemen feigned prudence, but in the garden was a different story. The property had an elaborate garden with a maze of high shrubbery and alcoves. Benches were tucked away at the edge of the path. Dory couldn't find a bench or niche where couples didn't steal a kiss or more. She longed to run as far away as she could. She wanted no part of this world she'd been born into. Skirting a man with shiny Hessians and a long mustache, she bumped into a rotund woman whose dress dipped low enough to expose the pink of her areola.

The woman smirked at her before returning her attention to a young man who kissed the top of her breast. Smothered by the flesh of her bosom, he moaned.

Dory excused herself and ran farther into the garden's dark pathways and towering shrubs. Her heart pounded and she trembled. Images of men and women in various embraces flew past her as she ran.

Thomas stepped in front of her, blocking her path.

She clutched her chest trying to catch her breath.

"What's wrong?" Dressed for Southerton's, he wore tan knee breeches and a crisp white cravat tied in the traditional style. He held his hat under his arm.

"N-nothing. Why would you think something is wrong?" Swallowing her panic, Dory pulled her shoulders back and clutched her satin reticule.

"Well, you were running as if the devil was chasing you. Were you running away from something or toward it?" His blue eyes bore into her.

"I have no response that will not make me seem like a complete fool."

His grin was addictive and revealed straight white teeth. Stepping in closer, he took her elbow. "You need not do this, Dory. I will not hold it against you if you have changed your mind."

Hartly's rotting, crooked smirk flashed in her mind. That image and the moments with Wormfield in the ballroom were more than enough to keep her mind made up. "I have not changed my mind. If you are still willing, I want to go with you."

He led her even deeper into the maze of shrubbery and paths. "Do you not even want to ask where I am taking you?"

"It does not matter."

"But it will at some point, Dory. You are afraid now. You want to get away from a terrible situation. I understand, but at some point, you will open your eyes from this nightmare and find yourself married to me. You will be Mrs. Thomas Wheel. If that is another kind of nightmare for you, then you have given up far too much to achieve it." He said it all like a businessman, but underneath was worry and sorrow.

Dory threaded her fingers through his. Even through their gloves, he warmed her. Tugging his hand, she pulled him off the main path and into a private niche cut into the shrubs. "You are not a nightmare, but my savior. Forgive me if I looked less than enthusiastic, but this is an insane thing we are about to do. I have always been a willful daughter, but this is something altogether different."

He brushed a stray hair off her cheek. "And again, I must say, you need not do this."

"The alternative is unacceptable."

"I agree, but perhaps you can talk to your parents and find another solution."

A wave of nausea swamped her. "You do not want to marry me. Of course, how could you? Forgive me for putting you in this position. I am a terrible person to have done this."

"Dory, marrying you is the only part of this plot I like. Believe me when I tell you that if I had a title to offer you, I would have proposed last year. My only concern is for you. This will ruin you. Being Mrs. Wheel is not the same as being the daughter of the Earl of Castlereagh. Marrying beneath your station will gain you nothing but the censure of the ton."

"Thomas, I want to marry you." Her head swam with emotions. This man could save her. Kind and handsome, he would stand by her no matter the consequences. She'd never had that from either of her parents.

Taking a deep breath, he closed his eyes. When he opened them, the intensity was enough to make her heart skip a beat. "Then I suggest we go before you are missed."

"I left a note for my parents. I don't want them to think you've kidnapped me. The butler will find it before Mother arrives home from the ball tonight." She hated the way her voice shook.

He wrapped a loose lock of her hair around his finger and leaned closer. "That was wise as long as the butler doesn't find it too soon."

It was hard to catch her breath with him so close and so large. He towered over her, yet there was no threat of him harming her. A perfect gentleman in every way, Thomas would see she was safe. Though the way his gaze devoured her, she doubted herself. "My parents' house runs like a clock, everything the same, every day. Ward, the butler, will check my father's study at precisely two in the morning to verify that it is tidy and the brandy decanter is full for when my father arrives home. On Wednesday, Father will pull in around three o'clock."

"And your mother?" His breath was warm and tickled the side of her face.

"I do not know what will happen tonight. Normally, we would return home at two-thirty, but when she cannot find me, I cannot say what will happen."

His lips grazed her temple.

The light kiss shook her soul and she had to grab his arm to keep her feet. The full moon illuminated the angles of his face, turning him into a creature of myth. She gazed into his eyes and his lips captured hers.

Just as it had in his study, the world collapsed into that moment in time. Lost in the kiss, nothing else existed. His lips were soft and strong and he wrapped his arm around her waist possessively. His other hand cupped her throat, caressing her flesh like she was a crystal goblet and might shatter if he applied any pressure.

It wasn't as if she'd never been kissed before. Several young men had stolen kisses over the last two seasons. But this was something else. There was passion behind Thomas's kisses that went beyond the physical. His lips made her yearn for more.

Her heartbeat tripled and her skin prickled calling for his touch. There was a soft moan, which she knew was her own, and a low groan from him.

He pulled back and she stumbled in his arms. "Dory, you are amazing."

"Thank you, though I have no idea what you mean."

Pressing his lips to the top of her head, he gave her a brief hug. "Come, I have a carriage waiting at the back gate."

This was really happening.

He offered his arm.

She hesitated before accepting.

"Dory, you are pale as a sheet. Are you certain this is what you want?" He led her through the gardens with the ease of a man who sneaked around often.

"I will not lie. I am terrified."

"Shall I return you to your mother?" He stopped at the back gate. They were alone with only the moon to light the way. He faced her. Placing his finger under her chin, he encouraged her to look him in the eye. They shone like sapphires in the night.

"If I go back my life is forfeit. My father has sold me to pay off his foolish debts. I cannot go back." Her voice caught, despite her determination to be brave.

He shook his head kept his gaze averted. "I was not sure you knew the circumstances of the arrangement with Hartly."

"Father is always forthright. He told Mother and me everything. He always tells everything. His fatherly advice included waiting a full month before I found myself a proper lover."

"He did not say that?"

"He did."

"I am sorry, Dory."

She drew in a long breath and squared her shoulders. "I am ready to go now, Tom."

"We have to wait here for another moment or two." He stepped close and held her. Lowering his head for a kiss, but stopping short and staring into her eyes.

It was difficult to gain enough breath to speak whilst in his arms. "Why? I thought you said the carriage was waiting."

"It is, but we need to do one last thing before we go. It is the thing that will keep your mother from tearing Southerton's apart tonight."

Voices filtered in from the left. Some familiar and some not.

Serena Dowder laughed and stepped into view. She nodded to Thomas and tugged Lady Pemberhamble's arm.

Pemberhamble stared open-mouthed at Dory and Thomas.

Thomas grabbed Dory's hand and pulled her through the gate, into the alley where his carriage waited.

He was clever to arrange for the most notorious gossip in London to see them leave together. It would cause a scandal, but it would also keep her mother from assuming a nefarious plot was at hand. She cringed at what would be in the paper once Pemberhamble spread the word, but it couldn't be helped.

Once in the carriage they rumbled down the streets of London. The silence between them loomed like poison.

Dory watched as the Southerton townhouse grew smaller out the window. She was not likely to be welcomed back again. Why should that bother her? She had never cared much for society balls and social clubs. She preferred to choose her own friends.

Still she stared at the card and the red embossed seal in the corner.

Thomas patted her hand. "You may yet have use for it, my lady."

She tucked it back into her reticule. "It doesn't matter. I do not enjoy those events much anyway."

"It is not the events so much as the invitations one misses." He'd captured it.

Hartly's hideous face and hunched body reminded her that this was the right thing to do.

She shrugged. "Are we going to Gretna Green?"

"No. I have had a better idea."

"Where are we going?" Her brother and Sophia adored Thomas, but what did she know about him? Maybe he would take advantage of her and leave her in some village to fend for herself. She was being an idiot, but she couldn't keep her mind from conjuring one horror after another.

"I thought you might like to have a friend present at your wedding and since we both have friends living in Scotland..."

"We're going to Kerburghe?"

He nodded.

Her dearest friend, Elinor, had married the Duke of Kerburghe. The two of them had moved to Scotland for the better part of the year. Her heart filled with joy. She would not stand alone at a foreign altar and speak sacred words with no family to hear them. Elinor would be with her. She leapt into Thomas's arms. "Thank you."

Laughing, he held her. "I am glad you are happy."

Clinging to him, she kissed his cheek. "I could not be more thrilled."

"I shall endeavor to keep you in this exact state of bliss for the rest of your days."

She knew he was joking, despite the solemnity of his tone.

Pushing away, she moved to take her own seat.

He held her and tucked her more firmly into his lap. "I wonder if you would let me hold you a few moments longer, Dory."

"If you wish."

"Because I am saving you?"

He was warm and comfortable. He filled her head with spice and manly scents that transformed into music inside her. She longed for a pianoforte or a scrap of paper. Breathing him in, she placed her head on his shoulder and her arms around his neck. "Because, this is nice and comfortable."

He relaxed. "I am very glad you think so."

"I have always liked you, Tom. As I told you before, I did not choose you on a whim, but with care and thought."

"Because I love music and will not hinder you playing." His tone was flat and his arms loosed around her.

Wishing for flowery phrases would not change who she was. Simple truth would have to do. "You are a good and kind man. You have done well in business. The gossip of you is always favorable. I like you more than most people and you never have been anything but respectful toward me. Also, my brother thinks the world of you."

He laughed but there was no humor in the sound. "Anything else?"

He wanted romance and she wished she could give that to him, but it wasn't the truth. "I know you are in love with Sophia and perhaps I might be a good substitute for unrequited love."

His entire body tightened at once.

She'd made him angry. Dory pushed away, but he held her tight.

"Dory, listen to me very carefully. I am not nor have I ever been, in love with our friend Sophia. I am very fond of her and delighted for her happiness with Daniel."

"I would like to go back to my own seat now."

He released her and she scrambled across the carriage. It was not better to be looking at him. In his arms, she could hide from his all-knowing gaze.

She smoothed her skirt. "You offered to marry Sophia. I know it was a secret, but she told me."

He closed his eyes, took a breath, and when he opened his eyes, there was a softness there that made her heart beat faster. "True. If Daniel had not married her, I would have prevailed upon her to marry me."

"And I am sure you would have made her very happy. It is lucky for me that Lord Marlton came to his senses. Sophia and I have much in common. Hopefully, I am a fair substitute and will make you content."

He rubbed his forehead and ran his hand through his shock of dark red hair.

"Perhaps I should not have said anything. We had said we would be honest with each other." This was a bad beginning. She'd misread him, thinking he was as forthright as she, and now he was angry. Her heart pounded as she waited for him to bang on the carriage and demand the driver turn them around.

He leaned forward placing his elbows on his knees and staring into her eyes. "Dorothea, I am not in love with Sophia and I have never been. I thought we might suit because I like her. At the time, she needed a friend and Daniel was being an ass. You are not a substitute for anyone. I would never place you in comparison with our friend."

"That is a relief, as I can never come close to Sophia's goodness." Dory swallowed the dread rising in her throat.

Shaking his head, he captured both her hands in his. "I wish you knew your worth, my dear." He kissed first the fingers on her left hand, and then those on her right before releasing her and sitting back against the bench cushion.

Chapter Five

Thomas longed to take her from the opposite bench and pull her into his arms where he would keep her for the remainder of the trip. The search for her will have already begun, making it impossible to stop and rest for the remainder of the day. She slept, though fitfully, and he watched her as he always watched her, from the shadows. His desire for Dory and the daydreams of what a life with her might be like had not included an elopement.

How could she think him in love with Sophia? He adored Sophia and had Daniel not married her, Thomas would have. But love her romantically? No. He never had nor did he suspect he ever could.

Dory shifted and the hood on her cape fell back. Her skin shone like gold and her hair a rich warm blond. Everything about her lured him in; petite, perfect, remarkable, and about to be his. It was madness to marry her, but she had asked and he was helpless to resist. The sight of Hartly ogling her was too much. He couldn't bear it.

The sunrise streamed in the carriage and filled the world

with orange and red. Thomas's heart stopped at the way her skin glowed in the daylight.

She listed to one side, catching herself, and her deep green eyes popped open. Cheeks pink, she righted herself.

Thomas moved to the other side of the carriage next to her. He wrapped one arm around her shoulder and pressed her to his side.

Stiff as an old oak when he first touched her, she relaxed and settled against him with a slow sigh. "Thank you."

He didn't deserve the joy erupting inside him. "My pleasure."

Relaxing her head against his collarbone and the crook of his neck, she returned to sleep.

Her hair filled his senses with flowers and her skin warmed him like nothing else. There was no point in denying he was smitten. She was everything he'd ever wanted in a wife and much more. If only he deserved such a person it would all be perfect. But he didn't, and there would be a price to pay for giving her what she wanted. He kissed the top of her head, her soft hair tickling his nose and cheek.

Between her maid, trunk, and harp they'd needed a second carriage for transport. It was a miracle they'd not been spotted already. The only thing saving them was that they took the road to Kerburghe and not Gretna Green. It would take them an extra half-day to arrive, but the spotters would be looking in the wrong direction.

Thomas closed his eyes for a few hours' sleep.

~

A s the sun cast long shadows from the west, Thomas instructed Mally, his driver, to stop for the night.

"Are we there?" Dory stretched her arms as far as the carriage walls would allow.

"I am afraid not. It will be another day and a half before we reach Kerburghe land."

"I did not realize it was so far."

"Quite a distance. I have ordered a stop for the night. I imagine you could use a soft bed and a good meal at this point."

Her eyes opened like green pools of panic. "Don't you think they'll find us if we stop?"

"I hope they are looking in the wrong place entirely."

The carriage pulled to a stop in the yard of a small inn. The quaint stone building was alight with activity. There was singing and stomping inside from a party of some kind. A boy ran from the barn to help with the horses.

As long as Thomas had known Dorothea, she had always seemed supremely confident. As a school friend of her brother, Markus, he had watched her grow from childhood to magnificence. In all that time, she had played music like an angel and men like a vixen. She had turned down the regard of men with twice his worth and not blinked an eye. She manipulated her father and brother with ease and even helped recover Daniel when he'd been kidnapped. The woman next to him didn't resemble that person. Eyes cast to the floor, she tugged her cape around her as if it were armor and crossed her arms.

The footman opened the carriage door and took down the step.

Thomas held up a hand. "One moment, Sam."

Sam closed the door and turned his back to the carriage.

"Dory?"

"Yes?" She looked at the empty vase attached the wall, and then at the leather cushion of the bench seat.

"Are you afraid of being caught, or is it me you fear?" His chest tightened, hoping it was the first.

Still unwilling to make eye contact with him she bit her lip and looked out the window where a boy chased after a dog. "I have made promises—"

"You mean to me? You mean the offer of your body in exchange for this rescue?"

She nodded and paled.

Dear God, it was him she feared. The air went out of him. At once desperate to ease her worry and furious at her. "I would never harm you. You must know that."

Finally, she braved looking at him. Liquid pools reflected his own warped image. "You are angry. I am sorry. I should be on my knees thanking you for what you've done for me, but I am afraid and want to run away."

"You are running away."

"From you."

"I see." The pain in his chest tore at him until he knew what people meant when they said their heart broke. "Nothing will ever transpire between you and me that you do not permit, Dorothea. I am not a monster."

"I know that."

It took a force of will to hold his temper at bay. "Then let's go inside and get some rest. You have trusted me this far, can you not take it a bit further?"

A knock on the carriage door. "Are you all right, my lady?"

Thomas sighed and eased the door open.

The maid's shoulders slumped and dark rings smudged beneath her eyes. She was as exhausted as her lady.

"We are fine. Can you see that your lady's trunk is unloaded—"

"Emily, sir. I will see to the luggage." Emily bobbed and walked away.

Thomas stepped down and helped Dory from the carriage.

The innkeeper introduced himself as Mr. Fine. He stood

more than a foot taller than Thomas and his expression went from grim to dour.

Craning his neck, Thomas stared the man in the eye. "My wife and I will need a room for the night. I also need arrangements for my lady's maid and three other servants."

Mr. Fine moved with slow deliberation a few seconds behind those around him. He spoke slowly and his welcoming gesture crept along. "I have space for you, sir. You'll have to forgive the noise though. We've had a wedding and the party guests will be at it for some time."

The common room was raucous with drink and laughter. The bride and groom laughed from high up in chairs, carried by the crowd and paraded around the room. "It is not a problem for us."

"Very well. I will have my wife show you to your room. I will see to your servants."

Mrs. Fine was as tall as Thomas. She wrung her hands and fidgeted as they walked up a flight of stairs and down a hallway. "The room is quite nice. I hope you'll be comfortable."

They entered a clean, serviceable room with heavy dark blue drapes over a sturdy wood bed. One chair in the corner and a table near the window overlooking the yard.

"Thank you, Mrs. Fine. This will do nicely," Thomas said.

Dory kept her face hidden by the hood of her cape but she twisted her fingers together.

"Should I have supper sent up?"

"Would you mind if we went down for a meal? We've been cooped up in that carriage for the entire day. If the wedding party would not mind a couple of strangers, we'd love to eat in the common room."

Mrs. Fine brightened. "Of course. Come down whenever you're ready. I will have a fine meal for you."

He had hoped the knowledge they would not remain in the

room until morning would lessen her worry, but she stared out the window as if death himself were coming for her. His rage got the better of him. "Dorothea."

She spun toward him, eyes wide, mouth open, and hand clutching her chest. Her hood fell away.

In two steps, he crossed the room and dragged her into his arms. Crushing her to him, he ordered his temper back and kissed the top of her head. "I am sorry. I should not have raised my voice. The fact that you are terrified of me does not bode well for our future. I will endeavor to change your mind about my character."

"I am afraid, but your character is not in question, Tom." Against his chest, her voice vibrated into his soul.

He ran his hand along her back. "You cannot question your own?"

Pulling away, she turned to the window. "Can I not? I faced the ultimate test of our society and failed."

"Is that what you think?" He was at a loss for what to say to such utter bunk.

"My father needed me to save him and I ran as far and as fast as I could. Now they will endure the scandal I created. Is that not failure?"

He sat in the lone chair. "Here I thought you were afraid I was going to ravage you."

She spied over her shoulder. "Yes, there is that too."

She was magnificent and he couldn't hold back a laugh. "I shall tell you what I think and you may listen or not. Your father put you in an untenable position. He created a debt too high to pay and was willing to sell you to clear what he owed. If you had married Hartly, not only would you be miserable, but your father was likely to continue his gross spending until another debt hovered over his head. What do you suppose he would sell then? I can only imagine. He is your father and I shall offer him my respect after we are married, but it is a mystery to me how you and your brother turned out with such fine characters with parents who are repulsive. Forgive me, but I wonder where on earth you came from."

She sighed. "I have often wondered the same thing. Mother is—difficult, and Father is a nightmare, but Markus is all that is good in the world."

"You are as well, Dory."

She blushed and the sight tightened his groin to the point of discomfort. He adjusted his seat. "As to your other worry, I will not touch you unless you permit it, my dear. I realize I am the means of escape for you, but to me, *you* are quite precious. I would never harm you in any way."

A knock sounded on the door.

"Come in," Thomas said.

The footmen carried in Dory's trunk and Emily deposited a small harp next to the luggage. "Will there be anything else, sir?"

"No, Emily. Thank you. You may go eat then get some rest. It will be another long day tomorrow."

She looked at Dorothea, who nodded, and she left the room.

The harp was a third the size of a standard one. He touched the arch of the wood. "A lap harp?"

"I hope you do not mind my bringing it. It is my habit to play before bed and I do not know if I can sleep without it." She bit her lip again.

Warmth spread through him with a longing to hear her play each night. If this was the only benefit of their marriage, he would be lucky, wholly unsatisfied, but lucky none the less. "I do not mind. I look forward to hearing you play. Perhaps you might teach me at some point."

"You wish to learn to play the harp?" She pulled off her cape.

Strumming the strings produced a lilting chord. "I think I would."

"I have never heard of a man playing the harp."

"Nor I, but I see no reason why I could not learn to be adequate at the task."

The first smile since he'd told her they were going to Kerburghe lit her face. "You know, I have never heard you play, Tom. Markus says you are quite good."

"Markus is far too kind."

She cocked her head. "I would like to hear you."

It would be an embarrassment to play in front of such an accomplished musician. "Then you shall hear it at the first opportunity."

Dory crossed and lifted the harp. She strummed out several melodious chords and looked him in the eye. "Will you always agree to everything I ask?"

He stepped behind her and placed his hands over hers as they strummed. Between her heady scent, the music, and the way her bottom fitted against his thighs, he floated in a kind of euphoric state. "If I can, I always will."

She plucked out a sad melody and leaned deeper into his embrace. "Why are you so good to me? I have ruined your life, Tom."

Kissing the shell of her ear, he whispered, "I am quite taken with you, Dorothea Flammel. I have been for some time. A fact I am sure you knew before you made your decision to enlist my assistance."

The notes fell from her fingertips like tears on a pillow. Soft and encompassing. "If you knew I was manipulating you, why did you change your mind and run away with me?"

"That is just it. I could not resist even though I was aware of your game."

Her long deep sigh pulled her even deeper against him, but then, she stepped away and put the harp down. "We should go to dinner before it gets too late."

As if a piece of him had been severed, he missed the feel of her in his arms. The person he wanted most was steps away, but he would wait for her to want him as well and pray that time would come before he died of longing. The table held a washbowl and pitcher. He poured some water in the bowl, took off his jacket and cravat, and tugged his blouse over his head.

The bed creaked.

She sat watching from the edge of the bed. Her eyes wide, she gnawed on that poor lip again.

Longing to kiss that lip, Thomas washed his face. The cool water helped to douse the flame growing every time his gaze fell on her.

She touched his back.

He stilled, not realizing she had left the bed and crossed the room.

She traced a path from his shoulder blade to almost the center of his back. "You were hurt?"

"It is an old scar. When I served the crown, a French spy got the better of me."

Flattening her palm on his back, she skimmed to another war wound near the top of his breeches. "And this?"

"An arrow." He picked up the towel and dried his face and neck. "You know, when you touch me, Dory, I long to touch you."

She snatched her hand back. "I apologize. My curiosity got the better of my good sense."

Turning, he took her hand and kissed the tips of her fingers. "I hope this will not be the last time."

Stained bright red, her creamy cheeks were delightful.

It took all his strength to pull his clothes back on. "I will let you get cleaned up. Come down to the common room when you are ready."

The common room was still bustling with wedding celebration. Mr. Fine met him at the bottom of the stairs and escorted him to a corner table. It was out of the commotion, but no place was quiet with the wedding revelry. "I apologize, but this is the best I can do."

"This will be very good, sir. My wife and I are hungry and a good wedding is always enjoyable."

The food arrived just as Dorothea stepped into view. She'd changed into a dark green gown that made her look like the queen of the woodlands, regal and worthy of respect.

Mr. Fine was at her service as well and led her to the table. She thanked him.

Thomas stood and held her chair for her. "How is it you manage to still look grand even after all this travel and little rest?"

"You are being too kind." She sat.

He offered her some crusty bread and honey, which she accepted.

The mutton was overcooked, but the gravy exquisite. They ate and watched the party fun. It gave them an excuse to say little.

Dory grinned as the crowd walked the bride and groom to the door of the inn. The partygoers followed into the yard. The door closed, and the room fell silent.

"That was quite a party." Thomas's attempt at light conversation.

"I love country weddings. I tried to get Mother to allow me to marry in the country, but she insisted on St. Georges, of course." Realizing her mistake, she clamped her hand over her mouth. "I am sorry."

"You have nothing to apologize about. You and I both had lives before last night. We have been friends but not confidants throughout our lives, Dory. It will take time, but I want to know all there is about you." The truth of that gnawed at his gut.

She shrugged. "There is little to know. I love music and didn't want to marry an old codger."

"I am certain there is much more than that."

"My mother has been nagging me to marry for three years. I am notorious for chasing off perfectly acceptable offers from men of high standing and thus found myself at your doorstep begging you to marry me. What more is there to say?"

Perhaps it was too soon to get her to open up to him with more than this attempt at levity. "How did you and Sophia meet?"

At the mention of their common friend, Dory gave him a smile that lit her eyes and warmed his heart. "She rushed to Elinor's rescue during that silly scandal with Michael. Sophia did not even know Elinor yet she rushed to her aid after reading the account of a kiss with Sir Michael in the paper. At first I was mistrustful, as I usually am, but then Sophia spouted a breathless argument about whether I was always mean and sarcastic or if I was protecting Elinor. After that, I could not resist her with all her American charm and missteps. She's wonderful."

Sophia had once told him the story, but it was interesting to hear it from Dory's point of view. Sophia had made Dory out to be the protector, and now he saw their friendship was equal in many ways. "I agree."

She popped a piece of bread in her mouth. "How did you meet her?"

"At a picnic. She performed her mimicry and entertained the entire group."

Dory laughed. "You liked her because she can imitate people?"

"No, it was not that. It was that the moment we were introduced, I could read on her horrified face she could not remember my name. She was so open and untainted by London and the ton."

Dory sighed. "Yes. Amazingly, she's still like that."

Incredible, Dory had no idea how magnificent she was, or maybe she did and didn't care. Whatever the case, it intrigued him beyond any other woman. "Why did you turn down all those other men who offered for you? I know quite a few of those hearts you broke. Some very eligible lords have fallen in love with you."

Putting down the bread she'd just torn off, she sighed. "I wanted to play."

"And you think marrying means you must stop?"

"Mother has made it quite clear that once I am married my attention must refocus on my husband and not composing music." Her voice took on that grating sound of a mother scolding her child.

"Is that what she does?"

The bridge of her nose scrunched up. "Who, my mother? What do you mean?"

"Does your mother dote on your father? Is she very attentive? Does she run to do his bidding at every moment of every day?"

"As you can imagine, my parents' relationship is less than ideal. Father has his life and wants little to do with ours."

Thomas pushed his plate back. "Your father is a notorious philanderer. Please do not mistake anything I say for approval of abhorrent behavior. I cannot help but wonder what part your mother played in his behavior."

"You think his affairs are my mother's fault?" Her cheeks turned bright red.

"No. I think he would have taken lovers no matter the state of his marriage. I wonder about the way he goes about it. He intentionally flaunts his behavior and waves it in your mother's face. It occurs to me there is a reason for it, which we are not aware of."

Her anger quelled, she cocked her head, popped another morsel of bread in her mouth and swallowed. "I see your point. I had not thought of that before."

"There are many mysteries to what happens in another person's marriage. Perhaps it is as it should be."

She stared down at her half-eaten plate of food. "Indeed."

The wedding party sounds drifted away. Mr. and Mrs. Fine returned and cleaned tables with the help of two women and a young man.

Thomas had so many questions he longed to ask her about her life and what she wanted out of it. Bombarding her with inquiries would only put her further on edge.

Mrs. Fine arrived at their table. "Are you finished with your dinner, Madam?"

"Yes, thank you, Mrs. Fine. Everything was delicious." Dory beamed at her.

"I am glad you liked it." She picked up the plates and bowls from the table and carried them into the kitchen.

"Shall we go up?" Thomas asked.

She bit her lip, but nodded.

Chapter Six

Dory took his arm and walked up the steps to their room. She had made a complete mess of her life. No, her parents had a hand in it as well. Trying to lighten her spirits, she focused on Thomas's profile. His lips turned up in a satisfied expression. Her gaze had the opposite effect. She shuddered at the thought of giving herself to him or anyone. Not that she didn't like Tom, she did.

He unlocked the door to their room and gestured for her to precede him inside. Once in, he locked the bolt.

Her heart skipped a beat. She rushed to the opposite side of the room and sat on the chair.

He cocked his head and tugged off his jacket. Placing his fingers between his cravat and throat, he pulled the cloth loose until it hung around his exposed neck. "Dory?"

She met his gaze. "Yes?"

"You know I will not touch you unless you want me to?"

"Yes." She did know. He was a gentleman and nothing like her father or Hartly. It was the reason she'd chosen him.

"Then why do you look as if I am about to devour you?"

"I don't know."

He crossed the room and crouched in front of her with his hands on her knees. "Perhaps it is your own desires and wishes you fear and not mine."

Once he backed away and sat on the bed she breathed again. "I wonder if you might give me a few moments to change?"

He nodded. "I will send Emily to you."

"No need. I can manage this dress myself if you will release the hook at the top." Standing, she pointed to the hook at the back of her gown.

He closed the distance until the heat of him permeated her clothes and warmed her back, buttocks, and legs. She pointed again over her shoulder. "It's just there."

"I see." Light calluses brushed against her shoulder at the edge of the fabric and traced a path across her back. He rubbed her spine with his thumb before pushing her hair aside. His lips touched her neck where it met her shoulders.

"Tom?"

"Is that 'Tom, stop' or 'Tom, that is quite nice'?"

She had to swallow to clear the tightness in her throat. "I hardly know."

With a low chuckle, he unhooked her gown and stepped back. "Honesty is always best and I thank you for it. I will wait in the hallway until you have changed."

The moment he shut the door she was at once sorry for his loss and grateful to relax. It seemed like a lifetime since she had a proper bath. She stripped off the gown and washed at the basin. Perhaps she could have a real bath at Kerburghe. That would be wonderful. In the meantime, the soap and water would be a treat after a full day on the road. Once dry, she pulled her nightgown over her head and went to the door.

Her heart pounded. No man had ever seen her in her nightgown. Even her father had not seen her in such a state of undress in ten years. Cracking the door open, she peeked out.

Thomas leaned against the wall, one knee bent with the bottom of his booted foot on the wall. A bit of dark red hair shone through the open tie on his blouse. The cuffs were rolled up, exposing muscular forearms and tanned skin. It was no wonder the mothers of the ton made a fuss over him and were desperate to attach him to their daughters. He looked at his watch and then put it back in his pocket before seeing her at the door.

"You may come back in now."

A slow smile spread across his face. He pushed off the wall and crossed the hall.

Dory backed away from the door, crossing her arms over her chest. Rather than gawk at him while he undressed, she went to her trunk and retrieved her hairbrush. Once seated at the table, she pulled pins from her hair until it fell in tangles down her back. Sleeping in the carriage had made a mess of it. There was no help for it, so she pulled the brush through, bearing the pain of pulling through knots.

His hand covered hers and removed the brush before clasping her hand.

Looking into his deep blue eyes, she lost her breath. "Is something wrong?"

He'd tugged his blouse from his breeches and removed his boots. Shaking his head, he led her to the bed.

Her heart was about to pound out of her chest. Should she scold him and pull away?

He sat and she did too, facing him. He ran his finger along her jaw. Then he held her shoulders and turned her so that her back was to him. With utmost care, he pulled the brush through her hair from root to tip. When he encountered a snag, he eased the brush better than any lady's maid.

Heart steady and breathing back to normal, she relaxed and enjoyed the process of his pampering. "However did you learn to do this?"

The brush stilled. His breath was warm on her ear. "This is the first time I have ever done such a thing. Am I adequate to the task?"

Warmth infused her cheeks. "It's lovely, Tom."

He resumed brushing in long, smooth strokes. "I love to hear my name on your lips. I hope you do not mind my saying so."

Goosebumps prickled her skin. "I think if we are to be married you must say what you think and not worry as much about my sensibilities being offended."

The brushing stopped, his arm wrapped around her waist, and he hauled her back against him. "I think that is where you are wrong, Dory. Your sensibilities, feelings, wants, and needs should be at the forefront of my worries. You have made this arrangement to escape a perilous marriage, but you will be my wife and I want you to be happy."

Everywhere his body touched hers sparked with fire. She wanted more of him, more of this. Leaning her head back against his shoulder, she breathed him in. "I would like to make you happy as well if that is possible."

"Of course, it is." He kissed her temple.

"Maybe." The derisive way her mother always looked at her father clouded the moment.

"Will you tell me what you want from your life or is that too personal a question?"

"I am sitting in your lap, at an inn, in the middle of the night. What could be more personal?"

"Tell me then, Dory."

Her name came out of his mouth on a breath. She wished

she could bottle the sound. "I want to compose music and play."

"To what end?"

"What do you mean?" She turned and met his gaze.

"Do you play just for the joy of the music or do you have loftier goals?"

"You are teasing me." Anger roiled in her gut.

"No. You must have some dreams about where your music might take you."

"Take me? I am a woman living under his majesty's rule. Where can it take me? I play for the love of music—any other goal would be fantasy."

"Put the restrictions of society aside and tell me your wildest dream."

In all her life, she had never voiced the desire he asked for. She had never told her closest friends or family what her heart yearned for. "You will think me a fool."

"Never."

She breathed as if she'd run around the building a few times. "If I could have anything, I would play an original piece for the king and the academy of music. They would see me as a musician and not a woman for one hour in time."

He smiled and passion filled his eyes. "Now that is a wonderful goal."

"It's a foolish dream."

He shrugged. "Maybe, but I adore that you shared it with me."

"You are the only person I have ever told. It's a ridiculous idea."

Eyes closed, he took in several long breaths. When he looked at her again, fire burned in him. "Not ridiculous at all. I am honored to be in your confidence."

Her heart expanded so far that it ached inside her,

pounding against her breast. "I suppose we should sleep if we are to travel again in the morning."

Thomas watched and waited for her to say more. When she didn't, he rose, placed her brush on the table, and turned out the lantern. Only the moon shining in the window gave any light.

Dory braided her hair and climbed under the blanket. Careful not to look at him, she faced the wall and tried to breathe normally. She must be crazy to have imagined she would have more time to get use to the idea of a man in her bed. They were eloping. Of course, he wanted to take advantage of his rights as her husband.

The bed dipped and she gripped the edge to keep from rolling closer to him.

"Dory?" His whisper hung in the darkness.

"Yes, Tom?"

"I wonder if you would permit me to hold you."

She rolled over.

He sat on the edge of the bed in only his blouse, which hung to mid-thigh. He stared down at the floor, his shoulders slumped. Where was the bold Mr. Wheel who always knew what everyone was thinking and had a witty remark in every situation?

"If you like. I have already told you I will give myself to you." Her voice shook along with the rest of her.

His eyes filled with so much emotion she had to hold back tears. "I know, and it is a very generous offer, but I think it best to save that particular honor for after we are married."

"You don't want me? Then why are you doing all of this?"

Leaning over her with a hand on either side of her, his mouth was an inch from hers. Their breaths mingled. "I have never wanted anything as much as I want you, Dory. Make no mistake. But should you change your mind before we reach

Kerburghe and can arrange a marriage, I will not take what is not rightfully mine. I also hope that by that time you will offer with more enthusiasm and less obligation."

"It is the only thing I have to compensate you, Tom. I know this marriage and scandal is not what you want." Heart pounding from his nearness, she struggled to get the words out before having to gasp in another breath.

He shook his head looking away. When he refocused on her, a ferocity lingered in his eyes. "If I might just hold you until you sleep, I would be very pleased."

Her breath shuttered despite her resolve to be brave. "Of course."

He stared at her, as if attempting to read her thoughts.

As soon as he lifted his arms, she rolled toward the wall.

The bed dipped and rocked until he was under the covers.

When he touched her hip, she flinched.

"I do not suppose promising you I will not ravage you would put you at ease and make you relax." Tom wrapped his hand around until his palm lay flat against her abdomen then he drew her back to him.

"No, but I appreciate the thought." This entire scheme was a mistake. She should have stayed at home. Oh, but then, she'd be attending her engagement party in two days. There was no good resolution for her.

His chest was hard and warm and her back fitted against him like they had been designed to match. With his hand around her waist and her head resting on his other arm, he curled his legs in behind hers aligning their bodies.

Trying to relax only made her stiffer and her muscles shook from strain.

"If you trust me just a little, I promise you will be more comfortable." His whisper tickled the back of her neck and ear.

A trill of energy shot through her and settled between her

legs. Was this the excitement Elinor had told her about? She settled into his warm embrace. If he broke his promise, then she would deal with the consequences. "May I ask you something?"

"Anything."

"My mother once told me that my father behaved as he does because men cannot help themselves. I knew it was not true because my brother would never take a mistress. He adored Emma too much. But I had always believed at least part of what she said was true. That it was a grave mistake to allow a man liberties as he would lose his sense of propriety. Was Mother wrong about this as well?"

His chest expanded against her back with a deep breath. "Men and women can both be driven by desire. Some men refuse to control their impulses, but that does not mean they are incapable of using good sense, only that they choose not to."

"Then my father could control his behavior if he wished?" Did either of her parents ever tell her the truth? She'd been raised on lies. It was no wonder her brother moved to the country and avoided their parents. Her younger brother rarely came home during his breaks from school, preferring to stay with friends. Only she was subject to a constant strand of lies.

"I am sure he could."

"I see."

His thumb rubbed just under her breast and he kissed her hair. "I am sorry if that is not what you wanted to hear."

"I want the truth. It seems my life has had little of it. If you could always be honest no matter the consequence, I would appreciate that very much, Tom."

"Then you will have it if I may request the same." He squeezed her and placed another kiss behind her ear. "Everything is going to be all right, Dory. I will take good care of you. I promise you will want for nothing."

Letting his pledge flow over her, she relaxed, and his muscles yielded as well.

~

Dory woke with a sense of loneliness she'd never experienced before. Alone in the bed, she sat up searching for Tom but found only an empty room. Perhaps he'd come to his senses and rode off in the night. More likely, he had gone down to see to the carriages and given her time to wash and dress.

Orange hues of daybreak filtered in the window and a chill nipped the air. She forced herself to push away the warmth of the covers and brave the chill, which only worsened from washing with cold water. Pulling on a serviceable day-dress, she brushed out the skirts as best she could. Unable to tie the back, she left it open and found a pair of stockings and boots. She placed her nightclothes and gown in the trunk.

A scratch sounded at the door.

"Emily, is that you?"

Emily opened the door. "Good morning, my lady. I thought you might need help dressing."

"Thank you. I cannot tie the back of this dress properly."

With a deft hand, Emily laced and tied the dress. "Shall I do your hair?"

"If you can just give it a better braiding and pin it up, that would be sufficient."

Emily usually chatted about the goings on in the household while she tended to Dory's hair. Her silence was unusual.

"Is everything all right, Emily? Did you sleep?"

"I am fine. I had a nice clean room for the night. Mr. Wheel's men were housed above the barn but I was here on the top floor."

"Good. I am glad it was acceptable."

Emily tugged Dory's hair affixing the braid to the crown of her head. "Are you all right?"

Understanding dawned on Dory. "Mr. Wheel was a perfect gentleman. You have no need to worry."

Placing the last pin in the coil of hair, Emily let out a long breath. "I am so relieved. I worried about you half the night."

"You may stop, as this was my choice and the alternative is worse by far. Mr. Wheel will be good to me."

With a nod, Emily smiled. "The men are waiting in the yard for you. Shall I have them collect your things?"

The lap harp rested next to her packed trunk. For the first time in years, she hadn't played before bed. She always needed an escape into music to clear her mind enough to sleep. Perhaps it was exhaustion that allowed her to sleep without a distraction, or maybe Thomas was distraction enough. She ran her fingers over the strings releasing a soft vibration. "Yes. They can load my things. I am ready to go."

Mrs. Fine met her at the bottom of the stairs. She handed her a basket. "I have put some bread and cheese in here for you, Madam. I hope you have a safe journey."

"Thank you. That was most kind of you."

Mrs. Fine bobbed and lumbered across the common room and into the kitchen.

Dory stepped into the cool morning, gripping her pelisse for warmth.

As if out of the ether, Tom appeared at her side. He took the basket from her and offered his arm. "It will be a fine day for travel, my lady. The sun just needs a chance to warm things up."

Taking his arm, she let him lead her to the carriage. "I am sure you're right."

"I have taken the liberty of having a warm stone placed in

the carriage. It should keep you comfortable until the temperature improves."

"Thank you, Tom." Would he always think of her needs first? Did her father ever take such fierce care of Margaret? Would Thomas's affections wither with time? She shook herself. It was not affection, only an agreement they had come to. The man had to marry eventually and she needed help. That was all. Though the memory of his arms around her and his breath on her skin would not fade anytime soon.

She climbed in and waited for the men to load the luggage.

Thomas sat across from her. "The servants' carriage has been loaded and we shall be underway in a few moments."

"Do you have a valet?"

"I am a gentleman, Dory. Of course, I have a valet."

"I am sorry. It's just that I have not seen him, and your butler in London is, well, unconventional."

"Porter, my valet, is with Emily in the other carriage and more in line with the ton's description of a servant. I admit, I have little need for him due to my time on the continent. Crowly is an exception." Crowly had served the crown, and when his injuries kept him from continuing in that position he'd needed employment. Thomas felt it was the least he could do, and the slight limp was not a problem in his current capacity as butler to a gentleman.

"Crowly was with you in France?"

The carriage jerked into motion.

"He was a soldier."

"You were not?"

"Not officially, no." He did not meet her gaze.

"If you would prefer not to speak of this..."

"No. It is not that. I rarely speak of those years." He sighed and leaned back against the cushion. "Perhaps that is where we all went wrong."

"Who?"

"Markus, Daniel, Michael and I."

"Where did you go wrong?"

"When we left university, we went to work for the crown but not as soldiers. Soldiering is honorable. What we did holds no honor. We became spies. Each of us had our own specialty."

She'd known her brother worked for the government for several years before settling down with Emma. A spy, Markus—she couldn't imagine it. He was so open. "What was yours?"

"I collected information. Crowly's assignment was to protect me for several missions. He saved my life when he was injured and rendered unfit for duty. With little skill beyond fighting, he had little chance of survival. Training him as my butler was the least I could do."

"I find it hard to believe my brother was a spy."

"But not me." He laughed.

"I hope you are not offended, Tom. There is an air of mystery surrounding you. You laugh often but it does not always touch your eyes. You watch people more closely than is customary. Markus is not like you." She held the windowsill as the carriage veered to the left.

"Markus has his own skills and did his duty to our king, but those are his stories and I will not share them."

"You sound as if you are proud of Markus's accomplishments but not your own."

"I have done things I am not proud of. I cannot speak for my friends, but I wish we had never joined up. That kind of life leaves a mark which cannot be erased."

Her chest tightened. "I am sorry."

He shrugged. "The choice was my own. I must live with it."

"I know it is none of my business, Tom, but I am certain that whatever you did was necessary at the time. You are a good man and I do not believe you could ever engage in odious behavior unless it was with good reason and with no other alternatives."

Staring out the window, he ran his hand through his hair.

Boldly, she crossed to his side of the carriage and wrapped her fingers around his other hand where it rested on his knee.

He looked down at their hands, and then, into her eyes. "I appreciate your confidence."

Why should holding his hand make her heart beat like a drum? It was silly that gazing into his eyes had her aching to repeat the kisses they'd shared. Honesty was what they had agreed on. "Do you think you might like to kiss me now?"

He cupped her cheek in his palm, lowered his head, and captured her lips.

Warm and wet, he made love to her mouth as if it were the most wondrous candy in all of London. She wanted to be that sweet and opened for him, allowing his tongue entry. It was wicked and wonderful and she touched her tongue to his, drawn into the passion. Clutching his jacket, she hauled herself closer to him.

He pressed her back until she came up against the hard side of the carriage with his chest pressed to hers. His hand slid across the side of her breast and her insides tightened with yearning. He nibbled on her bottom lip, kissed her cheek, her eyelids, her nose, and her lips once more. "You are more than I could have ever hoped for, sweetheart."

Everywhere he kissed burned with the brand of his lips. The endearment lodged in her heart, leaving an impression she could not ignore. There was no answer to a compliment of that magnitude.

When he sat up, she did too.

He took her hand and threaded his fingers with hers. Such a small gesture, but so comfortable.

She leaned in to his side and found him warmer than the

heated brick at her feet. "Thank you for saving me. I do not think I really thanked you, Tom."

"Your thanks is beside the point. I am getting a far better bargain than you, sweetheart."

The carriage rumbled along hour after hour. Dory dozed, snacked on the bread, then dozed again. Late in the afternoon they stopped to change horses. Getting out, she breathed in the cool air. It was another inn, but they were only there for the horses. She took a turn around the yard just to stretch her legs.

Thomas ruffled the stable boy's hair. He spoke to the innkeeper. Handed money over to the man at the barn. With each person, he started a rapport and treated them as an equal. He made no fuss over his wealth as her father might have. Of course, Geoffrey Flammel was an earl, but Dory didn't think that would matter to Thomas. Even if he were a duke, he would treat everyone like they too were noble.

She let the footman hand her back into the carriage as the horses were harnessed.

Once Thomas had shaken the stableman's hand, he joined her and they were moving again.

"Tom, are you parents alive?" She knew little about him.

"My father died when I was a young man. My mother remarried and lives in Kent. We can visit her after the wedding if you like."

Oh dear, his mother would reject her. Any mother would reject a girl ensconced in scandal. "I suppose we should pay our respects."

He kissed her fingers. "She will love you."

"Do you have a country house?"

"A small estate in Middlesex. When my mother remarried, I closed the house as it was unused. As a bachelor, I never saw the need and my friends have always been very generous to invite me when I need to get out of town for some fresh air. I have great plans for expansion and farming. I noticed quite a lot that needs doing in the area last time I toured the grounds. I hope to help the village quite a bit. Perhaps we can open the house back up. Would you like that?"

"You need not change your life to suit me. I don't want to be a burden. I came to you with no dowry or anything to offer and don't want you to spend your money because of me."

He turned in his seat to face her. "Dory, I would not have agreed to this marriage if I did not want it. I am very fond of you. Even if you did not know it before, which I suspect you did, you must know it by now. I am not sure what to do to make you believe me in this."

"I am fond of you too." Oh lord, why did her voice shake?

"As I have told you before, everything is going to be all right."

She wished she believed him.

They did not stop to rest when the sun went down. Dory curled against Thomas's side and slept.

Chapter Seven

Thomas hated to wake Dory, but they were on the drive at Kerburghe Castle. She fit against him like the piece he'd been missing all his life. He squeezed her shoulder. "Dory, we are arriving in a moment."

She sat up, stretching.

There was something missing as her touch fell away from him. He was in deep trouble.

"The sun is up." She squinted out the window.

With a quick look at his pocket watch, he said, "It is five minutes before eight o'clock."

"Goodness, I slept a long time. You must have been horribly uncomfortable with me crowding you all night."

Telling her how much he loved having her close would not help his situation. She need time to adjust without him crowding or frightening her. "Not at all. I managed a few hours' rest as well."

"Look at that." She gaped at the castle.

It was impressive from a distance. The rundown castle the king had given Michael along with his title was something out of a fairytale, complete with moat and machinations. At least the moat no longer stunk of bile. Michael must have had that cleaned out in the last year.

The Dory of London was always so in control and aloof, it was strange to see her amazed by anything. Actually, the Dory he'd swept away from Southerton's did not resemble the woman he'd watched grow into a stunning young lady. She hesitated more and worried far too much. "You knew it was a castle, did you not?"

"Yes, but this is far grander than I imagined."

"When I was here last year, it was run-down, the moat reeked, and Michael blew up the servants' entrance in the rear."

Her smile set him afire. How she managed to muddle his brain with just a look, he didn't know.

The carriage slowed and crossed the bridge. They went through an arch that had once been the portcullis. It was less foreboding with the gates no longer in service. As they pulled into the yard, the Duke and Duchess of Kerburghe stepped out the front door. Elinor ran down the steps, clapping her hands. Michael had a more reserved approach. He waved and followed his wife.

As soon as the steps were down, Dory flew from the carriage and fell into her friend's embrace. The two women cried.

Thomas stepped down and shook Michael's hand. "I suppose that is happiness?"

"I have only been married a year, but I believe they are quite happy."

"Will I ever understand women?" Thomas didn't know if she was crying for joy at seeing Elinor or if she was just glad to be out of the carriage. His chest tightened at the possibility that she was overjoyed to get away from him.

"No. I don't think so." Michael's grin spoke volumes about his current state of happiness in marriage. "I got your message. Is it improper to say I was somewhat stunned?"

Thomas slapped Michael on the back. "No. I should have written more details. Were you able to do as I requested?"

The women broke from their tearful embrace. Dory curtsied. "I apologize, your grace. Good morning."

"It would be a much finer morning if you would not call me by my title. We have known each other since you were a baby, Dorothea. I hope you will do me the honor of using my Christian name."

She smiled and her shoulders relaxed. "Thank you, Michael."

He smiled at her. "I have the vicar waiting in the chapel as requested."

Dory's smile faded and she bit her lip.

Elinor frowned, shuffling her feet.

A boy with blond hair and long legs ran down the steps.

A wild scream followed him from within the castle.

Carrying a toddler, a woman in a black dress and white cap rushed out the door. "Jimmie Rollins, you come back in here this minute. You haven't finished your meal and your face needs washing."

Jimmie careened into Michael's legs and Michael scooped him up. "I think your nanny is calling you."

He was lanky and a smudge of dirt marred his cheek. "She wants me to eat porridge. I hate porridge."

"That is a problem, but I think if you asked for spoonful of jam for the top, you will find the porridge much more to your liking."

Jimmie's eyes lit up. He lowered his voice, but the whisper was still loud enough for everyone in the yard to hear. "Do you think Mrs. Douglass would let me do that?"

"I am sure it can be arranged. Now, do you think you can act the gentleman and meet my friends?" It was amazing how Michael, a soldier, had fallen into the roles of husband and father. It suited him. He placed Jimmie on his feet. "Jimmie Rollins, this is Lady Dorothea Flammel and Mr. Thomas Wheel. Mr. Wheel and I have been friends since we were younger than you."

Wide-eyed, Jimmie stood straight and offered Thomas his hand. "Mr. Wheel." He bowed to Dory. "My lady."

"It's good to meet you," Thomas said.

With more energy than he could contain, Jimmie shuffled from foot to foot.

Mrs. Douglass stepped down and curtsied.

Elinor made the introductions to both the nanny and Sarah, their three-year-old adopted daughter. Sarah leaned over and reached for Thomas as if they were old friends.

He took her. "Hello, young lady. What are your feelings about the porridge?"

Sarah scrunched up her nose and patted Thomas's cheek. "Play?"

"Perhaps later. Right now, Uncle Thomas has an appointment he cannot miss. Do you think you'd like to play this afternoon?"

A wide grin spread across her face showing off several new teeth. "Play!"

Mrs. Douglass took Sarah back from Thomas. "John went back to sleep, my lady."

"Thank you, Mrs. Douglass. Perhaps you can take Jimmie and Sarah in to break their fast and ask Cook for some of that jam she made the other day. It seems the porridge is somewhat bland."

"Yes, my lady." Frowning all the way, Mrs. Douglass trudged up the wide stone steps with the two children.

The party followed and Michael led them into a parlor to the right of the towering foyer. The furniture was old and faded but everything was clean and orderly compared to Thomas's last visit.

Thomas turned to Elinor. "You are looking well, my lady. Motherhood seems to agree with you."

Several strands of pale blond hair escaped around her flushed face. Elinor beamed. "It has been a wonderful year. We've adopted Jimmie and Sarah. Jimmie is so bright and Sarah is the sweetest child. John was a surprise, as we didn't think we would have any children of our own. It has been quite a year."

"I can only imagine." Thomas had thought Elinor silly when Michael began courting her. She had shown herself to be extraordinary when Michael needed her and again when kidnapped by a dangerous enemy. The new Duke and Duchess of Kerburghe smiled and looked at each other as if all the constellations had aligned. Under normal circumstances, the sight would have been repulsive, but he hoped Dory would look at him that same way. He was sure his fate was sealed even if the lady didn't notice.

Dory put her arm around Elinor. "Are you going to adopt more children?"

Elinor nodded. "I think so. There are so many who need homes. I want to enjoy these three for a little while, though. Jimmie still has nightmares over losing their parents. He wakes up screaming. If Michael or I am away from the house for too long, he panics."

Michael sat next to her and patted her hand. "It will pass. He has come a long way already."

Dashing away a tear, Elinor smiled. "He has."

Dory fiddled with the edge of her bodice.

"Shall we call for tea? Are you hungry or do you want to go directly to the chapel?" Michael held his wife's hand.

Since all of this was at her request, Thomas looked at Dory for a response.

Blushing, she asked, "Do you think there is time to relax before we see the vicar? I would not mind a walk in the garden. It has been a while since I have been out of that carriage."

Thomas couldn't tell if she was sincere or if she was stalling. "I do not know. Michael, what have you heard?"

"Dory's parents have sent runners to Gretna Green to stop you. Even if they make Kerburghe their second stop, they will not arrive for another day or so." Michael looked from Thomas to Dory.

Dory ran a finger over the faded red brocade of the chair. "I cannot imagine they will go to much trouble. Father will be angry but only because his debt will go unpaid. Mother will only be angry that I am disobedient."

Michael opened his mouth, but a quick jab from Elinor and he closed it again.

Thomas looked at his watch. "I suggest you rest and do whatever you need, Dory. I will await you at two o'clock at the chapel."

She gave a nod and rose.

Elinor got up. "I will show you to your room, and then we can take a turn around the garden. I want you to meet John."

Without looking back, the ladies left.

Michael crossed to a desk but sat in one of two chairs in front. "Are you sure about this, Tom?"

Thomas sat opposite him. It was good to have Michael there to share some of his burden. "Do you know Lord Hartly?"

He pulled a face. "Unfortunately."

"I could not let her fall to that fate." He tugged off his jacket and tossed it on the back of the chair.

"But to marry a woman because you want to save her from a miserable marriage to someone else is not a great recipe for a successful marriage. I know she's Markus's sister, but that does not obligate you to save her."

"That is not why."

"Oh, are you fond of her beyond your responsibilities to a childhood friend?"

"I have admired her for some time. She is above my station so I kept my feelings to myself. There was no point in pursuing the daughter of an earl." Thomas hated the truth even as he spoke it.

"Yet you intend to marry her and expose yourself to censure."

Thomas couldn't stand the chair's confinement. He stood and walked to the window. The sun streamed through, warming his face. "She showed up at my door and proposed. I did the right thing and said no. Then I saw that lecherous pig drooling over her and my idea of the right thing changed. Sometimes the right thing is wrong."

Michael nodded. "A lesson every good soldier learns the hard way."

"Yes. I think so."

A maid walked in with a tray of coffee. The bitter scent warmed him. "You're an excellent host."

With a laugh, Michael poured two cups. "I know how you love your coffee and I expected you would not have any yet this morning. If you are going to be married, we need to get you feeling your best and maybe knock some of the road dust off you."

"When that note came from Thomas, I was sure Michael had misread it. I made him read it aloud, no less than ten times, and then read it myself. You really plan to marry Thomas Wheel?" Elinor tucked Dory's hand through her elbow and they walked the garden path.

There was a lovely winding path through a kind of wilderness in back of the house. "It's either this or I must marry the Earl of Hartly and pray every day for his demise."

"Your mother cannot have approved Hartly. She's always been difficult, but she had your best interest at heart." Elinor moved them away from a pile of rubble that looked to be part of the castle, which had collapsed.

"I am not certain Mother had any say, but she jumped on board just the same. Father's debts have put them in a bad position and his unwillingness to change his lifestyle will continue to hurt them. Markus was smart to make a few of his own investments years ago."

"It is unfortunate you do not have the same opportunities."

"Indeed."

Elinor squeezed her arm. "Still, I hate to see you marry this way."

She shrugged. "Mr. Wheel is a nice man and I think he holds me in high regard."

"And you? What do you feel about him?"

The path wound away from the house. It was good to be out of the carriage, but she longed to think of anything other than her impending nuptials. "He is nice, loves music, and most women find him handsome."

"Is that enough?"

"It must be. I cannot go back. Besides, look how thoughtful it was for him to bring me here instead of Gretna Green. I was sure he would rush me up there and marry me before I had time to change my mind."

"I, for one, am thrilled to have you here and be able to attend your wedding even if it is untraditional. Thomas is very accommodating and will be kind to you. I am sure you can be happy with him if you wish."

"Perhaps he hopes I will change my mind and get him out of this mess." Dory forced a laugh.

Stopping in the path, Elinor jerked her to a stop. "First, you realize he is getting the better end of this marriage. You are not only wonderful, but the daughter of an earl. Second, Thomas Wheel is a wealthy and well-respected gentleman. He has no reason to commit to you. He risks his own reputation by doing so. If he did not want to marry you, he would not have agreed or rushed in like a knight in shining armor to rescue you."

It was a fair description. Tom was her hero. So why was she so afraid of the next step? "I do not wish to cause his ruination. He was the only man I could think of when faced with my situation. He always likes to listen to me play. I thought perhaps I had some value in that, at least with him."

"I doubt he is marrying you so he can have more opportunity to listen to the pianoforte. Besides, I understand he can play very well."

"I have not heard him play, but I have seen him watch me. I thought without a dowry, my playing and my body might be trade enough for his protection."

Elinor gaped at her. "Is that how you put it to him?"

"No. Not quite so crude as that, Elinor. This is a strange arrangement, but I had little choice. Who else would take me without any dowry?"

Putting her fists on her hips, Elinor stared Dory down. "You chose him, which says you must like him at least a little. He has always been very kind, even dancing with me when I was ruined and no other men would talk to me. Thomas offered for Sophia when it looked as if Daniel would turn his back on her. He made me save Michael from himself when he'd gone to duel last year. Shall I go on?"

"You and your lists. No. I know he is virtuous. But, Elinor, I am not in love with him. I do not think I can ever love anyone. He is a safe harbor." She pulled her shoulders back.

Elinor raised her eyebrows. "If you say so. I suppose if you are going to marry Mr. Safe Harbor we had better get you inside and dressed for your wedding. I have ordered you a bath."

Her heartbeat sped, but not at the idea of her wedding. The thought of a bath was wondrous. "Yes, a bath. I would love a real bath."

Laughing, Elinor led her back inside through an odd door that was newer than the rest of the castle. They passed the rubble again and walked up several stairs in what must be the servants' area before coming to a long hall and returning to the room made up for Dory's and Thomas's wedding night. She brushed the idea aside at the sight of the deep copper tub steaming in the center of the room. Emily brushed out Dory's pale blue gown.

Elinor left her at the door with a pat on the shoulder and a kiss on her cheek.

❧

A week ago, Thomas had no intention of marrying. Standing at the front of the Kerburghe chapel with Michael and the vicar, he panicked with the idea that Dory would not show up. He had given her time to change her mind. Instead of taking the shortest route to Scotland and marrying in a traditional elopement, he'd taken her to her friend. The last thing he wanted was for her to back out, but he also wanted her to be sure.

He flinched when the door opened.

Michael put his hand on his shoulder. "Steady, Tom."

Dorothea and Elinor stepped inside. Dory's pale blue gown shimmered in the afternoon sun shining through the windows. Her hair rested in curls around her shoulders with much of the soft tresses braided with pearls and tiny white flowers. Her green eyes shone as she met his gaze.

Thomas rushed toward her, passing Elinor, who headed toward the altar.

Dory's eyes widened the closer he got until she looked up at him as if he were the wolf and she the lamb. "I think you are supposed to wait at the front."

"You look beautiful." His heart pounded and excitement boiled inside him.

"Thank you."

Taking her hand, he tried to calm his breathing. "I wanted to tell you that if this is not what you want, we shall seek another answer. Just the fact that you have gone to this extreme might be enough to change your parents' minds. I do not want you to do this if you are not sure."

Her deep breath pushed her breasts up and accentuated the low neckline of the gown. "Do you want me to say I have changed my mind, Tom?"

"No. I want to marry you." He had never wanted anything more.

A hint of a smile pulled at her lips. "Then I think you should offer your arm and walk me up to the vicar."

Heart in his hand, he did just that. Twenty minutes later, they were pronounced man and wife.

Elinor and Michael congratulated them and said they would have Cook prepare a special dinner.

He leaned down and whispered in her ear, "Michael told me of a lovely walk along the river. Will you go with me?"

She nodded.

Hand in hand they exited through a door in the garden wall and walked across a pasture to the river. The water bubbled by and the sun created diamonds in the ripples. "Is there anywhere you would like to go for a honeymoon?"

"I had not thought about it. It would be nice to stay here for a few days, if that would be all right with you. Though, I expect you must have business to get back to. I do not wish to hinder you."

He slid her hand through the crook in his elbow and they strolled along the river. "You do not hinder me, Dory. You are my wife."

"Thank you."

Where the river turned, he stopped and knelt in front of her. "I feel we did this out of order and it should be corrected."

"What are you doing?"

He pulled his mother's ring from his pocket. A diamond surrounded by emeralds, it gleamed in the sun but paled in comparison to Dory. "This is the ring my father gave my mother. She gave it to me a few years ago, in hopes I would find a woman who I wished to share my life with."

"And instead I lured you into a notorious elopement."

"I cannot be lured, Dory. If I was opposed, no amount of pressure would have forced me to marry you. Will you honor me by wearing the ring?" An enormous weight pressed against his chest and his shoulders ached from the strain of waiting for a reply.

"The honor would be mine, but you are too good to me."

He slid the ring on her finger. "Hardly."

"If you do not stand up, I will have to join you on the ground and ruin this dress."

He laughed and stood. "We cannot have that. You are even more stunning in this dress than you are in any other."

"Will you always be so good?"

Leaning down he kissed her lips and brushed her hair back from her shoulder. "I will try."

A gasp escaped her and she wrapped her arms around his shoulders, pulling herself against him.

Everything he could have ever dreamed of was wrapped in his arms and he worshiped her lips with his own. Her sighs and moans thrilled him and his reaction reminded him they were in the woods and she was an innocent. "I think we should return to the house before I ravish you on the ground."

She stepped back. "I am your wife, Tom. Your property."

How he hated that notion. "I will protect you with my life, Dorothea, but you need not subjugate yourself. I like you as you are: strong, talented, and formidable. Please do not feign some simpering twit because you think it is what I want. The woman who brazenly came to a bachelor's townhouse and proposed marriage is the woman I want."

"I do not make the rules." Her eyes narrowed on him.

"Why can we not be in this together? Must it be me conquering you?"

"I have no idea what you want of me." She stepped away her back straight as the tall oak she leaned on.

His temper flared and he cursed himself. "Forgive me. I am not angry at you. Hopefully, with time and trust, you will see me as your partner and not your master. I do not wish to master you, Dory. I do not wish to change anything about you."

Chapter Eight

T en minutes earlier, Emily had gone to bed, leaving Dory to worry about her wedding night. Her wedding night. She couldn't believe she had gone through with it. She was Mrs. Wheel and any moment Thomas would arrive in their bedroom and take her virginity. She shouldn't be nervous. Elinor and Sophia had told her, in great detail, what happened between husband and wife. She should calm herself and do what was right. He had sacrificed his bachelorhood and his reputation to rescue her. Sex was the least she could give in return.

Why did her heart beat as if it wanted out of her chest? Taking up her lap harp, she sat on the chair near the fireplace and plucked the strings. It sounded as stilted as her emotions. She took off the constricting wrap and placed it on the arm of the chair. She closed her eyes and drew her fingertips along the strings.

All her love had poured into her music and she had no more to give.

The harp rewarded her with a gentle vibration that filled

the room with sound. She played Bach's "Sonata in G" and wished she had a full-sized harp to give it all it deserved.

The door opened and she stopped mid-stroke.

"Please do not stop." Thomas entered and closed the door behind him. Still in his clothes from dinner, he was elegant and handsome.

She should have left her wrap on. "I have never played for someone while wearing only my nightdress."

He grinned and sat in the chair opposite her. "I would not think you had."

"I am embarrassed." She swallowed down her fear and met his gaze.

"Finish the piece, Dory. Please. I would love to hear it and I am a great admirer of Bach."

Her expectation was for him to barge in and demand his husbandly rights. His quiet request for her to play for him surprised her. Calming her heartbeat, she focused on the curved neck of the harp. She ran her hand along the wooden shoulder and down the soundboard. With her eyes closed she began the piece from where she had stopped. Her left hand brought depth while her right pulled out the melody.

The music vibrated through her, around her and to the depth of her soul.

She plucked out the last notes and placed her palms against the strings, silencing the harp.

"You are magnificent." Thomas leaned forward with his elbows on his knees. His eyes, the color of the summer sky, shone in the lamplight.

Dory placed the harp on the table. "The piece is wonderful. I am only the interpreter."

"I think you do not know your value in the equation. Will you show me something on the harp?"

She giggled. "You really want to learn to play harp?"

He raised an eyebrow. "I realize it is uncommon for a man to play the harp. I feel secure in that what happens in private with my wife will remain private."

Picturing him behind the feminine instrument amused her more than it should. "What if our secret gets out and all the ton learns that you are learning to play harp?"

"I am secure enough in my masculinity to survive that as well." His smile was warm and alluring.

Shrugging, she pointed to the floor in front of her chair. "Bring that ottoman here."

He did as she commanded.

"Sit and pick up the harp. Place it in your lap so that the soundboard rests against your chest."

Once he sat, she inched forward until her chest pressed to his back.

He stiffened.

Her nightdress scrunched up at her thighs and the pose was more intimate than she intended. Unwilling to back down, she wrapped her arms around his shoulders and took his hands. She placed them near the strings. "You must relax."

"You are not making that easy to do." His muscles eased in spite of his claim.

"Keep your elbows up and your wrists down." She lifted his elbows then pressed down on his wrists.

"Like this?" He did as she instructed.

"That is very good. Now point your knuckles at the corner where the wall meets the ceiling with your thumbs up." His closeness infused her with heat and made it difficult to concentrate on the lesson.

"This is the G and this the B." She plucked the strings, one then the other.

"It has a lovely sound."

She had to catch her breath. Her thighs quivered and she

struggled to think what to tell him next. "When you play, you pull your fingers in to your palm and your thumb covers your first finger." She plucked three strings creating a chord.

He tried it and the sound was successful, though harsh rather than soft and lilting as the harp should be.

"You need to relax your hands, arms, and shoulders." She rubbed his back and shoulders, kneading the tight muscles.

He put the harp on the table. "My dear, Dory, as long as you are pressed to my body as you are now, I shall never relax."

She pushed back sucking in her breath. "Forgive me."

He turned so he faced her with her legs on either side of his. Sliding his hands along her thighs, he gazed into her eyes. "There is nothing to forgive."

"I do not wish to offend you, Tom, but I think I should tell you, I am quite terrified." It was foolish to be so afraid, but her heart lodged in her throat and she worried she might vomit at any moment.

With his hands on her thighs, he gripped her and pulled her forward until she was in his lap with her legs over his. Her most intimate spot pulsed against the ridge in his breeches. "As you just instructed me, you must relax."

"I do not think it is possible." Torn between fear and curiosity, she yearned for more, but the idea was too foreign.

Gripping her bottom with one hand, he ran his knuckles down her face with the other. "I shall practice on the harp."

She forced a smile through her fear. "I will become accustomed to this kind of intimacy with you."

He cupped the back of her head threading his fingers through her hair. "I sincerely hope so, Dory."

"Strange, but I hope so too."

The kiss was no more than a whisper. He rubbed his lips over hers and a moan rumbled in his chest.

Dory's skin hummed with desire as if the kiss was everywhere all at once. He'd kissed her before, but this was different. He wanted something from her beyond the duties of a wife to her husband. This kiss asked for permission, for partnership and for equality of desire. She wanted more from this man who didn't laugh when she'd told him her most sacred dreams. He almost made her believe she could do things a man did, just as he'd taken the first step to play the harp. She pulled his bottom lip between hers.

A long, low moan rumbled up from his chest and vibrated against her mouth. He imitated what she had done but with her top lip.

Her breath and a bit of her soul mingled with his.

His tongue slid inside her mouth.

Warm and exquisite sensations flowed down her body and settled between her legs. She pressed her hips forward hoping for some relief, but the want only increased with the pressure. Gripping him with her legs she pulled him tighter. Like a bolt of lightning, the additional contact shot through her.

Releasing her legs, she pushed back. "You must think me the most terrible wanton."

Holding tight to her back and bottom, he did not let her go far. "I can hardly think at all, sweet Dory."

"Is that wise?"

"Imperative." He kissed her lips, tilting his head so they fit together.

Brimming with excitement, Dory pushed her fears aside.

He slid his hand along her thigh, where the nightgown bunched to her hips.

She shivered with the intimacy, wanting more but not knowing how to ask.

Still farther his fingers traveled along her inner thigh, his thumb finding her most intimate spot.

Gasping with shock and a hunger for more, she rocked forward. The reward was immeasurable.

He slid his fingers along her crease sending jolts of delight through her.

She clutched his shoulders and neck wanting to participate, but being unable to put a plan into action. Instead she bucked against his hand and reveled in the fervor his fingers created.

With one finger, he breached her where nothing ever had before, stretching her with a second finger.

Sounds she had never heard from herself cried from her lips and she stilled against his penetration.

He rubbed his thumb against her bud and her world exploded.

Crashing waves of ecstasy washed over her. She thrust her hips tight to his hand, her body clasping his fingers. More waves ebbed and flowed and he held her through the physical storm.

He cooed in her ear and stroked her back as he kissed her neck. "That was the most beautiful thing I have ever seen."

As her rapture ebbed away, her face burned with embarrassment. "I do not know what you mean."

Him standing with her in his arms forced her to hold on with her legs around his hips. He walked toward the bed. "May I make love to you now, Dory?"

"I thought that was what you were doing."

His grin stirred her desire once again. A second before she'd thought herself spent, but now she longed for more Thomas Wheel.

"That was only a taste." She might have been a china doll, the way he eased her onto the mattress. Beside the bed, he removed his clothes while never taking his gaze from hers.

Naked, he was magnificent. Hard planes and a splattering of red hair. Even his shaft, though terrifying, was glorious.

Boldly, she touched the ripple along his ribs.

His skin quivered under her touch.

Placing her palm on his stomach, she closed her eyes and let his warmth infuse her. She explored his chest and arms, down the side of his torso to his hips and legs. There were scars, too many to count, but she wanted to hear the story of each one. She fingered a puckered mark just above his knee. "How did you get all of these?"

"That was a pistol in the South of France when I was escaping capture."

Her heart hurt. "You were captured?"

Taking her hand, he smiled. "For a short time."

"Will you tell me about it?"

His eyes became distant and lost the warmth she associated with Thomas. "I will tell you, if you want."

"I would like to know you."

He crouched in front of the bed before her. "Then we will spend the next few days getting to know one another." Reaching on either side of her, he gripped the edge of her shift and pulled it up over her breasts.

She lifted her arms and let him undress her. Crossing her arms over her chest like a shield, she wished she was braver. She shivered.

"Are you cold?"

"No."

"Frightened still?"

"Yes." She sounded like an idiot.

"You have nothing to fear, sweet Dory." He went around her and lay back on the bed. "Will you come and lay with me?"

This was the price of her freedom and it was time to pay. However, what they had done in the chair had not felt like payment. He gave her pleasure before taking his own. Her mother said men always took their pleasure. She eased down next to him, exposed and trembling

He rested his palm on her stomach. "You look braced for attack."

Relaxing was not an option. Her muscles quaked with strain. "I am sorry."

"It is my responsibility to make you comfortable. I will do my best." He rested his head on her shoulder, hugged her waist, and crossed his leg over hers.

Trapped, she closed her eyes and braced for the pain that would come. "I think trying to make me comfortable is a futile effort."

He kissed her chin. "Do you know how beautiful you are?"

"My only saving grace, according to my mother, is my good looks."

Popping up on his elbow, he frowned at her. "What do you mean?"

"For the better part of my life it was made clear my purpose was to marry well and better my family's position. I knew it and now I have failed. I did so willfully, of course, but it is failure nonetheless." Years-old pain and disappointment swelled in her chest.

Thomas sat up and pulled his knees up so he leaned on them with his wide back facing her. His muscles bulged along his shoulders. "Dorothea?"

She had no idea why anger rang in his tone. Going over what she had said, she could think of nothing that should have upset him. She hadn't even been speaking of him. Perhaps he didn't wish for her to mention her mother while in bed. That was understandable. She leaned up on her elbows. "Yes."

"Do you mean to tell me that your parents verbalized their intention to use you to better their place within the ton since you were a child?"

When he put it that way, it sounded awful. Still, it was her place, always had been. "I am not a son; therefore, my purpose was to be pretty and accomplished."

"Markus will inherit. What is Adam's use?"

"My younger brother will help Markus, and should anything happen to him, Adam will take his place."

"He is a spare." Fury shook in his oath.

"I do not know what you are so angry about. These are my parents' edicts, not mine. They are not so far off from what society expects of a daughter and a second son." Sitting all the way up, she pulled a pillow in front of her and hugged it.

He faced her. "How did I not know this? I have known your family since Markus and I were ten years old."

"You came in the summer for a few weeks. You were very young and your attentions were on riding, hunting, fishing, and seducing the girls in town. Why should you have noticed?" She had loved it when Markus's friends would come and stay with them. Their presence eased the pressure in the house. Father would cavort with the boys and Mother hid away from the noise of three extra boys in the house. Even at that young age, Dorothea appreciated them leaving her in peace to practice her music or play with the nanny.

"You were only a baby the first time I stayed at the Flammel estate in the country."

"I do not remember the first time. The first year I remember you and the others staying with us, you were twelve and I was five."

"You parents are unbearable, Dory. You deserved a childhood filled with love and affection."

Her heart pounded. "I had a very kind nanny. I am not injured."

"It is a miracle you have become this warm, kind woman. I have no idea how it happened. I want to rage at your mother and father." His knees pressed against hers and he took her hands and kissed each one.

"To what end? They are what they are, Tom. Asking more of them would only bring failure. You have saved me from the fate they designed. Let that be enough."

"Markus never mentioned anything was amiss besides your father's propensity toward multiple mistresses and overspending."

She shrugged. "Because for him that is the most troubling aspect of their behavior."

"Did he know your plight?"

"We have never spoken of it, but I imagine he knew."

Thomas gazed at the wall. "Perhaps I should have spoken to him prior to our marriage. I suppose I might have at least sent a note."

"What if he had disapproved?" Dory inched back toward the head of the bed.

Grabbing her calves, he hauled her forward until their knees touched again. "I am not saying I would have done anything different, Dory. Only that I should have informed my friend of my intentions toward his sister."

His erection drew her attention. She longed to explore his body, but fisted her hands around the pillow instead. "I...I am glad of that."

He followed her gaze. "You are free to touch me, Dory. I am yours as much as you are mine." His eyes branded her with his passion.

Putting the pillow aside gave the heat in her cheeks time to ease. Wanting to be worldly and brave and being so were two different things. She touched the corded muscles along the side of his neck and ran her fingers over his shoulders. His arms bulged and indented like a diamond cut along his flesh. She traced the pattern before continuing to the soft hair smattering his forearm. Long, graceful fingers and strong hands, it was no wonder he was a musician.

His intense gaze captured her.

She slid her hands down along his chest and her thumbs slid over the taut nipples.

He drew a sharp breath.

"How do you stay so fit? I thought all gentlemen were soft and flabby."

His smile lit his sapphire eyes. "I ride and fence to stay fit."

"You look as if you lift trees for a living."

"Sometimes I go to the docks and help load my ships. It keeps me strong and gives me a chance to know the men who work there."

She trailed her fingers down his ribs, each one like a key on the pianoforte. Desire burned inside her and she longed for more of his touches. She swallowed the lump in her throat. "You are a strange man. I have never heard of a gentleman doing manual labor."

"Perhaps more should."

She couldn't argue with that. The men of the ton were often soft and spoiled. "Perhaps."

Without breaking eye contact she let her touch drift to his shaft.

An intensity built in his gaze. It was at once terrifying and powerful.

She didn't know what she'd expected, but the soft skin in contrast to the rigidity of him surprised her. Lightly, she caressed the length of him from tip to base.

His chest rose and fell faster and his Adam's apple bounced up and down.

Her courage bolstered, she took him in her hand and massaged his shaft.

He closed his eyes and groaned low. "Dory, you are amazing, but I cannot take any more of that."

She stilled.

Taking her hand from his rod, he stared into her eyes.

Blood rushed through her pounding heart and every touch of his skin to hers was pure delight.

He leaned forward until he was on his knees and she back on the pillows. His weight pressed her to the mattress and she braced for the pain to come.

With his shaft perched at her opening, he kissed her lips. His hand slid along her thigh, and as he eased to one side, his fingers dipped between her legs.

Intense delight shot through her. Sounds spilled from her lips, but she only knew she wanted more.

He rubbed a circle around between her nether-lips until she bucked against his hand. His fingers stretched her then slid out and teased the bud.

She tried to regain her senses but his fingers drove her to the brink of madness. "Tom."

He pressed her thighs apart, took his fingers away, and placed his shaft at her entrance. "Dory, look at me."

Strain pulled his face taut. His eyes shone with the sun's intensity. She braced herself.

"Sweet, you have to relax. I promise the pain will subside quickly and will never return." He eased forward and pulled back.

Trying to control her breathing, she sucked in a deep breath.

He thrust forward.

Tearing, burning pain shot through her. He'd ripped her in half. Tears streamed down her face.

Thomas didn't move. With his weight supported on his elbow he wiped her cheeks and cooed, "I am sorry. I promise there will never be pain in our bed again. Just this once it is necessary to make you mine."

The agony eased to a dull ache. She wiggled back to remove herself, but he stayed with her. Her treacherous body responded to him despite the dwindling pain. The next time she pulled back, he let her, but the delight forced her hips forward again.

"Are you all right?" His voice was strained and tight.

Amazingly, the pain had gone, leaving behind longing, desire, and pleasure. "I think so."

He slid out to the tip of his shaft and then eased forward again.

Her body clutched at him and she grabbed his shoulders. "That feels good, Tom."

Still straining, he smiled. "For me it is heaven."

Pulling out and thrusting in caused his pelvis to rub her in the most amazing way. Wanting more, she lifted her legs and gripped around his waist. It was just enough and more delight followed. Nothing existed beyond him and her and the bed. Her world collapsed into that small space and the pleasure he delivered. Clinging to him she played counterpoint, her hips to his, until the dam broke and rapture engulfed her.

He stilled, holding her tight. As soon as her body relaxed he pumped into her fast and hard, spilling his seed inside her. His body jerked and took her through another pop of pleasure.

Dory collapsed on the mattress, legs and arms spread with Tom on top of her still intimately linked. She caught her breath. "That was..."

"What?"

"Unexpected."

He burst out laughing and rolled to the side taking her with him until she lay on top of him. "You are amazing, and if I did not know it would hurt you I would wait five minutes and make love to you again."

She tingled at the notion. "Is that possible?"

"Not tonight. You will be too sore." He rolled again and gentled her onto the mattress as if she were the most delicate crystal.

In spite of the pleasure he'd shown her, there was an ache between her legs and exhaustion blanketed her.

The bed dipped as he got up. Maybe to sleep in another room. Wishing she could convince him to stay, but even too tired for that, she closed her eyes.

Warm and wet, she woke to someone bathing her. Thomas had a cloth and he cleaned between her legs and her inner thighs. Nothing could have been sweeter. She wanted to tell him so, but again she dozed.

His arms enveloped her and she snuggled against his hard chest. Whatever he was saying, her brain only processed a low hum and the steady cadence of his breathing.

Chapter Nine

In his entire life, nothing had been as wonderful as waking up with Dorothea in his arms. She slept soundly and the steady rise and fall of her chest was better than any lullaby. He pulled her in closer and she nestled against him.

The sun peeked through the curtains.

Dory stretched long, her legs brushing his, and her arm pushed up along his face. "Good morning."

He caressed her silken skin from just under her breast to the curve of her hip. *Mine.* "Did you sleep well?"

"Mm. Too well. Usually, I wake several times and must play to relax enough to find rest again." She snuggled back against him.

"I glad you slept, but I have to admit I would have loved to hear you play in the middle of the night."

"Shall I play for you now?"

There was something off about her tone. He kissed her shoulder. "Dory, you should always play for yourself. I may reap the benefits, but I would hate to think of you playing simply to entertain."

She rolled to face him. Her hair was a mass of waves, which had come loose of their braid. Those stunning green eyes of hers were wide. "Why would you say such a thing? Everyone wants me to play for them."

He longed to pull her plump bottom lip between his and then kiss every square inch of her luscious body, but he forced it aside because he longed more for her to be happy. He took a deep breath and pushed several stray strands of hair out of her eyes. "The times I have enjoyed you play the most have been when you did not know anyone was listening. You are free with your emotion and it shows in the music. I hope someday you will play thusly when an audience is present."

With unfocused eyes, she stared at someplace on his face below his eyes. She brought her gaze up to meet his. "Elinor has told me something similar."

"I am in good company then."

"Indeed."

Perhaps it was time to change the subject and lighten the mood.

"What would you like to do today? Shall we get up and find something to break our fast, walk in the garden, or would you prefer to stay in bed all day?" He lifted his eyebrows several times.

Her stomach grumbled and she giggled.

He peeked under the sheet toward her complaining belly. He meant to be silly, but her breasts were delectable as was the rest of her naked form. A growl rumbled up from his chest. "I know you are hungry and as a good husband I should whisk you down for whatever the cook has prepared, but I cannot look at your stunning body and be unaffected."

Slipping her hand under the covers, she ran her fingers along his ribs.

Her touch sent his blood rushing to his shaft. Another growl followed.

Continuing her path down his body, she tickled her way to his growing erection. "Perhaps your wife is hungry for more than just food."

"That would make me quite happy."

She gripped him and worked her hand up and down.

When he could take no more of her gentle ministrations, he pulled her hand away and rolled on his back, taking her with him. His rod perched at the entrance to heaven.

Wide-eyed, she stared down at him. "This is...unexpected."

"There are a great many ways we can make love together, Dory. I hope you will find pleasure in many of them and always tell me what you like and most certainly what you do not." Hands on her hips he edged her up until the tip of him entered her. The rest, he left up to her.

She pressed her hands against his chest, closed her eyes, and slid down until he was deep inside her. Her mouth opened on a cry and she lifted her hips and settled again.

Wanting her to find power in their lovemaking and being able to resist the need for a faster pace warred within him. He grasped her hips and quickened the pace.

She leaned forward and a sharp cry filled the room.

His body tightened like a bow pulled back to fire. Slipping his hand between them, he found her bud and rubbed the wet folds.

Her orgasm flowed around him pulling at his own until he erupted.

Gasping, she collapsed on his chest. "My word, Tom. That was wonderful."

Joy that would last a lifetime bubbled inside him. "Yes, it was."

Her stomach growled.

He ran his hand from the rise of her buttocks along her spine and up the supple curves of her shoulder blades. Every inch of her was exquisite and unmarred. His body was as tarnished as the stars in the sky yet she didn't seem bothered by his imperfections. "Shall I ring for our breakfast or would you like to go downstairs?"

She propped her head on her hands where they rested on his chest. "That was not what you were thinking."

"How can you be so sure?"

"You were very far away, and then you asked about my desires."

"You are very astute." He should hide his feelings better. Practiced enough at the game, he could keep the darkness away from his innocent bride. Yet, something rang true in her seeing through his disguise.

"Will you tell me where you went? What were you thinking about?" Dory watched him, her face a mask of concern and curiosity.

He kissed her nose. "I wondered what you thought when you look at my scarred and beaten body."

Cocking her head, she smiled. "Mind you, I have no other male forms to compare yours to, but you look very nice to me."

"You are being kind." His chest burned with years of regret for service he had always accepted.

"No." She touched a puckered scar on his shoulder. "Each one of these wounds shaped you and made you the man you are, Thomas Wheel. It occurs to me that I am an extremely lucky woman to have married you."

"What makes you think so?"

There was just the hint of a smile in her eyes. "What do you want most out of our marriage?"

"To make you happy." The response was immediate.

"There, you see? How could any woman want more than

that? I will never be able to thank you enough for marrying me." She pressed her forehead to his chest and the first cool tear dripped on him.

Keeping one hand around her back, he threaded his other through her hair and forced her to look at him. "You must never thank me for that, Dorothea. I am yours as much as you are mine and believe me when I tell you I have bartered a far better deal than you have. All of England will think I stole myself a treasure and they will be right, even if they are wrong about where your value lies."

"I do not care what anyone thinks. You saved me from a horrible life with a troll of a man. How am I not to be grateful?"

"Because I would not have married you if I did not want you for my own reasons. If I did not care for you, I would have left you to your fate."

She dashed away her tears. "It is a good thing you love music and I can play. At least for my sake."

Sighing, he closed his eyes. "One day you will know your own value, sweetheart."

Her stomach growled so loud he felt the rumble against his own belly. Her eyes widened and her cheeks pinked.

God, she was stunning.

With a laugh, he rolled her to the bed. "I'd better get you fed or you will wither away. Shall I ring for food?"

"Let's go down, if you don't mind."

He sat up with a touch of regret because he wouldn't be able to keep her to himself. "As you wish."

～

The midday sun helped to warm the garden. It was more chaotic than an English garden. Paths wound through the wilderness with no obvious sense. Yet in its madness, there was order and Thomas admired the juxta-position.

Dory's shawl slipped from her shoulder.

He caught the silk and replaced it before taking her hand.

"Thank you."

Children's laughter tinkled in the distance and they walked on toward the sound. They reached a small grassy clearing and found the source.

Jimmie and Sarah played with two other children. They kicked a ball around the grass while the nanny watched and held John in her arms.

"Be mindful of Sarah, Jimmie. She's just a wee one." The nanny called to the oldest Kerburghe child.

Jimmie peered through a wave of chestnut hair and gave her a nod.

Dory dropped his hand and crossed the grass to the nanny and John. "May I hold him?"

"Of course, madam." She passed the bundle of arms and legs over.

Dory sat and took John in her arms. She pressed her lips to his head and closed her eyes as if breathing him in. "There is nothing like the scent of a baby."

"Yer right about that, madam." The nanny grinned.

"What is your name?"

"Gertie."

Thomas strolled over keeping an eye on the boisterous play and Dory at the same time. "You look quite natural with that baby in your arms."

Her eyes lit with delight. "Do you think so?"

"I do." His heart clenched longing to fill his house with babies for her to hug. He'd never seen anyone or anything more beautiful. Everything about Dorothea lured him in and held him captive. If they had not been in the company of the children and Gertie, he would have taken her right there in the soft grass. Would she like adventure in their lovemaking or was their bedroom the only place she would allow him liberties? Not that it was something to complain about, but he longed to make love to her in every room in all of his houses.

"Oh aye, madam. You look stunning holding a bairn. You'll be a fine mother to your own babes in no time." Gertie smiled but kept her gaze on the four children tumbling across the grass.

So caught up in his fantasy of Dory giving him children, he was late noticing her bright red cheeks.

She cooed to John.

If he watched her much longer, he would embarrass himself. He turned to the play. The ball forgotten, all four were going head over heels like little balls of cloth and flesh. "What's the game?" Thomas called across to the children.

Jimmie stood at the far edge of the clearing. A lanky, sturdy fellow, he had eyes much older than his years. "Tumbling and I win."

The other three groaned and ran to stand near Jimmie.

"It's a race then?"

Jimmie cocked his head. "You want to play with us, sir?"

"I have tumbled a time or two in my life. There's no need to look skeptical."

With a shrug of his thin shoulders, Jimmie arranged everyone in a line at one end of the field.

Thomas removed his jacket and cravat and tossed them to the grass before lining up next to the children.

"Too big." Sarah pointed, her lips in a puffy frown.

"Maybe so." Thomas crouched next to her. A quick glance at Dory confirmed her rapt attention.

"Go!"

All four children tumble-salted in drunken lines toward the finish.

Thomas put his head to the ground and pushed off. He came down on his back with a thwack but rolled to his feet.

Feminine laughter trilled toward him.

By the time he reached the opposite end, Jimmie celebrated his victory and Dorothea was gasping for breath. She laughed so hard she held her stomach with one hand and Gertie reached for the baby bouncing in her arms.

Getting up, he brushed off his clothes.

Sarah stared up at him. "See. Too big."

He scooped her into his arms and tickled her tummy. "You think I am too big?"

Wiggling and giggling, Sarah hugged him around the neck. Sunshine and grass mixed and wafted from her, as he'd expect. For the first time in his life, he longed for children of his own.

Gertie called for them to come do their lessons.

Thomas knelt in the grass and placed Sarah on her sturdy little legs. "Learn all there is, little one. I see big things for you."

Her eyes matched the sky but ringed with dark lashes. Chestnut curls stood out in every direction. She patted his cheek and followed it with a wet kiss on the other before toddling toward the nanny.

Thomas's heart clenched. What had Jimmie and Sarah endured before they found a home at Kerburghe? They had lost their parents in a fire, a test of courage for anyone, let alone two children. Dory walked toward him, so he stood.

She bit her bottom lip ready to burst out laughing. "You shall need to practice if you are to compete with that bunch."

Gertie bustled the four children toward the castle door.

Grabbing Dory around the waist, he jerked her tight to his body. "Are you saying I am not a good tumbler? As my wife, you're supposed to root for me."

A joyful bubble of laughter escaped her luscious lips. "I have failed miserably then. I was hoping Sarah would make a run for the win."

He leaned in. "I had the same hope myself."

Laughing together sparked the most dangerous thing inside Thomas. Hope. He married her because he wanted her and couldn't bear to see Hartly touch her. His own feelings had grown with such speed, his head spun. Dare he dream she could ever love him? Warnings rang in his head. He released her. "Shall we collect my clothes and resume our walk?"

An instant of confusion passed over her face before she steeled her expression. "Of course."

~

The curve of the lap harp in his arms was not as unnatural as he'd expected. Sensuous in a way a pianoforte could never be, he liked the feel of it as he practiced the motions Dory had shown him. Unlike the other instruments he'd played, the harp vibrated harmonically from the first stroke. It was not music, but the sound pleased the ear even from his unskilled hands.

"You are doing well." Dory entered from the dressing room. Her chemise and wrap left little hidden.

His body bolted to attention. "I have a good teacher."

"Try the chords I showed you."

He obeyed, producing the chords one by one as she'd shown him the night before. "Do you think you might like to teach music?"

Grabbing the edges of her wrap, she turned toward him. "You mean besides teaching you the harp?"

"You are a very good teacher." He demonstrated several chords together and produced a lovely phrase.

"Are we in need of additional income, Tom?"

He put the harp aside, stood and took her hands. "No. Our financial situation is good. I thought you might enjoy teaching."

"I have never considered the notion. Ladies do not take on a profession, they do not play all day without regard to their duties, and they do not compose concertos when their households require attention."

"Your mother, I presume."

"Yes."

"May I make a suggestion?"

She nodded.

"I propose we have a different kind of life together. I know there are rules that society expects and as part of that society we are obligated to comply, but I am happier when I ignore those mandates."

Hands flat against his chest, she pushed away. "I am not sure what you mean."

Keeping his hands on her hips, he didn't let her go far. "I mean that if you wish to teach music, you should do so. If you take a notion to apply to the Royal Academy, you will have my full support. If I gave a damn about what society thinks, we would not be here in Scotland as husband and wife, sweetheart."

"May I be honest?" She gazed at his chest, his nose and over his shoulder, but not in his eyes.

"Always."

"I have never considered the possibilities beyond playing and writing at home. Of course, occasionally I wonder what if I was a man."

"And, what if you had been born a man? Though I shudder at the idea."

Her cheeks pinked as he'd hoped. "I would be playing for kings and queens."

"Is that what you want?"

"Not really, but do you not think it interesting as a woman I am locked out of certain avenues and as a man I would be locked in to the very same? I doubt that would have made me happy either. I believe I would hate to be commanded to play at the whim of a sovereign."

"A very astute observation. You have an uncanny ability to place yourself in another's shoes, Dory. Most people do not share the ability or the desire."

"Elinor's influence, I imagine. She has always been empathetic and I have always been self-absorbed. I will give your idea some thought, Tom. I enjoy teaching you. Perhaps there is a less selfish path for me and the music."

He kissed her cheek just under her left eye. "What you can do is a gift and no more selfish than the nightingale's song. Your mother has done you a disservice by attaching guilt to the thing that has made you different and special. Perhaps she did so out of an effort to protect you, or maybe she is jealous of your talents. Either way, you are a grown woman and must overcome those backward ideals."

Wide-eyed she stared back at him. He'd expected her to defend her mother, but she didn't agree or disagree. She wrapped her arms around his neck and hugged him. "I think I am a lucky woman to have married you."

His shaft tightened to full alert. He lifted her into his arm and carried her to the bed.

Chapter Ten

Dory sipped her tea while Elinor nattered on about the children's artwork. Not that Dory didn't care about how talented Sarah was, but she was distracted by the half-scolding from Thomas. What an odd man she had married. His views were nothing like the rest of the ton. He cared little for the rules that governed their lives. Though he had turned down her proposal at first, citing the ruin of reputations if they married. She couldn't figure him out and usually people were easy to read.

"Are you listening to a word I am saying?" Elinor tucked a strand of pale blond hair behind her ear. The high-backed chair surrounded her like a throne in her private parlor. The upstairs, which had been converted into a ladies' parlor, was close to the nursery. Elinor had checked in on the children several times since they'd come in for tea.

"I am sorry, Elinor. I was thinking." Placing her cup and saucer on the inlaid wood table, she focused on her friend.

Elinor put her own cup aside. Flouncing back into her chair, she grinned and pinked. "About your husband?"

Desperate Bride

Dory traced the damask rose pattern on the settee cushion. The afternoon sun shone in the window filling the room with light and warmth. "He is very kind, far more so than I had expected."

"You proposed to a man you were not certain would be kind to you?" Elinor stared with wide eyes.

"Do not say I proposed. It makes me sound desperate."

"But you did propose, Dory. And, if you are honest, you were desperate to do so."

"I suppose that's true."

Elinor nodded. "Didn't you think he would be kind?"

"I hoped he would be, but to be honest, anyone would have been better than the curmudgeon my parents had picked." She shuddered at the thought of being married to Hartly.

"Thomas seems quite taken with you, Dory."

"Don't be ridiculous. He is kind and so he saved me. He is making the best of the situation, just as I am."

"Actually, I thought him smitten with you long before you married. He has watched you for some time." Elinor smoothed her skirts and swung her legs.

"It is only the music that interests him. I am not even sure why he married me besides the that he loves to hear me play." She put up the familiar walls that kept her safe her entire life. Dangerously close to exposing herself, the conversation with Elinor rang her warning bells.

"I think he is interested in more than your music." Elinor narrowed her eyes. "If I had to guess, I would say you like him, Dory."

"Of course I like him. He is a nice man and a gentleman. Why wouldn't I like him?" Her heart pounded and a lump formed in her throat. No one would ever hurt her the way her parents had. She had trusted them, loved them, and they had sold her off at the first sign of trouble. Love was not for her.

A.S. Fenichel

"I have known you all our lives and never seen you take to anyone the way you have Thomas. Perhaps you might be in love with him?" Elinor leaned forward with her elbows on her knees.

Love would only lead to disaster. "No. I am not like you, Elinor. It is not possible for me to fall in love. I must be content to have a husband who treats me with kindness and respects my art. More than that is impossible with Thomas Wheel. I do not love him and I never will."

❧

Thomas had only intended to pop in on the ladies and tell his wife he was going for a ride with Michael and would see her at dinner. The nature of their conversation had halted his progress. He should have announced his presence, but found himself rooted to the space just outside the door of the parlor eavesdropping like a spy. That was what he was or, at least, what he had been.

"I do not love him and I never will."

Her conversation echoed against his heart and twisted until the pain was unbearable.

He walked away. Had anything ever hurt more than knowing Dory would never love him? He could remember a dozen war wounds, which were mere scratches compared to the pain tearing at him. What had he expected? His marriage came about for reasons having nothing to do with romance. She needed an escape and he loved to hear her play. They each had an agenda in which love was irrelevant. Still, hearing her say it burned like an iron poker just out of the flame.

He stormed through the house, out the front door, and to the barn.

"What in the hell is wrong with you?" Michael tightened his saddle.

The gray stomped and blew out his nose.

"Nothing is wrong. Why would you ask?" Thomas took the reins from the groom who led a chestnut mare out of the stone building.

Michael mounted. "You have the look of a man about to gut someone. Did something happen in the last thirty minutes I should know about?"

"No. At least not anything I was not prepared for. I was acting the fool and now I see the light. I will not make the same mistake again." He adjusted the stirrups and tightened the saddle. Giving the horse a pat along her neck soothed both the beast and his own pounding heart. There was something calming about horses.

"Care to elaborate?"

Mounting, Thomas gazed across the field to the north. The harvest was done and the ground lay dormant for spring planting. "I overheard our wives talking and learned more than I bargained for."

Michael shook his head and nudged his horse away from the stable. "Eavesdropping is a bad habit and one you should endeavor to break if you do not intend to work for his majesty in the future."

"I know, but I had hoped to gain insight into my wife. She is difficult to read. Always so guarded." He followed, walking his horse along a path that circled to the west of the field.

"And what you learned put that scowl on your face?"

"She does not love me nor will she ever. I was a fool to expect anything different. Ours was never a love match. She needed help and being smitten by her charms and talent I complied. In the last few days I thought we had developed a mutual affection, but I was mistaken." He shrugged and urged his mount into a trot.

Michael pulled alongside. "Perhaps it was just more of her guardedness, Tom. Do not give up hope. She seems to like you. Elinor describes Dorothea as cynical and damaged. Her parents are both selfish nightmares who think of nothing but themselves. Going off to school saved Markus. You know that. He had us to protect him. You must remember how different he was whenever forced to spend time with his mother and father. It would take weeks to bring him back from their influence. I pity Dorothea with no means of escape for all those years."

"More reason for me to keep my emotions in check. She might not be capable of reciprocation." The idea broke his heart but it didn't make it less true. It didn't change what he'd heard in that parlor.

"Maybe it means you need to use more patience and caring. She has had little affection in her life, Tom. Elinor is the only constant in her life who has not demanded and destroyed. I would imagine her faith in people is tentative at best." They trotted along the path between the field and a small stand of trees.

"So, you suggest I risk my heart?"

Michael pulled his horse back to a walk. "That depends."

Slowing down, Thomas turned in the saddle to meet his gaze. "On what?"

"Do you love her?"

The idea pounded in his head like the report of a bullet in a valley. Did he love her? Was it too late to save himself from the pain she could inflict? Her father was selfish and ruthless and her mother cross and bitter. Dory's beauty blinded him to many of those same traits. Yet when she played, her emotions lay her bare to her soul. "There are times when I think I do."

Michael raised an eyebrow. "Either you love her or you do not. One does not love from time to time."

She had injured him with the words not meant for him to hear. Her ability to inflict injury must mean he cared. Not ready to admit more to Michael or himself, he kicked his horse into a gallop.

∽

"I think we should return to London tomorrow, if that will suit you." Thomas interrupted her harp playing.

"Did something happen during your ride with his grace?" His distance since returning from his ride had sent up warning flags in Dory.

"No. It seems a good time to go back and face the music, as it were." He nodded to the harp.

Her gut twisted and her shaking hand vibrated on the strings. She put the harp aside. They had planned to stay in Scotland for another week. Her parents had not come to find her, which wasn't surprising. "If that is what you wish, I have no objection."

He removed his cravat, placed it over the back of the chair near the hearth, and then leaned against the back of the chair. "Our marriage will keep you safe from you parents' plans. I see no reason to delay. The deed is done."

"Fine." Their life as a married couple in Scotland had been so pleasant, she dreaded returning to the realities of London.

"Frankly, I am surprised your parents have not found us here. I would have expected them to come here after Gretna Green. After all, my friendship with his grace is well known." None of the warmth she associated with Thomas lived in his matter-of-fact delivery.

She stood. "I am sure they had better things to do than chase after me."

"So it would seem." His eyes softened for a moment before returning to the hard stare.

"Have I done something to upset you, Tom?" Stepping forward, she touched his hand where it lay on the blue upholstered chair.

As if burned, he pulled back. "Of course not. It's just time to go home. I have a few things to take care of before I come to bed. We will leave at first light. I suggest you try to sleep."

She stared at his back as he retreated from the room. The ache in her chest intensified and she stumbled back into the chair. Reality had finally barreled its way back into her life. She'd been a fool to believe even for an instant it would be any different in her marriage than it was in her father's house. Marriages like what her friends enjoyed were rare. Cool disinterest was more common among the ton. Desperation had led her down the path and now she would make the best of it. She dashed away the tears that had escaped and rang for her maid.

∽

Two days in a carriage with a man bent on not speaking to her was unbearable. The Thomas who smiled with his eyes and touched her at every opportunity was gone. A stoic, soldier-like man sat in his place.

"I don't expect we will receive many invitations. Do you have a busy schedule when we get back to your townhouse?" London loomed in the distance from the carriage window.

"I have a business to run, Dorothea. You may do as you please. Compose and play at will. I have a very fine pianoforte." He closed his eyes and leaned his head back. "You should be able to entertain yourself."

It should have sounded like heaven. Play and compose, wasn't that what she'd always wanted? Thomas Wheel offered her the dream and yet it came across as a prison sentence. Disappointment pushed up from deep in her gut where she had been keeping it in check. "Clearly, you are angry with me."

He opened his mouth.

She held up a hand to stop his lies. "I cannot listen to you lie again, so please spare me the everything-is-fine speech you have been making for the last few days. I do not know what I have done to upset you, so I cannot mend the situation. At some point, if the fancy strikes you, and you wish to tell me, I will listen. Until then, I agree, we should live our individual lives. As I said, it is unlikely we shall receive any callers or invitations beyond our small circle of close friends, so our need to be in each other's company should be limited. I thank you for rescuing me. I will always be grateful for what you have sacrificed."

Staring back wide-eyed, he closed his mouth and gave her a nod before closing his eyes once again.

The carriage turned down London's cobbled streets with slow precision, winding its way until they reached Thomas's townhouse. They entered the foyer and Crowly, the giant of a butler, took her pelisse and gloves. "Thank you."

Thomas offered his arm. "Shall I give you a tour of the property?"

She placed her hand on his forearm. Heat seeped through his clothes and infused her despite his chilly exterior.

He opened the double doors to the right revealing a large ballroom. "I have never given a ball, but the room is nice."

She left his side to stand in the center of the cavernous room. "This is exquisite, Tom."

"I am glad you like it. The house is far too big for me, but I can afford it and I like to aggravate the peerage by having a larger house than many titled men." He led the way out to a long veranda shaded by several willow trees as tall as the house.

Despite their size, the low hanging leaves gave an intimacy to the outdoor space. "I love this."

His lips twitched but the smile never appeared. "I can give you a tour of the gardens later."

She followed him around the house, peering inside three parlors, his study, and a dusty library. He took her down to the kitchens and introduced her to more of the staff. She arranged a meeting with the cook and housekeeper later in the day. "How many bedrooms do you have here?"

Holding her elbow, he guided her up the steps to the second floor. "There are six besides the master suite, which connects to the lady's chamber. Feel free to take whatever room you prefer."

Her heart pounded and she had to swallow down the lump in her throat. "Is the lady's chamber in use?"

Opening a door, he revealed a feminine room with cream walls and a pastel rug. It was clean and her trunk already placed near the wardrobe. "No, but I want you to do as you please and not feel hemmed in by society's rules. You should hire any staff you feel necessary. I am sure I do not have the appropriate staff for a lady in the house."

"I do not wish to be a burden to you." She ran her hand along the lace of the bedspread.

"It is no burden. My room is through there. You are not required to enter, but you are welcome." The cordial invitation paired with his cold stare and clipped tone held no allure.

Why had he changed from the man who had made love to her and wanted to play the harp? She opened the door to his room. In stark contrast to her bedroom, his had hard surfaces and masculine colors of autumn. It was like stepping from spring into fall to walk between the two. Perhaps it was a testament to how different they were. A door to separate what should never have come together.

He stayed in the doorway. "Take a parlor for your own and decorate it as you see fit. Actually, you may redecorate anything you like. The house is as I found it. I have no eye for such things and it suited my needs."

Vanilla and spice, along with a scent she couldn't place, filled her senses. She touched his bedding and slid her fingers across until she reached his pillow. Sorrow swamped her and she pulled her hand away. "I did not see the music room."

A slow smile lit his face. "I saved the best for last."

It was the first time she had seen him smile in days and the effect shot through her as if he'd caressed her from head to toe.

Returning downstairs, she followed him down the main hall to the back end of the house.

He pushed open the doors, revealing a long room with the most stunning pianoforte as the centerpiece. A harpsichord filled the back corner and scattered around the room were violins, violas, a cello and several other beautiful instruments. To the right of the door was a harp carved with Greek figures. It gleamed in the light filtering through the curtains.

She ran her hand along the curved wood.

"A wedding gift." He shrugged.

"It's beautiful. Thank you, Tom." She hugged him. It was an impulse of the moment.

His arms wrapped around her and for a moment he was himself again. Then he stiffened and dropped his hands to his sides. "No one will disturb you here. I have a small writing desk where I piddle with composing. If you do not mind sharing, feel free to use it in that capacity. Of course, my compositions are nothing compared to yours, but I enjoy the process."

"I am thrilled to have a place to play and write." Her voice was so small, she didn't recognize herself.

"I have work to tend to. Should you require anything, just let one of the staff know. They have orders to get you whatever you need." He left the music room as if it was on fire.

With a sigh, Dory went to the pianoforte and sat. She ran her fingers down the keys letting them caress her fingertips. Sitting up straight, she ran through several exercises to loosen her fingers. She let all the fear and sorrow of the last few days pour into her playing. Tears dampened her cheeks, but she played on.

Losing track of time while playing happened all the time. Eyes closed, she let the music flow from her. When the door opened, delight surged through her. Perhaps Tom liked the music enough to return.

She opened her eyes.

Anthony Braighton smiled from the other side of the instrument.

Disappointment sank like bad eggs in her belly. She rose and curtsied. "Mr. Braighton."

His dark hair fell over his forehead as he bent his lean tall body into a bow. "Mrs. Wheel."

Confused and curious about his arrival, she pointed to the chair a few feet away. "Have you come to call on me?

"I would claim it, but my purpose was to see your husband. He stepped out and I was waiting for him. I confess the music drew me down the hall. I am sorry to intrude." His American accent made every word harder but reminded her of his sister, Sophia.

"Tom went out?" He hadn't even bothered to let her know he was leaving.

Fiddling with the lace on the red velvet pillow, he clutched it then put it aside. "The butler said he would return momentarily."

Everything about Anthony Braighton made her like him

almost as much as his sister. He was open and everything he thought produced a corresponding expression. He could hide nothing, not even his nerves over being alone with her. "How are you enjoying London?

A wide grin spread across his handsome face. His olive skin bloomed with a slight blush. "There is always a distraction here. I like it very well."

"Will you stay or return to America?" She pressed the fingers of her left hand to the keys, tapping out a light tune.

Glancing at her fingers, he said. "I hope to stay. I have enlisted a partner to run things in Philadelphia. Strange as it may sound, I miss my family when I am away."

She stilled her hand. "Why should that be strange?"

With a stiff back, his glance darted to the high ceiling before returning to her. "Men are supposed to be strong and not care about sentimentality. Still, I find that after a few weeks without seeing my mother or my sister a malaise sets in over my heart. You probably think I am a fool."

No one missed her from day to day. It must be wonderful to have that kind of family connection. "I think that is the nicest thing I have ever heard. You are lucky to have such a family."

His blush deepened but he shook his head and grinned at her. "When I am not longing for my sister's company, I generally want to wring her neck."

Dory burst out laughing. "Do not say anything bad about your sister. She is one of my closest friends."

"Then you know how stubborn she is."

It was not a secret that once Sophia set her mind to something, it was impossible to sway her decision. "She has a firm idea of what she wants."

"Well put." Anthony laughed and slapped the arm of the chair.

"You two look to be having a fine time." Tom strode in, his

face a mask of indifference but his back stiff and his fist clenched as if he might challenge someone to a fight.

Anthony jumped to his feet. "I was waiting for your return and Mrs. Wheel was kind enough to keep me company."

Tom glared from one to the other.

Was it jealousy burning in his eyes? Impossible.

"What do you want, Braighton?"

Either indifferent to Tom's attitude or uncaring, Anthony's expression blossomed with excitement. "I have a business offer for you, Wheel. I think it will be good for both of us."

"You had better come to my study, then, and tell me all about it." Tom followed Anthony out the door looking back once at the threshold.

Heart beating twice the speed of a metronome, Dory poked at the keys until her breathing steadied and she pushed away everything but the music.

Chapter Eleven

Once Tom heard Anthony out and showed him to the door, Tom returned to the music room. In the hallway, he leaned against the wall listening to her despair. Obviously, being married to him brought her nothing but sorrow, but the deed was done. All he could do was give her what she wanted and hope they'd tolerate each other. His heart broke with every minor note weeping from the instrument.

By the second bridge, he couldn't stand it any longer. Shaking his head to clear away the sorrow, he strode down the hall toward his study. The music followed him.

Papers, letters, and contracts overtook his desk. In his absence, his secretary had organized the piles of paperwork for Thomas to go through. With a sigh, he sat and started with the letters.

Crowly appeared in the doorway. "Sir?"

"Yes, what is it?"

Silver tray in hand, Crowly crossed the room. "These messages arrived for you while you were on your honeymoon, sir."

Three notes lay on the tray. The first was an invitation to a dinner party at the Earl of Marlton's townhouse. Dory was correct about one thing. They were likely to only receive invitations from their closest friends. However, when one had friends in high places, things could turn around.

The other two notes both had Dory's family seal.

"When did these arrive?"

"The thick one came three days ago, the others just this morning."

"Crowly, would you ask my wife to join me? You will find her in the music room."

"Yes, sir. I can hear that." He lumbered out of the room.

Thomas placed the notes on the desk in front of him. One was twice as fat as the other.

The music stopped. It was both a pity and a relief. Perhaps one day she would play something less sorrowful.

Soft footsteps sounded down the hall, and then the door to his study opened. Dory stepped inside. "You wanted to see me?"

"We have an invitation to Marlton's for dinner tomorrow night."

Dory sat across from him in one of two chairs facing his desk. "Leave it to Sophia to make sure we are not ignored."

"We are lucky to have such good friends. Would you like to attend?" He loved the way her hair fell in ringlets around her face and neck. Just looking at her made his heart pound faster.

"Of course. She is throwing the party for our benefit. We must attend." Her gaze bore into him as if daring him to disagree.

"I will write directly and accept the invitation."

"Was there anything else?"

Did he see hope in her eyes? It must be the lighting. "We have two other messages and both carry your family seal."

She gripped her hands in her lap. "What do they say?"

"I have not opened them, Dory. I thought you might prefer to read them." He passed them across the desk.

She took them and read the address on the envelope. "They are addressed to you, Tom."

"I noticed."

"Why would you hold them over for me?"

Thomas wished she could see what he saw when he looked at her. Maybe that was the key to fixing what lacked in their marriage. Standing, he hoped for something brilliant to come to him before he rounded his desk and sat in the chair next to her. "I know I am not what you wanted, Dory. However, I would like for us to find contentment with our situation. I like you. You are an intelligent and sensitive woman. I saved the letters for you because you are my equal and will be treated as such. If my family wrote to you under these circumstances, I hope you would act in a similar fashion."

"You are a strange man, Tom."

He laughed. "And you mean that in the kindest sense."

A smile lit her eyes. "Which one shall I open first?"

"Crowly tells me the fatter of the two came three days ago, and the other this morning. Perhaps it's best to start with the first. I suspect it will be the worst of the two." He leaned back.

With shaking hands, she broke the seal and opened the letter. Tears filled her eyes but did not fall. After a moment, she turned the page, and then looked at the second sheet of scribble. With a sigh, she closed her eyes. "Shall I give you the short version or would you like to read it yourself?"

"You can just tell me what it says." He braced for a scathing put down from her father.

"My father says I am dead to him and you are a scoundrel. No gentleman would have done what you did. He claims you have stolen his property and ruined him and my mother. It goes on and on and he uses language I have never heard before. His English is not very good, but you should probably read it yourself. There is mention of money in more than one place." She handed him the pages.

Tom folded them. He didn't give a damn about the earl's feelings. Dory's eyes had filled with hurt and that he cared about. "What of the other one?"

With a sigh, she broke the other seal. "It is from my mother. She would like to call when we return."

"Is that a good sign or bad?"

"It is hard to say. At least I am not dead to her. Father was probably drunk when he wrote the letter. I can tell by his scribble he was less than sober."

"Will you respond to your mother?"

She nodded and folded the letter. "If you do not object, I will tell her we are at home and look forward to seeing her."

"I do not object at all."

"Thank you." She stood.

He rose and stepped closer. "Dory, I hope you know that this is your home and you may do as you please here. I am not your master. We are in this together."

"That is very kind of you."

Longing for the warm woman he'd had in Scotland would not bring her back. "If you would not mind, I would like to discuss one other thing with you."

With a nod, she sat again. "What is it?"

"You and I both know your father had planned to pay off a debt by marrying you to Hartly. I feel obligated to offer him compensation. He indicates our actions damaged your family monetarily. That does not sit well with me."

Her eyes narrowed. Every muscle in her body was tight and ready to snap with the least bit of provocation. "No. He has squandered his money and wanted to use me as a pawn in his game. I would not like it if you paid his way. He will only do the same thing again."

"I see." He understood her anger at her father's selfish motivations. "I will give it more thought."

Her breath was fast and hard, lifting her breasts in the most tantalizing way. She might never love him, but he could not deny his attraction to her. Her conversation with Elinor rolled around in his head and cooled his desires.

She stood. "If there is nothing else, I will respond to my mother, and then speak to the cook."

Rising with her, he pushed away the wild need to wrap her in his arms. "As you wish."

She spun on her heels and strode from his study.

Collapsing back into the seat, he rubbed his face. How was he going to make this work? She was a puzzle, and he had to figure her out before they fell apart. Even knowing she would never have tender feelings for him, he still longed to make her happy. He'd vowed to do as much.

~

Late that afternoon, he was still wading through the work left on his desk when Crowly announced the arrival of Lord and Lady Castlereagh.

"Show them into the formal parlor. I shall collect my wife and greet them there."

"Yes, sir."

Thomas waited for Crowly to leave, and then waited another few moments for the couple to reach the parlor. He didn't want them to see him searching for Dory. One thing Thomas had always hated was not knowing what would happen next. He prided himself on controlling his surroundings and being prepared for whatever might come. Since eloping, nothing had been in his control.

He knocked on the closed music room door.

"Yes," she called from within.

Pushing the door open, he found her sitting with her head over the small desk. She scribbled notes wildly across the parchment.

Unable to resist, he eased over to her and gazed over her shoulder. A miraculous stanza of notes in B-flat stretched to the next and the next. He heard the music in his head, and though sad, it was also brilliant. "Forgive the interruption. I long to hear you play this beautiful creation more than you can know. However, your parents are here."

She brought her head up. "Already?"

"I suppose they were eager to see you."

"My father is here as well?"

"Yes. It would seem so."

She lay the pen down, covered the ink bottle, stood, and brushed out her pale blue skirts. Patting her hair into place, she licked her lips and swallowed several times.

He took her hand. "It will be all right, Dory. You look lovely."

Her forced smile never made it to her eyes. "Thank you, Tom. You are always here to save me, like a white knight on a charger."

"I am no hero, Dory. But as I told you before, we are in this together."

In the hallway, she stopped several times and he had to nudge her along.

Crowly stood outside the formal parlor and opened the door as they approached.

No turning back now.

Like a warrior, she pulled her shoulders back and tipped her chin up before entering.

He had no right, but pride filled him as it never had for any other person. She faced her fears more boldly than most soldiers. Magnificent.

Geoffrey Flammel leaned against the wall near the fireplace as if he might fall without the extra support. He still wore his morning coat and had his ascot tied in an intricate knot. His nose and cheeks burned bright red and he flexed his fingers and fisted them over and over.

Margaret Flammel sat on the settee with her hands folded in her lap. Her mild expression continued as she regarded her daughter from head to toe. "You look well, Dorothea."

Dory made a curtsy then kissed her mother's cheek. "Thank you, Mother. It was kind of you to call." She turned to her father. "Hello, Father."

Castlereagh grunted and stared at Thomas, who had stayed near the door. He stepped forward and bowed to Margaret. "How do you do, Lady Castlereagh?"

Dory sat next to her mother. "I hope you are well."

"Tolerably so. Your father is under the weather but insisted on calling today. I suggested he remain home, but as you see."

"I do as I please, and the rest of you be damned."

"Can you stay for tea, Mother?"

"That would be very nice."

Thomas held up a hand, stopping Dory from leaving her mother's company. "I will make the necessary arrangements."

"I have heard you tend toward women's work." His lordship wobbled away from the stability of the wall.

"Geoffrey, please sit down before you fall and hurt yourself," Margaret said. She rolled her eyes.

Not offended, Thomas stifled the laugh building. "I think

our definitions of 'women's work' might differ, my lord." Stepping to the door, he instructed Crowly to call for tea.

"Is that why you have a gorilla for a butler? Need someone to do the manly work for you?" Geoffrey's speech slurred and he wobbled on his feet.

"Father, that is enough."

"Not nearly. This man is a thief." He pointed one bony finger at Thomas. "You've married beneath you and to a man known to be a conniving sneak who tore through the underbelly of France. You think him a hero, but he did not stand and fight. He crept around and skulked in dark corners. You cannot imagine what you have aligned yourself with."

Dory stood. "I am not property to be sold or stolen."

Margaret touched Dory's arm. "It is all right, Dory. He is in his cups, and what is done is done. Let him have his say."

Geoffrey stormed across the room with his arm raised. "I am the injured party. I am owed compensation."

Thomas stepped in front of the ladies before the earl could reach them. He wasn't sure what his intentions were with his arm raised to strike, but he would take no chances. Margaret had remained calm, but Dory flinched at her father's approach. That his Dory might have suffered abuse, beyond the emotional he already knew about, filled him with rage. "You will control yourself in my home, my lord, or you will remove yourself. I understand you are distressed. I cannot blame you. It was a shock to find out that Dorothea and I eloped. However, under the circumstances we felt we had little choice."

"I do not give a damn about how you felt. I was about to sign a contract with Lord Hartly. You do not know what you have done. I will be ruined because of you." He stuck his finger out, only an inch from Thomas's nose, and then looked at Dory. "And you have ruined your mother and brother as well. You will leave the entire family destitute rather than do your duty. Your mother raised you to be a hellion. This is your fault, Margaret, never controlling her willfulness."

"I see, Father. Everyone is at fault except you. You are blameless in all of this."

"I..." He stumbled, grasped for the high-backed chair to his left, and missed. Geoffrey hit the floor like a sack of potatoes and lay still.

Crowly entered.

Thomas turned to the ladies. "Tea will arrive in a few minutes. I will put his lordship in the next room on the couch where he will be more comfortable and rejoin you in a moment."

Dory's face blushed bright but she managed a tight smile.

Thomas and Crowly lifted Castlereagh and carried him to the small parlor.

The earl never stirred, but his breathing was even and strong.

Instead of returning, Thomas gave the women a few minutes to talk. He was sure they had much to say and didn't want to intrude too soon. When the maid arrived with the tea, he followed her in. "His lordship is resting comfortably. Those biscuits look delicious."

"Thank you, Mr. Wheel," Margaret said.

He snatched a biscuit from the tray and bowed to his mother-in-law. "As we are family now, I would be honored if you would call me Thomas, or just Wheel if you prefer."

Her lips twitched in a quick and rare smile before settling back into her normal stoic mask. Turning her attention to her tea, she looked over the cup rim at Dory. "I noticed you took your lap harp with you."

"Yes, Mother. If you wish it returned, I will have a footman put it in your carriage."

He hated the way Dory's voice shook and yearned to pull her into his arms and comfort her.

Margaret waved a hand. "No. It is yours. It is not as if your father would ever notice it missing. If you would like any other of your instruments, I shall have them sent over."

A tear slid down Dory's cheek. "My husband has a lovely array of fine instruments. I shall not lack for music."

"That is good to hear. I know how important your music is to you."

They spoke more like acquaintances than mother and daughter.

Markus was a warm, caring friend, but how he became that man was a mystery. It only just occurred to Thomas that all through school, Markus never spoke of his parents, though he often bragged about his sister and brother.

Thomas would do anything to end the misery Dory endured after a lifetime with these people.

Dory placed her teacup on the table. "If it wouldn't be too much trouble, I would like to have my flute and the metronome from the pianoforte."

"I will have them sent over tomorrow." Margaret put her cup down and stood, forcing Thomas and Dory to stand as well.

"You are leaving?" Dory kept her tone level, but a touch of panic hid behind her question.

Smoothing her skirts, Margaret nodded. "I have what I came for. You are well and in good hands. I know your father is angry about his losses, but I am glad you are not married to that old man, even if he would have given you a title. You will do well as Mrs. Wheel."

Thomas said, "I thought you wanted Dorothea married to a peer of the realm? If I would have suited all along, why did you push the marriage to Hartly?"

"Of course I wanted my only daughter to make a good match. That was my duty to her and to my husband. If she had accepted any of the perfectly fine offers she had in the last five years, all would have been well. However, what is done is done and you are a very wealthy man, Mr. Wheel. You are not titled and that is unfortunate, but Dorothea must have gone to great lengths to secure you in marriage and avoid the arrangement with Hartly. My liking the outcome is beside the point. I do not wish to lose my daughter completely. You must do as a son-in-law."

So much of what she said was offensive, he was at a loss for how to respond and remain a gentleman. "I suppose I should thank you, madam, but I find that difficult to do. I am glad for Dory's sake you will remain a part of our lives."

Margaret's lips twitched in half a smile. "An adequate response."

He bowed.

Dory blushed and shifted from foot to foot. "I am sure this is all difficult for you, Mother. I appreciate you coming here and not making a scene."

"I leave the scenes to your father. Wheel, if you will have a footman put his lordship in the carriage, I will take him home to rest."

Thomas bowed. "Do you need me to send a footman along to help you into your home?"

"No. The staff knows how to deal with these situations."

Dory took her mother's hand. "I am glad you came."

Margaret's stare lasted several beats longer than was natural. Perhaps she was steeling her emotions or deciding if more needed saying. "I am as well."

Neither woman was willing or able to force out the words that needed saying.

Thomas backed away on a bow and instructed Crowly to load his lordship as discreetly as possible.

As soon as the front door closed with her parents on the outside, Dory stumbled over to a small stool in the corner of the foyer and sank onto it.

With one look, Thomas cleared the staff from the area. He knelt in front of her. "Whatever else transpired today, Dory, you must see how your mother cares for your wellbeing."

She dashed away several tears. "Yes. I only wish she was loving like Sophia's and Elinor's mothers. I yearn for a conversation with her that leaves me feeling good and happy instead of tired and incomplete."

His heart broke for her, but he pushed away the emotion. "Wanting a person to be different than they are is a waste of your energy. She is who she is and neither you nor anyone else will change her. Wanting what she cannot give only sets your mother up to fail time and time again. It is not fair to her and is detrimental to you. Accept her. What she did here today could not have been easy for her. You and I broke all her precious rules and yet she is happy for you because she believes you are in a better situation than she could provide. Your mother loves you, Dory."

"I suppose, in her way, she does."

A change of subject was in order. "We talked about paying a visit to my mother in the country. Shall we go in a few weeks? Perhaps you might invite your brother Adam to join us there. I imagine he might like it more than a trip home."

She stared into his eyes for a long moment tears brimming her bottom lids. "You are a nice man."

He laughed. "You sound surprised. Was it not you who proposed to me?"

"No. Not surprised as much as—never mind. I think Adam would be happy to spend his break with us. Markus often invites him, but he still grieves for Emma, and with the baby he has enough to deal with."

He wished she would have finished her original sentence. Other than knowing she would never love him, he did not know how she felt. If she could like him, it might be enough. Maybe. His chest was on fire with his own wants and desires. It was too much. "I must get back to work. Will you be all right?"

She stood and he followed to his feet.

Swallowing down whatever else she might have said, she met his gaze. "I am fine. Thank you for your kindness to my parents. I know they are difficult and you were a perfect gentleman, even with Father. I will rest until dinner unless you require me for something."

Required her for something. He ached for her body pressed to his and to bury himself deep inside her softness. "You should rest. I will see you at dinner."

He waited at the bottom of the stairs as she climbed and turned down the hallway out of sight. Another ache tore at his heart.

～

Tom wished he could ease her worry as he watched Dory fuss with the lace on her gown. She would tear the delicate material before the carriage reached the Marlton townhouse.

He covered her hand with his. "Relax. These are our friends."

"Yes. I know. I am being ridiculous." Pulling her hand away, she sighed then smoothed her skirt.

Appearing in public as Mrs. Thomas Wheel could not be easy for her after being Lady Dorothea Flammel all her life.

The carriage pulled to a stop. London evenings were

growing cooler. Thomas waved off the footman and jumped down to offer Dory a hand down.

Thanking him, she took his arm and held her head high as they walked up the stoop.

The dinner party was lively, with more people present than Thomas had anticipated. He stifled a groan as Serena Dowder skipped over to them.

"Mr. Wheel, how wonderful to see you. I suppose I must wish you felicitations on your marriage." She curtsied.

Thomas bowed. "Of course, you know my wife, Dorothea Wheel."

Serena took Dory's arm and pulled her away. "I know we shall be even better friends now that you are married, Mrs. Wheel. It sounds so strange to call you that. It must be odd to hear it."

Daniel crossed the room and shook Thomas's hand. "I am glad you are here. I hope you do not mind that we invited a few people outside our usual crowd."

"I appreciate the invitation, Dan. I was worried we would receive none and Dory would be bored to death with only me for entertainment." They walked into the parlor and Daniel poured him a brandy.

Keeping an eye on Dory, he hated the frown she wore. Whatever the Dowder girl was saying, it was not pleasing.

Dinner was pleasant, though Dory sat at the other end of the long table. It was customary to seat married couples apart. Sophia did not usually adhere to the London dogma, but she was playing it by the book that evening. Probably to ensure no scandal would be attached to Dory and his married debut.

Miles Hallsmith was an amiable fellow and he chatted about his horse breeding operation throughout dinner. Why Sophia had to seat her brother, Anthony, next to Dory, Tom couldn't understand. He thought Sophia was his friend. Her brother was far too good-looking to spend time with Dory, and yet he always seemed to be there, churning up jealousy. Until she proposed to him, Thomas hadn't been jealous since he was a boy.

"Are you all right, Wheel?" Miles asked.

"Yes. Fine. How many foals do you have this year?" Tom turned away from Dory and forced himself not to look back.

Miles grinned. "Seven, and all fine stock. Do you think you might like to take a look?"

"Maybe. I have some other prospects with my land and the Westgrove lands. I need to sort that out before I consider more livestock."

"No rush. I do not want to take them from their mothers just yet anyway. Write me if you wish to make the trip to the country and see them."

"Thank you, Hallsmith. I will in a few months."

The remains of the evening went quickly, even though Dory was whisked away from him at every turn. Even after when they gathered for cake, that silly Serena Dowder pulled her into a corner and the two talked in hushed tones.

Dory stared out the window on the ride home, her expression mild and unreadable.

"Are you all right, Dory?"

"Fine." She sighed.

"What were you and Miss Dowder talking about so intimately?"

"You." She turned on the bench and stared at him. Eyes glowing in the moonlight, she was like a goddess.

"Me? What could Serena Dowder have to say about me?"

"She was wishing us well and saying how she thought it grand that you chose me as she was not certain that you and she would have suited at all. Your affections for her were clearly faint at best."

His gut twisted. "My affections for her? I have no affection for that ninny."

"Her father is wealthy and titled. She has a hefty dowry. You could have done much worse." Dory tugged the lace on her skirt.

"I suppose that is true, but I never had any intention of offering for her. Nor did I make any overtures that might have given the girl the impression I would."

Dory shrugged. "She saw it differently."

"Clearly. But it is irrelevant. I am your husband and that will not change." He meant to reassure her, but his annoyance with Serena Dowder rang in his tone and it came out harsh and cold.

"Indeed." The carriage stopped and she rushed to the door before Thomas could help her down.

Chapter Twelve

D ory played the new piece over again. It was missing
something. Perhaps it was the same thing lacking in her
marriage, yet she had no clue what that could be.

If Tom had married Serena Dowder he would have gained
quite a lot of clout in business. Her father was a Viscount but
since Serena was in her fourth season, a match to a rich
gentleman would have been accepted by society and a good
offer. Lord Dowder had many connections that would have
helped Tom as opposed to the damage marrying Dory had
done. Serena had gone into detail about all the gentlemen of
note who were likely to cut ties with Thomas for stealing Lord
Hartly's fiancée. It didn't matter that it was untrue. The gossips
had run wild with the tale.

If she could make him happy, it would be worth it, but he
was miserable and so was she. They had started out well, but
since leaving Scotland Thomas had grown more distant. With a
sigh, she struck the metronome and counted out the beat before
easing into the first notes.

The music room door opened, but she played on.

Thomas leaned against the pianoforte a look of pure bliss smoothing the worry usually etched on his face. He often hid in corners while she played. She knew he was there, but he chose not to step into the light. It was strange for him to walk in and stand so close.

The last notes trilled from her sonata and she closed her eyes. When she opened them, he was staring at her.

Whatever tenderness lingered in his gaze had disappeared an instant later. "That piece has come along nicely."

"Thank you. It is still not quite right, but there is progress."

He tapped a folded note on the top of the instrument. "We have an invitation to the Fitzwilliam ball."

"Really?"

He passed the invitation to her. "I am as surprised as you. It is rather late in coming. The ball is tonight. Shall I decline?"

"Lady Fitzwilliam is a close acquaintance with my mother. I am sure that is the reason we have not been shunned. It would be a mistake to say no to such a gesture."

"A close acquaintance?"

"Mother does not have friends." A sad fact that made Dory's friends even more precious.

"I will inform my valet we are going out tonight, then."

Before he could take his leave, she touched his hand where it lay on the fine wood. "Will you ever say no to me?"

His eyes widened before he could replace the mild expression he always wore. "Is that what you want?"

"I want the truth. I thought we had agreed to honesty." Her heart pounded as harp strings out of tune.

He cocked his head and took her hand. Leaning, he kissed her fingers. "I have not lied to you."

"No. You have said nothing. We have been in London for weeks and you speak only when there is no other choice. I wanted us to be friends, Tom, but I think you do not want that."

She wanted to say more, to complain that he had not come to her bed or invited her into his.

Without looking her in the eye, he traced a path along her fingers with his thumb. "We are friends, Dory. I am very fond of you. In answer to your question, I will deny you nothing within reason. My vow was to care for you, and I will do so to the best of my ability for as long as we live."

Her breath caught. What could she say?

"I will inform your maid you have need of her." Thomas strode out as if the room were on fire.

The plea that would bring him back to her lodged in her throat, tight with emotions she couldn't sort out.

~

Fitzwilliam's ball always drew a big crowd. It would be good for the ton to see them there. That was why she insisted they attend even with the short notice. Besides, she was sure her mother had gone to some trouble to secure them the invitation.

The announcement of their arrival came with quite a few whispers and many turned heads. Scandal would follow them until someone else provided society with a better story.

Thomas's expression was tight as he led her into the ballroom. They greeted their hosts at the door and endured coolness but not disdain. Not a bad beginning.

At the large fireplace, Thomas stopped but kept her hand threaded through his elbow.

"Why are you angry, Tom?"

His eyes darted around the room. "I have done business with many of the men in this room and made some of them quite a lot of money. I expect to be treated better and I expect my wife to be treated better."

She shrugged. "We broke the rules. You knew this would happen. In fact, you warned me about the eventuality. We are lucky to have been invited."

"Still, it aggravates me."

She stepped in front of him so he would look at her and not at the people still whispering behind their hands. "You do not even like these rule-following sheep. I have heard you say so many times. You despise their rules and their ways. Why should you care if they gossip about you?"

Eyes like steel, he stared at her. "I do not, but I care if they whisper about you."

Her chest tightened. "Your wrath is on my behalf?"

He nodded stiffly.

"Perhaps we should give them something to talk about."

A wicked smile tugged at his lips. She'd missed the expression in the past few weeks. "What did you have in mind, wife?"

The music changed to a waltz. "Dance with me?"

He bowed and offered her his hand.

They floated to the center of the floor. It was early in the evening and only a few couples had danced so far. Placing one hand at the small of her back and giving her the option to take his other, he smiled at her in the way she longed for.

Until then, she hadn't realized just how much she missed his regard. She took his hand, only their gloves separating skin from skin. Still the warmth of him infused her and spread to her toes, soothing everyplace in between.

He moved them around the dance floor with effortless precision. "Have I told you how lovely you look tonight, Dory?"

"Not yet."

"You are the most beautiful woman in the room. I am honored to be in your company."

"We should take up dancing at home." The idea was out of her mouth before she could stop it. Her cheeks heated.

He laughed. "Do you think so?"

She opened the door she might as well step through. "It would be nice to have this moment in private rather than in the company of the entire ton."

"I am surprised to hear you say that."

"Why?"

More couples joined the dance and the floor crowded with them. Thomas expertly maneuvered them around while keeping her safe and untouched by the more brutish dancers. He whirled her several times, leaving her breathless as the arched doors and vaulted ceiling spun by. The music ended before she had her answer.

He leaned in. "Thank you for the dance. I see that Lord and Lady Marlton have arrived. Shall we join them?"

As much as she wanted to see Sophia, she hated his avoidance in telling her why he thought her indifferent to his attention. "Of course."

They circled the room.

Dory stopped short. "Lady Pemberhamble, how lovely to see you. Do you know my husband, Mr. Wheel?"

The notorious gossip opened and closed her mouth several times like a fish out of water. "I have had the pleasure, Mrs. Wheel. Mr. Wheel, how do you do?"

He bowed over her hand. "Delightful to see you again, Lady Pemberhamble."

"How are you enjoying marriage, sir?"

Thomas grasped Dory's hand, pulled it to his lips, and kissed her fingers. "I could not be happier with my choice of bride or our life together."

"I am happy for you. I wish you both joy." It must have pained her to say it, but the public arena gave her only two choices. She either had to be cordial or she had to issue a set down. Clearly, she was unwilling to do the latter.

Dory guessed right. She suspected Thomas's wealth would keep most people in check. At least in public. "Thank you, my lady. Please excuse us. I see Lord and Lady Marlton have arrived."

With a quick curtsy, they stepped away.

Thomas leaned in. "That was quite a show."

"A calculated risk, which paid off. She and her cronies are compelled to be affable, at least in public. What they say in the back halls is not our concern."

"My wife is a clever one. I must keep my eye on you." Standing taller than he had when they first entered the ball, he actually appeared proud of her.

Heart soaring for the small taste of his approval, she greeted Sophia and Daniel.

Sophia's golden eyes narrowed with concern. "How are you, Dory?"

"I am fine. I saw you two days ago. Don't look so tragic."

With great difficulty, Sophia's expression changed to mild pleasure. It was impossible for the countess to keep her feeling from her face, but she was learning the ways of the English gentry and made the effort. "I know, but when I heard you were attending this ball, I worried it was a plot to publicly humiliate you and Tom. I could not bear that."

"It is my suspicion that my mother had a hand in securing our invitation, though I cannot imagine why she would go to the trouble."

Thomas and Daniel stepped away and were deep in discussion.

"How are things with Tom?" Sophia's mild expression slipped.

"We are fine. Nothing has changed. I write and play. He works and sneaks in listening to me play." The pain in her chest tightened.

Anthony joined them. He was in black with a buttery-yellow waistcoat and crisp white cravat. Playing the part of a proper English dandy came easily to him. "I hope I am not intruding, ladies."

"No, Tony. It's good to see you." Sophia kissed his cheek.

"This is quite a crowd. The music is fine, don't you think, Mrs. Wheel?" Watching the dancers, he clapped when the bandleader announced a La Boulangere. "As I cannot dance with my sister, would you do me the honor of this dance, Mrs. Wheel?"

He was too delightful to refuse. "Of course."

Leading her to the dance floor, he nearly came out of his shoes. They found their circle as the dance began. Tall yet light on his feet, Anthony showed more than average enthusiasm for the dance, which was delightful.

Dory had to hold back laughing at his exuberance.

"This is one of my favorites," he said.

Watching him was too much fun. "You dance very well."

Their circle turned and came together until the last strain played out, and he bowed while she made a curtsy.

Anthony offered his arm. "This was the highlight of the evening."

Placing her hand near his elbow, she laughed. "I am certain that is not true, but thank you for the dance. I enjoyed it."

They arrived by their friends as Daniel pulled Sophia out for the next dance.

Tom's frown deepened at Anthony, who bowed and stepped away.

Chin high and eyes focused anywhere but on her, he might have been a statue meant to go with the gilded walls and painted ceilings. "Are you jealous, Tom?"

With a snap of his head, he stared into her eyes. "I should hope not."

"Then why did you scare Mr. Braighton away?"

"Did I?" He crossed his arms and watched the dancers again.

"You know you did. It would be silly to be jealous of that young man. I have no interest and I think he is only being nice. Besides, you shall never have to worry I will betray you. I made my vows and will abide them. I could never hurt you with such a dishonorable act."

The lines around his blue eyes eased and he almost smiled. "Would you like to dance, Dory?"

"That would be nice, but perhaps we should wait a few minutes. We can get some lemonade and make ourselves seen."

"The sight of you in another man's arms did not please me. Not even if it is the brother of our good friend and I know he means no harm."

Looking over her shoulder at him, she expected to see amusement in his eyes, but what she found was much more serious. "To be honest, I am rather happy to hear you say that."

He grabbed her elbow and pushed her to a corner of the ballroom where a small niche offered them privacy. He backed her in and blocked out the sights of the room. Intensity shot from his gaze through her.

Her heart pounded against her chest with both fear and excitement. With no clue whether what she'd said angered him or not, she didn't know how to react.

When he leaned in, it trapped them in a bubble of intimacy. "Dory, we may not have married for love or even for more practical reasons, but make no mistake, I am yours just as you are mine. I would not like to find you in a compromising position and I will not break my marriage vows. Not now. Not ever."

A lump that could turn into tears clogged her throat. She took a deep breath, and then another. She touched his cheek but pulled back. "Tom, I would not blame you if you took a lover. Arrogance on my part, I suppose, but I hoped you would not. A bit of my father in me to think I was alone in commanding your attention."

His whisper struck right to her heart. "You are alone in that."

She was struck dumb. Nothing clever came to her as she dashed away a tear that insisted on escaping. She steeled her expression and met his gaze.

He stepped back and offered his arm as they walked to the refreshment tables.

At half past midnight, the lively music drew them back to the dance floor. If every night could begin and end with him holding her in his arms, she would be blissful.

Voices rumbled through the crowd like a disease spreading evil as it went. The dancers stilled, forcing Dory and Thomas to stop as well.

Lord Hartly, stooped and bitter, trudged through the crush of people. They parted for him as if he were poison, or maybe it was their eagerness to see the scene unfold.

Sanford Wormfield at Hartly's left shoulder wore an amused sneer and fixed his gaze on Dory.

Thomas bowed. "My lord."

Hartly pointed a crooked finger. "You are a thief and a scoundrel. You are no gentleman."

Standing straight and proud, Thomas looked him in the eye. He kept his voice low but firm. "I stole nothing. My wife is not property to be bartered like wool or tobacco. She made her choice. I regret any injury to you."

Hartly blinked several times and licked his thin, cracked lips. "Are you an imbecile?"

Thomas laughed. "I suppose to you it must seem as if I am."

Dory's heart beat so fast she thought she might faint. She

had been a fool to think once she married Tom all of this drama would go away. There was a price and no amount of manipulation from her mother would alter that fact.

"There was to be a contract and you knew it, yet you still took the girl and carried her to Scotland." Hartly continued to point his finger.

"True." Thomas's voice remained calm and even. The crowd leaned in to hear his softly spoken part of the altercation.

Hartly widened his deep-set, bloodshot, pale blue eyes. "You do not deny your injury to me?"

"I need not deny anything, my lord. The situation is what it is. You had not yet signed the contract and Dorothea chose to marry me. That you feel the lash of those facts is unfortunate but hardly my problem."

"You...I...I am an earl!"

"A fact everyone is aware of."

"I will crush you." Hartly shook his fist at Thomas.

Stepping closer, Thomas towered over the aging earl. His eyes were pinpoints of controlled rage. "You may try, my lord."

Hartly put up a hand.

Wormfield stepped forward. "You cannot make a scene here. We will deal with this *gentleman* another way."

If the situation was not bad enough, Dory's father stumbled across the ballroom, red-faced and with his clothes disheveled. Dory was an expert at keeping her feelings masked in public, but her resolve slipped. At the edge of the crowd her mother watched, shaking her head. Their gazes met and Dory recognized the apology in her mother's eyes. She turned away and stepped behind the fleshy form of Lady Drusilla Monkford.

No help would come from that quarter.

Dory took a deep breath and pulled her shoulders back. "Hello, Father. You look unwell. Perhaps you should find a quiet place to sit down."

For a few seconds, he looked at her as if he had no clue who she was or what she had said. "I have nothing to say to you, daughter."

It was a cut direct. Dory kept her chin up. "I understand. Since there is no need for us to speak again, I shall oblige you from this point forward."

Geoffrey's back stiffened but the reaction caused him to teeter, and he grabbed hold of Hartly's shoulder to steady himself.

The crowd remained riveted on the scene.

Hartly's frail frame couldn't support the drunken lord and the two listed to the left.

Wormfield clutched Hartly's arm.

Thomas caught hold of Hartly's other shoulder and grabbed Flammel by his coat, righting them before they hit the floor. The event brought them all close together. "Gentlemen, you are both out of order. Dorothea is my wife now. I understand your dispute, but it is unforgivable that you have created this scene. I shall settle with you in private or not at all." He stared into Hartly's eyes. "If you attempt to harm me, my family, or my business, I assure you, you will pay the price and it will be far higher than an embarrassing few moments in a ballroom. I am not some upstart to be threatened. I advise you to keep that in mind."

Father blinked several times as if the threat did not penetrate his drunken haze.

There was no mistake Hartly understood the threat.

To Dory's surprise, a flash of fear crossed his face.

A guttural noise close to a growl issued from Wormfield, but Tom ignored the thug and kept his focus on Hartly. Stepping back, he raised his voice so the people close to them could hear. "Good of you gentlemen to seek us out. My wife and I appreciate your well-wishes more than you can imagine. I hope to have you both to dinner in the near future."

Daniel reached the musicians and an instant later the music started again. The crush of people backed away and the murmur of gossip dimmed.

Hartly stomped away mumbling something while her father stood dumb staring at them.

Thomas pointed at Margaret, who stood watching near the doorway. "Your wife awaits you, my lord. I think she is ready to retire for the evening."

With a last look at the couple, Lord Castlereagh stumbled away.

Thomas turned to her for the first time since Hartly interrupted their dance. His eyes were wild with passion and danger. Grabbing her around the waist, he pulled her close and kissed her on the lips.

Dory clutched his shoulders to keep her feet. The contact was intense and shot through her like a lightning bolt.

The music changed to a promenade.

Thomas broke the kiss, his eyes closed for a moment before he bowed to her and offered his hand in dance.

A new round of mumbling rushed through the ballroom.

Unable to put a sensible thought together, she accepted his hand and curtsied. The voices faded, leaving only her and Tom moving around the room, as if in a bubble. Even when the dance took her away from him, their gazes never faltered. People would say they were rude, but she imagined that was the least of what they would say of the couple after the scene they'd been the center of.

As the last strain faded he bowed low to her. "Shall we go home?"

She took his offered hand and they eased through the crowd without speaking to anyone. Sophia watched from the refreshment table and Dory gave her a nod as they passed the arched entrance.

Sophia smiled and raised her glass.

Waiting for her pelisse in the foyer might have been the longest wait of her life. She tried to seem oblivious to the gawking from the next room or the people who felt the need to walk past the doorway more than once. It was difficult to keep her mouth shut and her eyes focused on the door.

Thomas leaned in and kissed the top of her head. "Another moment, my dear, and you may breathe. Just hold on."

She'd put on a public facade dozens of times in her life. Still, it made it easier to know he understood and supported her.

When the footman arrived, it took an act of sheer will not to snatch her wrap and run for the door. She allowed him to place the satin and fur over her shoulders, watched as Thomas accepted his hat, waited for the door to open, and for them to make their exit.

The carriage was close, which was a great relief. Thomas called up to the driver to keep his seat and handed her inside himself before joining her in the dark compartment. Instead of sitting across from her, he took the spot on the bench next to her.

Dory didn't know what to say. Her proposal had caused all of this. He must be embarrassed beyond tolerance. She wouldn't blame him if he sent her away to the country at first light.

The carriage rumbled forward, winding its way around the crowded drive until they cleared the party traffic and sped up. The nearly full moon was the only light offered and gave little illumination inside the carriage. Clutching her hands in her lap, she closed her eyes and prayed they would arrive at Thomas's townhouse before he erupted in a fit of rage.

Even when he shifted on the seat, she refused to open her eyes. If she could get to the house she'd be able to hold her emotions in check. Shame and remorse built behind her eyes trying to push out tears, she did not want him to see. She wouldn't have it. The matter of her marriage was no one's business and what was done, was done.

Thomas's long, strong fingers wrapped around her hand and tugged it away from the other. He threaded their fingers together. "Sweetheart, none of that was your fault. You must know that."

Swallowing down the lump in her throat, she turned and focused on his strong silhouette. "This is all my fault. I dragged you into this mess when you were perfectly happy as a bachelor. I knew my father's behavior would damage your reputation and still I enlisted your help. I am sorry, Tom."

He laughed.

It was the last thing she'd expected and she looked at him. "I thought you'd be angry."

Cocking his head let the moon shine on the side of his face like a romantic character from one of those silly novels Elinor loved so much. "I am not thrilled with the behavior of those two gentlemen, but I certainly do not hold you accountable for their bad behavior. You behaved admirably under untenable circumstances this evening. I was very proud of you."

"You are the strangest man."

"Why do you say that?" He rubbed the back of her hand until the tension fled.

"I thought we were getting along well in Scotland. I even hoped we might tolerate each other well as husband and wife. Then you have barely spoken to me since we returned to London. You were a perfect gentleman with my parents, despite their horrendous behavior. You never yell at me, though I know you must want to. You defend me in public, when putting me aside would be in your best interest. I do not know what to make of you, Thomas Wheel." She hadn't meant to let all the things she'd thought over their weeks of marriage tumble out at one time, but she couldn't stop herself.

The carriage pulled to a stop in front of his townhouse. He called it home, but Dory didn't know what that word meant. The houses she'd grown up in were places of great anxiety to be better, perform well, and meet other peoples' expectations. Nothing about living with Thomas was like that. It was all unfamiliar and scary.

He jumped out, pulled down the steps, and handed her down without waiting for a footman.

Dory wished the ride had been just a few moments longer so she could have gotten the response to her statements. As it was, they would climb the steps and he would tell her good-night as he had every night since they arrived in London.

In the foyer, she handed her gloves and wrap to the footman before stepping toward the stairs.

"Mrs. Wheel?" Thomas's use of the formal address drew her attention and stopped her in her tracks.

She took a deep breath ready for whatever might come next. "Yes, Mr. Wheel?"

"I wonder if you would join me in my study for a few moments?"

Heart beating out of her chest, she walked down the short hall to his private space, which she'd entered only when summoned.

He dismissed the staff and followed closely behind. Once inside, he shut the door. "What do you want from this marriage, Dory?

"I beg your pardon?"

"What do you want? Do you want a husband who is constantly solicitous? Do you want a partner in bed? Someone to play counterpoint in the music room? A friend to talk to? A hero to protect you from your father?" He leaned against the door in a relaxed state, but the muscle in his jaw ticked.

Where had this come from? He had said he wasn't upset with her, but clearly that was not true. "I do not know what you are talking about."

He slammed his fist back against the door. "I am trying to be the husband you want. I agreed to this marriage and hoped to be a good husband to you, or at least a good friend, but now I doubt what it is you want from me."

"I want you to do as you please. Whatever the source of your anger, I want you to discuss it with me before it becomes this poison spewed out in years to come when we are bitter and hateful. I do not know what I want from a husband. How can I know?" She rounded the chairs to put some distance between herself and him.

Pushing off the wall brought him to his full height. His eyes flashed and his posture stiffened as he stalked toward her. Only the chair separated them. "I heard you in Scotland. You told her grace that you could never love me. If tolerating me is the best you can do, perhaps a friendship will never be possible."

All the tears she'd been holding back bubbled from her eyes. "That conversation was not meant for your ears."

"But you do not deny saying them."

"No. I said them." What a fool she had been.

"Did you mean them?" He passed her his clean, crisp handkerchief.

She dried her cheeks. "I would never lie to Elinor."

"That is what I thought too."

"We did not marry for love, Tom." Defending herself came easily as the only reasonable course of action.

He crossed his arms over his broad chest. "No. Still, the

question remains. What do you want from me? Because our current situation leaves me unsatisfied."

Of course, that was what this was really about. "I never chased you from my bed."

He was around the chair in a flash, wrapped his arm around her waist and pulled her tight against him. "You chased me from your life, Dory. No one has ever hurt me as much as when I heard you say those words. Knowing they were not for my ears did not matter. I heard them and you hurt me."

"I am sorry." She held his shoulders for balance. "I never wanted to hurt you in any way. I like you and have always admired the friendship you and Sophia share. I hoped you and I could have a similar relationship."

"Impossible." He lowered his head a fraction.

It was as if he had taken hold of her heart and twisted the life out of it. "Why? I know I have made mistakes and have put you in a terrible position, but I would hate to think there is no hope for us."

He placed one finger just under her eye and wiped away a tear before tracing a path along her jaw. "I could never have that kind of camaraderie with you because I have long been in love with you, Dory."

The room closed in on her. His whispered confession vibrated through her soul more loudly than any scream. They sliced her painfully. "I do not know if I am capable of returning such feelings, Tom. I wish I could return the sentiment, but I have never felt such an emotion."

He closed his eyes and dropped his forehead to hers.

Pushing against his chest, she tried to free herself before he could react.

He held on and pressed his lips to her skin. "I think you underestimate yourself, sweetheart. Perhaps you will never return my feelings, but the way you play tells me those emotions simmer inside you with far more intensity than most people experience."

"It is only a trick of the music." Her throat was so tight she had to swallow down the lump. Where his lips touched set her on fire and shot bolts to her most sensitive places.

He kissed her cheek. "No one can fake such passion."

She hummed with desire and lifted her lips up to him.

Chapter Thirteen

Her eyes drilled into him like nothing and no one else. If he gave in and took her to bed, he'd be physically satisfied but no closer to having what he wanted from her. Perhaps he asked too much of her. She had little experience with human passion. Her romance came from music.

She brushed a stray hair from his forehead. "It might be best if I retired to the country. Then I would not risk hurting you further."

Losing her was not an option. Not this soon. Not without one hell of a fight. "Dory, will you play me the piece you have been working on?"

Blinking, she licked her lips. "It is not finished."

The pink of her tongue darting out to wet her lips drove him to distraction. "I know, but it's lovely, and if you wouldn't mind, I would like to hear it."

"I do not usually play a piece in public until it is complete."

"This is not public. Only your husband will be in the room."

She nodded and pushed on his chest.

Letting her go in that moment was one of the hardest things he'd ever done. It went against every instinct to release this extraordinary woman, but he did it, and then followed her out of his study and into the music room. Closing the door, he let the room embrace him. He had only practiced the harp since his marriage and he missed the warmth of the drawing room. He'd brought in several groupings of chairs and couches for comfort and done away with the standard of placing lines of chairs along the walls. Changing the arrangement of the room made it more organic and therefore a more creative venue.

"This is my favorite place in your house." She opened the pianoforte and sat.

"It is our house and I love it in here." Standing beside the instrument, he admired the curve of her shoulder, down strong arms to her tapered fingers, poised on the keys. His heartbeat tripled.

She cocked her head. "You never come in here."

"I wanted you to have total access to the room without my interference. I am never far away though."

"I could never wish to drive you away from your own music, Tom."

He sat beside her on the bench. "May I tell you something?"

"Yes."

"I am fascinated to the point of distraction with the way you play. The sound of it has become an obsession for me."

Her eyes widened before she looked away and dropped her hands to her lap. "Perhaps you should play for me instead."

Not knowing what to say was not a state he found himself in often. "I—you are a far superior musician."

"You will not play?"

Was there anything he wouldn't do for her? It was a small

request. "I rarely play for anyone, sweetheart, but I shall play for you."

She scooted a few inches over so he had more of the bench and better access to the instrument.

Laying his hands on the keys, he played her composition as he had heard it for the past few days. Note after painful note poured from his heart as the sorrow of the melody passed through the air. He dared not look over, afraid she would censure his lack of talent. At the coda, the key changed and he plugged on to a brighter section and through to where she'd left it unfinished. The last note vibrated away leaving them in silence.

Unable to resist, he looked at her. He'd expected her utter mortification but she stared down at the instrument. "Forgive me, Dory. I know I am not up to the task."

"Your play is excellent. You should never apologize for it." Still she didn't gaze at him, only at the keys with the most peculiar look, almost confused, worried, or a mixture of the two.

"Thank you. The piece is extraordinary. I should not have dared play it for the composer."

"I am flattered that you did."

He pivoted toward her. "If I may, you do not look flattered."

She raised her head and met his stare. "Would you mind if we tried something?"

"What?"

Standing, she said, "Play the piece again but in B-flat."

He did as she asked, letting the notes fall in that soulful key.

She sat on his right and added an entirely new melody to the construct. This was light and filled with air, as if breathing life into the sad composition. At the keys their hands came close but never touched.

Every note, tone, and vibration soared through Thomas like

the first time he'd ever heard Beethoven played. It was as if he were discovering music for the first time all over again. Her shoulder pressed to his seared him with warmth just as her composition branded him with love. Sweat poured from his forehead. Tears leaked out and ran down his face as the music drew to a close and all four of their hands stilled.

Half-afraid, he turned to her, and she, too, was crying. No other person had seen him cry since he was a small boy, but somehow this was right. He could not have helped his emotion anyway. "Shall we write this down?"

Her throat bobbed up and down and she pulled his hand into hers. "Do you mind? I know it's late, but realizing this is a duet is a huge breakthrough. I have never written a duet before. Everything I have tried before has been for one musician, just for me. Hearing you play my music, it was as if a lantern lit inside me. Suddenly, the missing pieces fell into place."

He longed to drag her into his arms and carry her up the stairs to his bed. But the music. "Shall I transcribe the original into B-flat?"

"You want to help me? You must be tired."

"I will not sleep for hours anyway. Let me do this, Dory."

They moved to the desk, where she scribbled the new section and he transcribed the old. Side by side just as they had been at the pianoforte they worked. Occasionally, she hummed the tune out and found the missing note. The entire time, his body burned for more of her, more music, more flesh. It had been too long since he'd made love to his wife and the sight of her creating a work of art, along with the memory of being a part of the creation, fed his desires.

Finishing the revision, he put the new pages aside just as the hall clock sounded six bells. The sun would be up soon, though the drawn curtains would let in little light. The candelabra had melted to stubs. Tom walked to the mantle and retrieved another and lit all three wicks before placing it near where she worked.

Her hand flew across the stanzas adding the notes that made up the masterpiece she'd created.

Leaning over her shoulder, he whispered. "Shall I leave you?"

His hand lay on the desk next to her and she covered it with her own. "Stay. I am at the end."

Heart pounding, he sat watching her scribble the last of it.

She put down the pen and stared at the pages strewn across the desk. "Will you make love to me, Tom?"

Had he misheard her? Was he hearing what he longed for since the first time he'd ever seen her? No. It was her voice. Her cheeks colored bright red at having asked such a thing. "I will do anything you want."

Turning, her gaze met his. "I want you."

Tom grabbed the base of her chair and yanked hard until she had to spread her knees to avoid them hitting his. Her full skirt lifted to just above her ankles from the unladylike position and her eyes were wide but with no fear in them. Pushing the fabric above her knees allowed him to lift her off her chair and onto his lap straddling him. "Do you want me to take you to our bed, Dory?"

She swallowed and clutched his shoulders. Only the thin fabric of her chemise and his breeches separated them. "I do not know if I can wait that long."

Cupping her bottom, he pulled her tight against his straining shaft. "As you can feel, I am in no position to argue with you."

She giggled then sobered. "I could not have finished it without you."

"I was honored to be a part of something so special." He

tugged her chemise up and found the silk of her thigh distracting from even the music they'd created.

Her eyes closed as he caressed her from knee to where she spread wide. Wet and warm, he longed to sink inside her and take his pleasure, but that was only half the satisfaction he yearned for. Grazing her sensitive bud elicited a gasp, and as he rubbed she moaned deep and satisfying. His rod jumped, wanting to join the pleasure but being denied at least for the moment.

"Tom." She threw her head back and cried his name over and over again. As her neck arched it exposed her throat and thrust her breasts forward until they strained against the scoop of her gown.

Keeping her seated meant his other hand secured the small of her back, but he licked along the flesh just above the taut fabric.

She cried out and tugged at the bodice until one perfect nipple was exposed.

Tom sucked the tight pebble into his mouth hard.

Arching further, she gave him more flesh to suckle and tease. Her pelvis ground forward against his hand, which was slick with her juices.

"Tom, please."

Licking circles around her nipple and tracing the same pattern around her sex, she bounced and moaned in his lap. Every movement bumped, caressed, and rubbed his shaft until the pleasure-pain was unbearable and unstoppable at the same time.

He'd intended to give her pleasure before taking his own, but she had other ideas. Her delicate hands tugged at the fall of his breeches, and then she pushed aside his smalls, took his cock in her hand, and worked the tight skin up and down.

Her breast popped from his mouth as pleasure pushed a moan from his lips. "Shall I move us to a couch, sweetheart?"

Thrusting forward she rubbed his shaft and her hand against where his fingers still teased her.

"Dear God, Dory." The feel of her wet sex against his burning rod was too much. He lifted her until she let go of him, positioned himself at her core, and let her body engulf him.

Their cries filled the music room.

Her feet didn't reach the ground, so he lifted her up and forward over and over again.

If there was a perfect moment, this was it. Her hair fell from its early state of grace and tickled his face. Her wet, tight body surrounded him with delight. Throwing her head back, she cried his name as her core pulsed around him.

Stilling himself as long as he could stand it, he let her orgasm cascade and relax before he redoubled his pace and let his own pleasure come. He had to close his eyes against the pure joy of it as the rapture took hold and he soared above the world before settling back into reality.

Dory pressed her forehead to his. "That was wonderful."

Still inside her, he stood lifting her and carried them to the couch near the far wall. A gold velvet upholstered screen blocked that area from the door should a servant come looking for them. Keeping them joined, he lay on his back with her on top of him. "It was. This entire morning, I shall count as one of the best of my life."

Her eyes darkened. "I am sorry it was tainted by the events of last night's ball."

Threading his fingers through her hair he forced her to look him in the eye. "Those things are not your fault, Dory. I wanted to marry you or I promise you I would not have done it. I know your reasons for entering this marriage were more practical, but mine were not. Do not worry about Hartly or your father. I shall deal with them appropriately."

"I do not approve of you paying my father's debt."

Sorry to lose the intimate connection he pulled away and sat up before pulling her onto his lap. He adjusted her gown to cover her breast and held her there enjoying the feel of her. Despite the intimacy they'd just shared, this tamer contact delighted him. "It is a debt owed and I have taken his only means of payment."

She pushed away from him. "My father intended to use me as currency. Will you do the same?"

The intimacy between them broken, he sighed with regret. "You put me in a difficult position, sweetheart. I respect your opinion, and you are not currency, but the debt is owed and our actions have injured your father."

Squaring her shoulders, she stood. "You must do what you feel is right. I have told you my wishes on the subject."

He rose as she did and ran his hands up and down her arms. "Please do not be cross with me. We have shared a wonderful morning together. Ruining it now over a silly disagreement would be a shame."

Arms crossed, she frowned. "It is not silly. However, I am not cross, I am tired. I think I will go to bed for a few hours."

"May I join you? I would love to hold you while we sleep."

Her cheeks pinked in the most stunning blush. "I would like that too."

Thomas let his breath out. He'd been sure she would deny him such an intimacy even after their lovemaking. He believed her when she said she would like to be held and it warmed him to his soul.

~

Desperate Bride

It had been weeks since Thomas had gone to Whites Gentleman's Club. Since the scene at Fitzwilliam's Ball, he and Dory had a steady stream of invitations. Everyone in London was keen for more gossip and some altercation that would make their affair stand out. The vipers were anxious for another ruckus to break out because the couple was present. Thus far, they had been disappointed. Hartly had not accepted any invitations and no one had seen Lord Castlereagh for some time. Dory's mother had called several times, but without her husband.

Thomas and Daniel opted to pass on the Berwick ball in favor of a quiet evening of cigars and brandy. The dark masculine environment suited Thomas, but his thoughts drifted to what Dory might wear and who she danced with while he was not at the ball.

Daniel leaned forward in the overstuffed chair and spoke in low tones. "How are things going at home?"

"Better." His wife wrote her music and allowed him to help. They got along well enough and even laughed from time to time. What more could he ask for?

"Is better good enough?" Daniel sipped his brandy.

Thomas flicked lint off the arm of the leather chair. "I am not unhappy, Dan. Do I wish for more? Yes. But it is unfair to expect more than Dorothea is willing to give. Perhaps in time things will change, but for now, we get along well and spend a good deal of time in the music room."

Daniel nodded, and then his attention shifted over Thomas's shoulder. He frowned. "Your father-in-law has just walked in and is heading this way."

Thomas remained seated and sipped his drink before setting the glass aside. "Does he appear inebriated?"

"I am afraid so."

It wouldn't do to get into a confrontation in the middle of Whites. All his attempts to meet with Geoffrey Flammel in private had gone unanswered. Apparently, he preferred public displays. "That is a pity."

"You!" Geoffrey rounded the grouping of chairs and pointed his finger. Distracted by his own hand, his glassy eyes lost focus and he stumbled to the left.

Thomas rose and bowed. "My lord, how are you this evening?"

"It was your plan all along, wasn't it? Well, you have done a fine job of ruining me. It is not to be borne." He stumbled the other way and blinked as if focusing. His cheeks and nose burned bright red and his expensive coat looked as if his valet had rumpled it into a ball before putting it on his lordship.

Most of the men in the room turned to gather fodder for the gossip mill. Some had the decency to turn away, but most gawked and whispered to their friends.

It was a chore to keep his temper in check. "This is not the place for a conversation of this nature, sir. I have attempted to meet with you and you have ignored me."

"I want no meeting with you other than pistols at twenty paces." Spittle flew from Geoffrey's mouth.

A gasp rumbled through the club. There was no mistaking that the Earl of Castlereagh had just called out Thomas Wheel.

Thomas's stomach clenched as his anger raged, but it would not do to feed the fires of this insanity. "My lord, perhaps you should return home and rethink what you have just said. It is a dangerous game you play."

Sweat beaded on Geoffrey's brow as he stepped so close to Thomas their noses almost touched. Fetid breath mixed with alcohol doused the air. "I have had plenty of time to think on your betrayal. I may never have satisfaction for what that bitch did to me, but you I will have satisfaction from. Are you a man, Wheel, or the simpering thief I have always taken you for?"

There was no going back. To decline such a direct challenge would ruin his reputation and to accept would end any hope of happiness with Dory. Thomas sighed, stepped back a pace, and bowed. "Have your second contact me with the time and place, my lord."

More whispers and mutterings went through the bevy of men who had heard the exchange.

Thomas stormed out of Whites. It was foolish, but he had no choice. He'd rather lose his life than his reputation. His skill with a pistol was unmatched, but killing Dory's father was not an option. As outrageous as it sounded, he had been outmaneuvered by a drunk.

Calling up to Mally in the street outside the austere front of Whites, he ordered the carriage home and climbed inside. Nothing was as it should be; even his carriage interior closed in on him. His life had never been what one might call normal, but it had never been out of his control before.

Before they'd moved an inch, he listed a dozen arrangements he needed to make.

The door to his carriage flew open, Daniel jumped in and sat across from him. In the privacy of the carriage the normal calm mask he wore fell away. Worry and disgust etched lines around his mouth and eyes. "You're not going through with this madness?"

"What choice do I have?"

Daniel ran his fingers through his hair. "You could decline the challenge. It's illegal to duel. Cite that as your reason."

"My reputation would be ruined."

"Better that than to kill your father-in-law."

There were things Daniel would never understand or agree to. Unable to lie to his oldest friend, he did the best thing he could for him. "Dan, it might be best if you stayed out of this mess. I shall find another second who is not so close to the situation. Besides, as you pointed out, dueling is illegal. Your involvement would be inadvisable."

For several beats, Daniel stared open-mouthed. "If that is what you wish."

"It is." It was the truth. He could not and would not involve his friends in the mess his life had become. It wouldn't be fair to damage their reputations with his own. Protecting those around him, those he loved, was paramount. It was all he had left.

"Very well. I shall leave you to your task." Daniel exited the carriage, slamming the door as he went.

Just another regret to live with. Thomas added writing a letter of apology to Daniel to his list of things needing his attention.

Chapter Fourteen

D ory's temper had gotten the better of her. She tried to be calm about Thomas paying her father's debt to Hartly, but he had completely disregarded her feelings. Looking for someone to calm and console her, she arrived at the Marlton townhouse and waited for Sophia to join her. It was early for a house call, so she waited in the front parlor while the lady of the house finished dressing above stairs. She'd brushed out her skirts a dozen times and taken countless turns around the room before resuming her seat on the edge of a fainting couch.

The door opened.

Dory shot to her feet. "Sophia."

Daniel held the door open for Sophia who entered first. Sophia rushed over and hugged her. "I had no idea what was happening until Daniel just told me."

She had hoped for a private conversation with her friend. Daniel was Thomas's friend and his presence complicated the matter. Yet it appeared Thomas had already shared their private matter with the Earl of Marlton. Her temper threatened to erupt in a very unladylike fashion.

"You know?"

They both stared at her with pity. Sophia had the good grace to blush and keep her eyes lowered.

"Is it today?" Daniel asked.

"Is what today? I believe he paid the debt several days ago." How long had Daniel known of Thomas's betrayal?

Sophia stared at Dory, and then at Daniel. "I have a feeling we are not all speaking of the same thing."

Dory gripped the back of the ornate chair she had put between herself and the couple. "I asked Thomas not to pay my father's debt, but he informed me yesterday he had done so anyway. My father does not deserve his charity nor do I appreciate being bartered about like livestock."

Daniel nodded. "I think he is settling the situation with your father because of the duel."

Dory's heart stopped. "What duel?"

Taking her hands, Sophia sat pulling Dory with her. "Your father issued a challenge to Tom at White's the other night."

"No. Father would never do such a thing. It is just a silly rumor." The ton loved to spread gossip and malice.

Sophia shook her head. "I wish that were the case, but I am afraid it is true. Daniel was there. Tom tried to stop your father, but he was drunk."

Daniel said, "I had hoped that the entire thing would blow over after Castlereagh sobered up, but if Tom is settling his debts, your father must have sent his second with the time and place."

Dory heard Daniel, but couldn't believe it. Thomas would kill her father in a duel. It was a story out of a bad novel. She refused to believe it. In spite of all their troubles, she still hoped they might be happy together. If nothing else, they had the music to keep them engaged. One day that might have grown into more. How would she forgive him after today? "Why did you not stop him?"

Daniel spread his arms with the palms facing up. "What could I do? I advised Tom to refuse, but it is a tricky matter when dealing with a man's honor. I do not know if I could have refused such a challenge made in public."

"Tom is going to kill my father." The horror shook the air and pounded her heart. Things had been getting better between them. The paying of the debt had hurt her more than she would have thought possible. She had begun to trust Thomas and his action had been a betrayal of that trust. Now all would be lost when he destroyed her family. Her gut twisted and a wave of nausea had her gripping the soft cushion for support.

"Shall I call for a tonic, Dory? You don't look well." Sophia stood and rang for the maid.

Mind racing, she pulled herself together. Tom would kill her father because he was the better shot and he would be sober. He'd gone out early before she'd awoken. She thought he was avoiding another argument about the debt. He might have already done the deed. "If he was planning to kill my father, why would he pay the debt?"

Thomas said, "Perhaps he wanted to do the right thing by your mother."

Dread washed over her. "He could have done that after the duel."

The butler opened the door. "My lord, this letter came by special messenger."

Daniel took the note and opened it. "Dear God."

Sophia rushed to his side. "What is it?"

"A letter of apology from Tom."

"Apology?" Dory gulped for air to slow her pounding heart.

"Is your carriage outside, Dorothea?"

"Yes. What is it?"

He grabbed her elbow and hauled her off the seat. "I will explain on the road. We have no time to lose."

Dragged from the house, she got in the carriage.

Sophia sat next to her and Daniel on the opposite bench.

The whack of information swirled around in her brain until it cleared to the only logical thought. "Tom is not going to kill my father."

"I do not believe so." Daniel frowned. He pounded on the roof for the driver to go faster.

"He plans to let my father kill him. That's why he paid the debt before the duel."

Sophia gasped. "My God." She pounded on the carriage. "Drive faster."

Dory stared out at the buildings as the carriage sped past. Thomas had left the house hours earlier. What would they find when they arrived at the dueling field? Perhaps they had both been arrested. Better that than the alternative. How could she bear seeing Thomas lying dead in the grass? She might as well have pulled the trigger herself. By manipulating his feelings for her, she had tricked him into a marriage doomed to fail.

The buildings gave way to countryside just outside of London. They bounced down the rutted road for an eternity before the carriage stopped next to a stand of trees.

Daniel flew from the vehicle followed by Dory. She lost her balance, but the footman caught her. As fast as her feet would carry her, she ran toward the clearing beyond the trees, holding her skirts up like a child. A mist still settled on top of the tall grass as if pulled out of a Gothic novel.

A shot rent the air.

She stopped. Her chest exploded with pain as if she was shot.

Too late.

Resuming her run, she crashed through the trees.

Daniel ran toward Thomas's body where he lay in the grass.

Dory turned away, her heart broken in a million pieces. What had she done?

Her father handed his pistol to another man and pulled out his handkerchief. He wiped his brow and then his hands before staggering forward.

Bradly Whitcolme shook his head and his unruly blond curls shadowed his face while he stared down at Thomas. "He never even aimed. Castlereagh fired, missed, reloaded, and fired again. All the while, Wheel just stood there looking across the mist. And we waited hours for that drunk to show up to his own duel."

Dory's feet were lead stumps dragging her closer to the scene.

Sophia ran past in a flurry of green and white skirts. "Tom."

"He's alive," Daniel said. "We need to get him home."

Alive?

"Whitcolme, call a surgeon. Bring the carriage!" Daniel waved toward the driver.

As if in a nightmare, she trudged across the field until she reached Thomas's side. His eyelids drooped closed and his color was pasty and gray. She knelt next to him and touched his cheek. "Tom?"

Daniel stripped off his jacket and pressed it against Thomas's waist. Blood seeped through the material.

"What have I done to you? Tom, I am sorry. I am so sorry. I never wanted to hurt you."

His blue eyes opened but paled compared to their usual brightness. "You should not be here, sweetheart."

The endearment crushed her soul. "I should be exactly here." She leaned close to his ear. "I love you, Thomas Wheel. Do not dare die on me."

He blinked and his eyes rolled up in his head before his head lolled to one side.

Heart hammering in her chest she prayed for him to open his eyes again. "No."

"He's lost blood, Dory. He's not dead." Daniel lifted Tom in his arms with the help of the footman and driver and they loaded him into the carriage.

Dory followed with Sophia.

Geoffrey Flammel staggered toward them. "Let him die. I might still get my money out of you, Dorothea. You are not pure anymore, but still pretty enough to draw a good price."

Dory stopped and turned. His ruddy face was bloated and he didn't focus his half-lidded eyes. She wanted to strangle him and make him feel the pain stabbing in her heart. Storming toward him caused him to stagger back a step. She slammed her palms against his chest, felling him to the damp grass. "You will never have anything from me, old man. Selfish and stupid is all you are. Keep away from me and my husband. I would rather prostitute myself on the streets than see you get another penny. Thomas Wheel paid your stupid debt, drunken fool, but if it had been up to me, you would have gone to debtor's prison. Keep your distance or I will see you burn in Hell."

He stared wide-eyed and open-mouthed as if he'd never seen his own daughter before. "You have no right to talk to me that way. That man is nothing. No title and barely any property. His money means nothing in our circle."

"You are not a man at all, while Thomas Wheel is the finest man I have ever known. Go back to your bottle and stay away from us." Dory spun on her heels and climbed into the carriage. Thomas remained unconscious for the entire ride, but his chest rose and fell evenly. She rested his head in her lap and Daniel held the bloody jacket in place. He had to live. Everything she had done had been for her benefit. Somehow, she'd believed having her in his bed would be enough compensation. Had she even tried to be a good wife? No. It had all been her music, her pleasure, her desire to not marry Hartly. None of it had been for the man who sacrificed everything for honor.

The surgeon, Dr. Revel, waited in the foyer when they arrived home. Once they carried Thomas up to his room, the dour-faced man barred all but Daniel and a nurse from the room.

"Dory, come downstairs. We can do nothing standing in the hallway," Sophia said.

"I am not leaving him." She pushed through the door.

Daniel blocked her. "There is much blood, Dorothea. You should wait until we've cleaned him up."

"He is my husband. I will stay."

Shrugging, he stepped back. "Do not faint."

She took a deep breath. Heeding the command, she rounded the bed. They'd cut away Thomas's coat and blouse, exposing a nasty hole in his side.

"It's a clean shot. The ball went right through. Lucky for him I will not need to dig around looking for lead. It was good work putting pressure on the wound, my lord, but he has still lost a lot of blood."

Dory brushed the damp hair from his forehead. "Will he live?"

The nurse handed a threaded needle to Revel. "I cannot say. If he is strong and his blood not poisoned, his chances are quite good. I will stitch the holes, and then we have to wait and see."

Kneeling at the edge of the bed, Dory prayed. She kept her eyes on the needle as it pulled through Thomas's flesh. Her stomach churned and her head was woozy, but she refused to look away or give in to the fear. This was her doing. She was to blame. The least she could do for him was to endure the gore.

The nurse bandaged the wound with Crowly's help and still Dory prayed to God to let him live.

Revel gave instructions to change the bandage and keep the wound clean. He left laudanum in case Thomas woke up in pain then closed his bag, bowed, and left.

"Dorothea, get off the floor before you become ill. How will you care for Tom if you are sick?" Daniel took her by the shoulders and lifted her into a chair near the bed.

"Thank you, Daniel."

"Crowly, give us a few minutes. You and Nurse Eve can wait in the hallway." Once they were alone Daniel leaned down so that his face was inches from hers. "I have always liked you, Dorothea. I will warn you now that if you do not eat and sleep, I will be back to see that you do. I will not have you doing what Sophia did when her father was ill."

"I would never—"

He held up his hand, stopping her, but it was the stern lines around his mouth and eyes that chilled her. "I know you care for Tom, even if the two of you are too stupid to tell each other. It is obvious to all who know you. Take care of him, but do not neglect your own health."

What did she care for her own health? Poor Tom could die and she was to blame.

Daniel pointed to the closed door. "Crowly is a devoted friend as well as his servant. He will let no harm come to Tom. Call on me if you require anything at all. I shall return tomorrow to check on you both." He rose to his full height, looked at Thomas still unconscious in the bed, and left the room.

Tears streamed down her cheeks as she leaned forward and took his limp hand in hers. "Wake up, Tom. Everything will be fine if you wake up and give me one of those smiles that always curled the girls' toes."

His eyelids fluttered. Perhaps he heard her.

Leaning her forehead on his hand she prayed he would wake and be well. She should have told him how much she cared for him but she hadn't known herself until she saw him lying in the grass. In that instant, when she thought he was dead, things became clear.

Dory had little experience with love. Her parents had been difficult from the beginning, but her mother was still dear to her. She had been fond of her nanny and loved her brothers though they were rarely at home. However, none of those relationships and emotional attachments compared to the devastation that pierced her at the thought of never hearing Tom's voice again or seeing the spark in his eyes when he listened to her play. The pain crippled her. Women spoke of a broken heart, but this went far deeper than her heart.

The door opened and closed several times, but Dory remained with her head down.

Someone lit the lantern.

"Madam, you must rest now. I will sit with him," Nurse Eve said.

Crowly touched her shoulder. "He will be fine, madam. If anything changes I will send for you. You must rest now."

Daniel's scolding rolled through her head. She must take care of herself to take care of Thomas. It was dark outside. She'd not realized how long she sat praying at his side. "Yes. I will rest."

Crowly helped her to the door where a maid waited.

Dory gazed back at Thomas's pale face. Throat clogged with emotion, she left the sick room for the lady's chamber and her own bed.

~

Before Dory was fully awake, the cook sent a tray up filled with her favorite foods. The smell of yeasty rolls had her stomach rumbling because she'd starved herself the night before. She'd eaten the entire roll with jam before she could stop to breathe. If the maid hadn't appeared so cross she might have run to Tom's side, but she forced down a few bites of coddled eggs before washing and dressing.

Sweat beaded on Tom's forehead and Nurse Eve placed a damp cloth there. "He has a fever. Could just be from the wound and loss of blood or might be his blood is poisoned. I have sent for Dr. Revel."

Dory's hopes of him sitting up smiling dashed, she approached and touched his cheek with the back of her hand. He was warm and clammy. "Go rest, Eve. I will sit with him until the doctor arrives."

Nurse Eve nodded and handed the cool cloth to Dory. "Try to keep him cool. It may bring the fever down."

Alone with Tom, she wet the cloth in a basin of water and wrung it out before placing it on his forehead and cheeks. His damp hair stuck to his skin and Dory brushed it away. "I know you must hate me now. I have brought you nothing but pain and humiliation. It was selfish of me to lure you into this marriage, Tom. I am sorry. I thought we would get along and I could play and compose. It never occurred to me my father would ruin us this way. I suppose it should have."

He moaned and became restless. Then he stilled, pain etched on his face.

"It is all right, my love. You lay still and heal. I do not think I could bear it if you die. I will make this right. As soon as you are well, I shall make all of this right."

Crowly arrived with Dr. Revel. Nurse Eve followed a few steps behind.

"Madam, let's leave the doctor to his work. I need a word with you if you don't mind." Crowly bowed and held the door.

Dory would return to hear what the doctor had to say, but she followed the butler from the room. "What is it, Crowly?"

"I think it would be best if we went to the master's study, madam." He lumbered down the steps.

Curious and confused, Dory followed him to the study. She turned and crossed her arms over her chest facing Crowly as he closed the door. "What is this all about?"

He shifted his gaze from side to side. "Mr. Wheel told me to wait until he was gone before I gave you a letter. I thought he was going on a trip. It didn't occur to me that he planned to let that bastard kill him. I know he's your father, madam, but his actions are unforgivable."

She waved off the insult. "I tend to agree about my father, Crowly. What happened on the dueling field was not your fault."

"No, madam, but I should have been with him. However, that is not what I wished to talk to you about." He pulled an envelope from the inside pocket of his jacket.

"What is that?"

"It is the letter meant for you after the master's death. I struggled all night over what to do with it and thought perhaps I should wait or burn it. I decided to give it to you now. Perhaps there is something in the writing that will help you or Mr. Wheel. Or maybe you'll burn the thing. I leave that decision in your hands." He bowed in his awkward way and exited the study.

The words "after the master's death" played over and over in her head. Perhaps the best thing to do would be to destroy the letter. She could put it in the fire and no one would ever know what was inside. If only Thomas would wake up, he could tell her himself. Stop being a ninny. She pulled open the parchment filled with Tom's elegant scrawl.

My Dearest Dory,

I am sorry to be writing this letter. I had very high hopes for our future. Even if it was only the music we had in common, I dearly loved listening to you play and learning from you. It would have been so nice to have a few children, teach them about music, and grow old watching them mature. I am afraid they would all have likely had red hair, but maybe we would have been blessed with one blond-haired little girl who could have stolen her father's heart just as her mother did.

I have loved you for a long time, sweetheart. Since long before you proposed, which is why I initially refused your generous offer. How could I marry a woman who clearly had no affection for me when my heart longed for her in ways I could never say? I was a fool to agree, but our choices were limited. I do not regret my decision, though I am certain you regret yours.

Your father will likely arrive to reclaim you as his property and sell you to the highest bidder. I told you I would protect you and I intend to keep my word. You will find the direction to my solicitor. He has all the papers to make you a very rich woman. You will never have to depend on anyone for money. I would be grateful if you would afford a living for my mother, but I leave it entirely up to you. I have no doubt you will do what is right and fair.

You can find someone you love and marry in your own time or not at all. If I might be so bold, I recommend you remarry. You are too pure of heart to never share that gift with another. I know you think you are void of deep feelings, but no one could play as you do without great love bursting to come out. I hope you will find a good and honorable man with whom to share all your love. If I have one regret it was that I was not that man.

Be well, Sweet Dory. Be happy.

All My Love,
Thomas

Tears streamed down her face, wetting the page in great drops of misery, smudging some of the writing. She would free him if he lived. That much she could do for him. Thomas made every sacrifice and she none. If she had been a dutiful daughter, none of this would have happened. She would be married to a man she hated and Thomas would be living his carefree life and charming all the women at the balls.

She did not deserve him.

A knock at the door roused her from her dark thoughts. She wiped her face and placed the letter on the desk. "Come in."

Dr. Revel ran his fingers through his shock of white hair. "I am afraid the news is not as good as I had hoped. An infection has taken hold. Being a young man in good health, I expected him to recover and wake up today. Instead he is in decline."

It was nothing she couldn't see for herself; still her gut knotted. "What can I do?"

He spoke slowly and with precision as if he thought out every word with great care. "All we can do is keep him comfortable. If he hadn't lost so much blood, I would bleed the poison out of him, but I fear he could not survive a bleeding. It is up to him to fight for his life, madam."

She stood and rounded the desk. The ache in her heart spread out until she wished to roll into a ball and have a proper wallow. There was no place for that. Tom needed her and she would not fail him again. "Thank you, Doctor. I appreciate your candor."

Revel nodded. "Call on me if Mr. Wheel's condition changes. I am at your service."

Dory saw him to the foyer, where he bowed.

Crowly held the door while Revel exited.

As soon as the doctor was out of the house, Dory leaned against the baluster and prayed for strength. Gripping the hard wood, she hauled herself up the steps and to Thomas's bedside.

She sent Nurse Eve away.

All day long, Dory cared for him. She only let Eve take over a few times while Dory ate. She stepped out of the room when Daniel came to visit. "How are you holding up, Dorothea?"

"I am fine."

"There is no need to lie. Charley has a cold. That is why Sophia has not come today. She sent a note." He handed her the folded paper.

"I am sure he will be better soon."

"Do you need anything?"

"No. It is up to Tom to make a recovery. All we can do is keep him comfortable and wait." She shocked herself with the steadiness of her voice. Inside, she screamed for someone to do something to make all of this a bad dream.

Daniel shook his head. His shoulders slouched and he didn't look like the Earl of Marlton. "I will visit tomorrow, if that is acceptable."

"Of course. Forgive me for not seeing you out. I would like

to stay with Tom." She left Daniel standing in the hallway. Crowly would see to him.

Tom tossed his head from side to side and sweat beaded on his forehead. He'd kicked off his blanket, exposing his bandaged side.

Dory rushed to the bedside and pressed his shoulder. "Don't fuss so, Tom. You'll rip your stitches. Then where will we be?"

He stilled at her touch.

"You know this was all foolishness. You should have called a halt to the madness. I thought you a much smarter man. How could you let my idiot father talk you into this? Now you must fight to come back, Tom. I will not have you dying, and leaving me a fortune is no answer to our problems. As kind as it was, it will not do."

Chapter Fifteen

Startled awake, Dory tossed off the bedding and grabbed her wrap. She rushed down the hall and into Tom's rooms. Nurse Eve, asleep in the window, never stirred.

Tom's skin was pale as death. His breathing low and intermittent.

Taking his hand, Dory kissed his clammy skin. "I forbid you to die on me, Thomas Wheel. I love you and you must give me a chance to make up for my mistakes. If you die now, how shall I survive the guilt?"

She climbed into the bed and rested against his good side.

A low moan pushed past his lips. Did he know she was there?

She whispered in his ear. "I love you, Tom. I should have told you sooner but didn't realize it myself. So sure I could never love anyone, I did not realize what we share is the best kind of love. A love that makes us equal and perfect together. In your letter, you wrote that you wanted children and I want to give you a house full of them. They will all play and sing and have happy childhoods. They will not grow up like I did.

Our children will know how much we love them. Our children will dote on their father. I cannot wait to go to the country and play in the fields. Is there a lake? I would like to teach them how to swim and we can all picnic at the edge of the water and have a lazy summer day. That would be lovely."

His chest rose and fell in a steady rhythm and the pain etched in the corners of his eyes eased.

"I love you, Tom. I shall love you until the end of time. Even if you put me aside, which you have every right to do after my behavior, I will still love you."

~

The light peeking through the blinds woke Dory. She pushed up from the mattress to get a better look at Tom's face. Was his color better, or did she just wish it to be?

Nurse Eve stepped inside with a fresh pitcher of water for the basin. She spared Dory a smile.

Dory's cheeks warmed with embarrassment. "I came in to check on him last night. I guess I fell asleep."

"He must have not minded, madam. His fever is down this morning. It broke an hour ago. I thought I might bathe him and clean away all the sweat. Cooling him down might lower the fever even more."

Dory crossed to the window and pulled the blinds back to reveal a sunny day. "Maybe we should leave these open. It might help him to know the sun is out and it's a beautiful day."

"As you wish, madam. I do not think it could hurt. I know I feel better with the sun shining in." She poured the water in the basin and dropped a cloth in.

"Shall I send Crowly in to help you? Mr. Wheel is quite heavy."

Eve smiled. "I can manage, madam. I have been doing this for a long time."

"Of course you have, and you do a fine job. I cannot thank you enough." Dory pulled her wrap closed.

Crowly knocked and stepped inside. In a rare show of emotion, his eyes were narrowed and his back stiff. He had his fists clenched as if he might be ready to fight someone. "Madam, Lord and Lady Castlereagh are downstairs. I have put them in the front parlor."

Her temper rose and she had to quell it. "It is very early for a call. They will have to wait while I dress."

"Yes, madam." He opened the door.

"And, Crowly."

He turned. "Yes, madam?"

"I will deal with my father. There is no need for you to take action. Mr. Wheel would not like it."

Crowly looked at Thomas. "No, madam, he would not. I shall keep my place."

Dory dismissed him with a nod. "Thank you. I will return as soon as my parents have left the house."

"Good luck, madam."

Dory laughed, but it was a sour, hollow sound. Rushing back to her room, she called Emily to help her dress and do her hair. It was still three quarters of an hour before she took the stairs down to the main level and opened the front parlor door.

One hand resting on the sill, Margaret gazed out the window at the street. The sun illuminated deep creases around her mouth and eyes that had not been there the last time Dory had seen her.

Geoffrey jumped up from the overstuffed chair and had to grab the edge of a wood inlaid table to keep from collapsing on the muted green rug. Distracted by his lost balance, he pursed his lips as if searching for what he wanted to say.

Closing the door, Dory said, "It is quite early for a call." She crossed the room and kissed her mother on the cheek. "Lovely to see you, Mother."

"Are you all right?"

"I am fine."

Father growled, "You are to pack your things and come home this instant."

A knot tightened in her belly. Screaming as she wanted to would do no good. She had ordered Crowly to behave as was appropriate for his station and now she had to follow her own advice. "My husband is ill. I am not going anywhere."

"You mean he is not dead yet?"

"Father, if you cannot behave like a gentleman, I will ask you to leave. It is already disgusting for you to call here, at Mr. Wheel's home, after your abhorrent behavior."

He pointed an unsteady finger at her. "You should know your place. You do not get to judge my behavior. I am your father."

She'd called him father out of habit. Nothing about his behavior her entire life granted him the rights of that honor. "My lord, you may consider your post in that regard relinquished. I want nothing to do with you."

"I am your father and you will come home as soon as that idiot dies. You will marry Hartly, as planned, and all of this will be right." He plopped back in the chair and the bounce of the cushion caused him to grip the arm and swallow.

She hoped he didn't vomit on the rug. "I will do no such thing. First of all, I know my husband paid your debts in spite of the fact that I opposed his doing so."

"What?" Margaret stepped away from the window. "You told me we were in danger of going to debtor's prison."

"I will not discuss this with you here, madam."

Margaret crossed her arms over her chest and narrowed her

eyes. "Dorothea, you said 'first'. I assume that you have more information. Please go on."

The intense satisfaction from having her mother's support surprised her. Maybe the earl had gone too far even for Margaret. "Thomas not only paid Castlereagh's debt to Lord Hartly, he settled all his debts to put an end to this madness. Despite that, Castlereagh challenged him to a duel in public. I am guessing you did it so you could not only have a clean slate, but also make a bit of extra money from selling me. The only trouble is, you came to the duel drunk, and although my husband never lifted his pistol, your shot was off and not fatal."

He pushed up from the chair. "I have it on good authority Wheel's injuries are fatal. He will likely die and you will be on the street. It will be a kindness for me to take you back into our house."

"Geoffrey, is all of this true? Did you intentionally arrange for your daughter's husband to die so you could profit? What has become of you?"

"I did it for us, Margaret. I wanted you to be happy again."

"You could not care less about anyone's happiness save your own. I am embarrassed and ashamed to be your wife."

The depth of his betrayal was astounding. Wanting her voice to be clear and firm, Dory took a deep breath. "You will not take me back nor will I ever live on the street. You see, my husband did not lift his pistol because he would not kill my father, a fact for which I am both grateful and disappointed. Before he met you on the dueling field that morning, he arranged for me to be a very wealthy widow. So you see, I do not need you and you will get nothing from me."

"It cannot be true. He only married you out of some strange sense of duty. You are nothing. Why would he give it all to you and not to his mother?"

"That is none of your business. I recommend that you ask

Markus to assist you with your finances before you lose all of his inheritance. Frankly, I think he could use something to distract him from his grief. Even Adam would do a better job than you have."

"You are the most selfish child. Ungrateful little cuss." He stormed toward her with a hand raised.

Dory backed up a step.

Margaret put her foot in his path and he tripped over it.

Crashing to the floor, he took a table and vase with him.

"I would not care a fig about you or your finances if not for my mother. Though, she will always have a place with me. Do as you like, my lord. Just do it elsewhere." She pulled the cord for the butler.

Crowly entered. "Crowly, please escort his lordship out."

Her mother remained standing with one hand on the back of a chair.

"Mother, you are welcome to stay. I can order some tea."

Margaret raised her eyebrows then folded her hands together in front of her. "That would be lovely."

Crowly bowed. "I will see to it, madam."

Father harrumphed and ambled to the door, followed by Crowly, who closed the door behind them.

Dory collapsed in the chair and leaned her head back.

Rounding the seating area, Margaret smiled. "Well done, my dear." She sat on the settee and placed her hands in her lap. "You handled that like a true lady."

"Thank you, Mother. I never thought I could do it."

"This was the first opportunity you had the power to get him out of your life. I wish I was half as brave."

Sitting up, Dory regarded her mother's stiff posture and sedate expression. Clearly, a facade she wore to fool everyone, and maybe even herself. After all the years she'd dreaded her mother's attention, she saw her differently. Maybe her mother felt the same way. "Mother, you are always welcome to remain with me. I do not believe Thomas would mind, and we have plenty of room."

Margaret smiled and she was lovelier than she had been in years. "That is very kind, Dorothea. I will give it some thought. How is Mr. Wheel?"

"Things were quite bad but I think he is better today. Father's bullet pierced his side and poisoned his blood, of which he's lost so much the doctor will not bleed him. All I can do is wait, and pray that he recovers."

The tea arrived and neither spoke until the maid placed the tray on the table, curtsied, and left the room.

Margaret accepted a cup from Dory. "And is that what you want?"

Dory's hand froze while holding the teapot over her cup. "I want Tom to recover."

"If he dies, you will be a wealthy woman." She sipped.

Refusing to take the bait, she poured her tea and placed the pot on the tray. "Tom risked his life to spare me the pain of losing my father. That would be extraordinary in any circumstance, but considering who my father is...Tom is nothing short of a saint. I want him to live."

"Then I will pray that he makes a full recovery."

"Thank you, Mother."

Margaret put her cup down and took a biscuit from the plate. She nibbled on a corner and put it on her saucer. "Are you in love with him?"

Could a woman like her mother understand such a thing? She couldn't imagine her parents were in love, but maybe they had been at one time. "I love him with all my heart. He is the best man I have ever known. Marrying me has cost him far too much."

Margaret nodded. "You could not have known what your

father was capable of. Frankly, I am surprised by the depth of his betrayal. It makes me wonder if Hartly and that Wormfield character are not behind it. Since your father has lost himself in the bottom of a bottle, he is easily influenced."

"You think that Hartly is behind the duel?"

She shrugged. "I think it is more likely than Geoffrey risking his life of his own accord. He never was the type."

Dory put her tea aside. "Do you think Tom is still in danger?"

Sipping her tea, Mother looked over the rim. "I cannot say. However, Hartly has never struck me as the kind of man who takes losing lightly. He courted your father about marrying you for over a year. I think he may have fouled a few of your father's business deals to create the need for the loan, which made you available as payment. Much of Geoffrey's gambling debt was owed to Hartly or Wormfield. Perhaps this was all a grander plan that you ruined by going to Mr. Wheel."

She had put Tom in more danger than she could have guessed. Her heart sank. "Have you heard anything else with regard to Tom?"

"I am sorry, Dorothea. Your father does not confide in me about his dealings. He never did." Deep creases formed around Margaret's mouth. "I would not have liked seeing you married to Hartly."

Heart in her throat, she couldn't believe her ears. "I thought you wanted me to marry the earl?"

"I wanted you to be a countess and you had already refused most of the eligible men of the season. Hartly solved the problem and the issues of money as well. He is an old man and I thought you would not have to suffer with him for long." She picked up her tea and sipped.

"Rather cutthroat, Mother, to take the money and then wait for my husband to die." She'd lost her appetite for the tea.

"Perhaps. In any event, you made your choice, and I am glad of it. I always thought Thomas Wheel a good man and he solved the other problem as well. He has no title, but you never cared about such things." Margaret took a bite of the biscuit.

"Did you love father at one time?" It was none of her business, but it was the first adult conversation she had ever had with her mother. Might as well take advantage of the moment.

Margaret placed her tea back on the table. Her chest lifted with a heavy sigh. "It was so long ago, but yes. When we first met, I was much taken with him. He was handsome and clever. He remained so until his father's death when the title fell to him. I think perhaps it was too much for him and he drank more and more. His behavior was repugnant and I suppose I was sharp tongued. We grew further apart with every passing year. Once he took his first mistress without even bothering to hide his infidelity...well."

"I am very sorry, Mother."

Her shrug was slight and she picked her tea back up. "If I may, I would like to see Mr. Wheel and then return home."

"I would like to reiterate that you are welcome to stay here." They rose and walked to the door and up the steps.

Margaret shook her head. "I will have my maid pack, and perhaps it is time I visit with Markus. I have seen little of my granddaughter and I am worried about Markus. He should be getting out more by this time."

Knowing her mother, she thought a gentle warning in order. "An excellent idea, though I recommend you are gentle with Markus, Mother. He took Emma's death very hard."

"Gentle is not in my nature, but I shall do my best."

Nurse Eve stood when they entered. "He seems better today, madam. His breathing is steady."

Margaret strode to the bed. "Has he woken?"

"Not yet, Mother." Dory rounded the bed and pressed her palm to his forehead. Warm, but not as much as the day before.

Taking a step back, Margaret paled. "It is unforgivable what his lordship has done. I cannot tell you how sorry I am."

Eve eased away with the water jug in tow.

Dory wasn't sure if her mother was apologizing to her or to Thomas. "It is not your fault, Mother."

"No, but I am still sorry for his pain." Shoulders sagging, she stepped out of the room.

Dory followed, asked Crowly to have a carriage brought around for her mother, and then saw her mother to the door. "I am glad you came, Mother. Even more pleased that you stayed for tea."

"Will you be all right? I can postpone my trip to the country and visit daily."

"I think Markus needs you more than I do. If anything changes, I will write you for help."

"Very well. I know you prefer the help of your friends to me, Dorothea, but do tell me if I can be of assistance."

Dory's chest tightened. Longing for a relationship with her mother, hoped leaped in like a waving flag. "Perhaps that will change in the future, Mother. We seem to have crossed into a new chapter of our relationship today."

"Indeed." Her mother kissed her cheek. "Take care of yourself, Dorothea. I hope Mr. Wheel will soon be himself again."

Crowly opened the front door and she swept out with her chin held high.

Dory sat on the steps and put her head in her hands. The morning had left her numb.

"Are you all right, madam?" Crowly asked.

She hardly knew. "It has been quite a day and it is not even noon."

"Yes, madam." His lips quirked in what might have been a smile if he hadn't held it back. Stoic to the last.

She took a deep breath and stood. "I will be with Mr. Wheel should anyone else call. Lord Marlton will return at some point."

"The Duke of Kerburghe is on his way from the country as well, madam. Lord Marlton mentioned it yesterday as he was leaving. I apologize for not mentioning it sooner."

Tom's friends ran to his aid just as he had run to theirs a dozen times. "I am not surprised. Did his lordship say if Kerburghe was opening his London house or staying with him?"

"He did not say."

"Very well. I suppose we will know if he brings her grace soon enough." She trudged up the steps, using the railing for assistance. All the emotions exhausted her. Knowing that she had put Tom in all this danger ripped at her soul, and not knowing if the danger was over broke her.

As soon as she was alone with Tom, she allowed the first tear to fall. Her chest ached with the sorrow she'd been caging up. "I am so sorry, Tom. If I had known what Father and Hartly were up to, I would have stayed away from you. I swear I would not have risked your life and your business."

Chapter Sixteen

P ain tore at Tom's head as the room came into focus. It was his own bed in his London home. His throat was so dry he struggled to swallow. Blinking drew moisture back to his eyes, but the room was lit by only one candelabra, making it difficult to see. He called for some water, but only a croak pushed from his parched lips.

Dory appeared before him like an angel in the darkness. "Oh, Tom. Thank God you are awake."

Were there tears in her eyes? Were they for him? He had dozens of questions, but he could voice none of them.

She ran away. A moment later, she reappeared and put her arm behind his head, lifting it enough for his lips to reach the water glass.

He gulped it as if it were manna from heaven.

"Not too much. Go slow." She pulled the glass away and eased him back down.

He pushed up, but pain shot through his side as if a knife stabbed. The duel came back to him in a flash of memory. He'd been shot. Dory had been there in the field outside London. He closed his eyes. How could he have been so foolish?

"You must not try to do too much, Tom. You will be all right, but you had to be stitched and if you pull those loose I do not know what will happen.

As he opened his eyes, her pretty face came into focus. Dark rings marred the underside of her eyes. "How long?"

"Five days."

Dear God. He'd been unconscious for five days. How could that be? "What happened?"

She leaned in so she was an inch from him and her breath warmed his skin. Her lovely scent wafted over him. It was like coming home after a long journey. "Do you remember the duel with my father?"

He nodded.

"Good. He shot you and you lost a lot of blood by the time we got you back here."

"We?" The idea of the Earl of Castlereagh carting him home after shooting him put a log in his gut. He fisted the sheets.

She touched his hand easing his strained muscles. Even that much effort soon exhausted him.

"Daniel, Sophia, and I brought you home. My father shall never interfere with our lives again."

He had many more questions to ask, but she blurred before him.

"Sleep a while, Tom. I will tell you everything when you are stronger."

The room blurred, dimmed, and then went dark.

The sun poked in around half-opened drapes, burning Tom's eyes.

"Do you want me to close them?" Dory asked.

"No. Leave them. I will adjust." His voice was more croak than speech. He squinted and blinked until he could tolerate the light and his vision cleared.

Dory sat in a chair, which would normally be placed near the hearth. Next to the bed, she leaned forward, watching him.

The other chair was near the window and in it a woman in a nurse's long cap. She slept with her chin on her chest in a most uncomfortable position.

"You are looking much better." Dory smiled.

"You look tired, Dory. Have you been to bed?" He reached out but couldn't quite reach her cheek.

After a quick look back at the sleeping nurse, she leaned toward him and accepted his touch. "I have slept and eaten under strict orders of Lord Marlton. It has just been a long few days."

It was no surprise Daniel had ordered her to take care of herself. He wouldn't have wanted a repeat of what Sophia had done while her father was ill. No need to worry about that. Dory's affection for him could not compare to the love between father and daughter.

Her skin was like silk under his fingertips, leaving him wanting more of the feel when she leaned back. "I am sorry to have given you so much trouble. You said I have been unconscious for five days. Was that last night we spoke?"

She beamed. "It was early this morning before dawn. At first you had a lot of blood loss, and then you had a terrible fever. The fever broke yesterday, so it is very reassuring that you have woken."

"Were you worried I would not wake? If I had died you would be a wealthy woman."

She crossed her arms over her chest and stared at his forehead, never meeting his gaze. "So I am told. Please do not do anything so stupid again, Tom. And leaving everything to me was ridiculous. You left nothing to your mother." Her scolding tone was nothing short of adorable.

"My mother has other means of living and I knew you would take care of her. I never doubted the extent of your kindness." He pushed up with both hands. Cringing from the pain, he dropped back to the soft mattress.

"Wait!" She shot from the chair. "Nurse Eve."

The woman was awake and across the room in an instant. "Do not tear those stitches."

"I want to sit up." The plea came across as petulant.

Nurse Eve smiled with her eyes if not her mouth. "I will help you if you will do as I say."

"Yes, ma'am." He hoped his smile was more teasing than baring teeth. The shock of pain made it difficult to know.

She nodded. "I am going to put my arms around you and when I say so, roll toward me, Mr. Wheel."

It was the strangest thing to have a woman not his mother or his lover wrap her arms around him, but she did it with no fanfare.

"Now, roll toward me."

Pain pulsed at his side, but much less than when he tried on his own. Once on his side she eased him to a sitting position.

Dory piled pillows behind his back and he leaned back against them.

His head spun.

Nurse Eve held his shoulders. "Look at me, Mr. Wheel."

He did. She had the most intense brown eyes and she narrowed them at him. He focused on Nurse Eve until the swirling of the room stopped. "Thank you. That is much better."

Showing her crooked teeth, she nodded and felt his forehead. Her hands were soft and warm. "It's good for you to sit up, and perhaps later today we will try a few steps. We can have Crowly help, if that's all right with you."

"If it will get me out of this bed, I will let the king himself assist."

"I am glad you are not going to be a difficult patient."

"That is yet to be determined." He winked.

Shaking her head, she took the basin of water and rag from the side table. "I will see if there is soup for you to try. I am sure you must be starving. We poured some down your throat, but it was not easy to get you to swallow."

Dory said, "Thank you."

As soon as the door closed, leaving them alone, he grasped her hand. "Are you sure you are all right?"

She settled on the edge of the bed and held his hand. "I am fine. Better now that you are awake. I will send for Doctor Revel to have a look at you. He's been here several times. Daniel has called every day and Michael arrived from the country yesterday and stopped in to check on you. I am sure they will both be back today."

It was gratifying his friends had called, but not unexpected. They had always been there for each other. "You said something this morning about your father not bothering us again. What did you mean?"

"I have sent him away. He and my mother called yesterday."

Fury rose from his gut but he was too weak to do anything about it. He gripped the blanket and fought for control. "He came to see if I was dead so he could take you away."

She nodded and patted his hand. "Do not upset yourself. I

explained that I shall always be independent of him and would no longer have any dealings with him. My mother knew nothing of what he had done beyond that ridiculous duel. She did not know you had paid his debts. It was clear she underestimated the depth of his flawed character and suspects Hartly's influence. She has gone to spend time with Markus and the baby."

It had only been he and his mother for most of Tom's life and all his adult life. He longed for a large family and hated that the incident had created a rift that might not be mended. "You did not have to disown your father on my account."

She cocked her head and several strands of golden hair fell across her cheek. "I did not do it for you. Everything he has done was selfish and harmful. He thinks of no one but himself. He is ruining his title and lands and will leave poor Markus nothing if he continues. I hope that Markus will snap out of his bereavement and do something about it soon. If he wants to preserve his birthright, he must."

"I agree that Markus should act, but if you did not disavow your father for me, then why?"

She stood and crossed to the window and drew back the curtains. Her pale blue dress was wrinkled, her hair pulled free from its chignon, her cheeks were pale and those dark rings still marked under her eyes. No one had ever been more beautiful. The sun rose above the roof line as midday approached. "For myself and maybe in part for my mother. I did it because you gave me the courage to do what had to be done."

"I was unconscious. How did I give you courage?" If he could have gotten up he would have held her in his arms and never let her go.

She watched him from across the room. "You stood in front of a loaded pistol to save me from losing my father. He was not worth your injuries, but you did that for me. It was the most noble thing I have ever known. Scolding Father for his behavior pales in comparison. It is not as if he has ever been a kind and caring father. At best, he is occasionally amusing."

His gut was in knots and not just because of hunger. "And what of your mother?"

"Mother stayed for tea after Father left. It was the most pleasant time we have ever spent together. She even came up here to see you."

He could not have been more stunned. "She did?"

Dory nodded. "She is glad I married you and not Hartly."

"I don't understand. She supported the match with the earl." His side ached and he tried to adjust his position.

Shrugging, she stood and took his arm in her hand. With more strength than he would have guessed, she assisted him in finding a more comfortable pose. "My mother is practical. She wanted me to have a title and money. It seems she was hoping Hartly would not live long enough to be too much of a bother."

Laughing shot pain through his wound. "She must have been disappointed to learn I was on the mend and would continue to vex you."

She stared at him, those green eyes alight with passion. "No. I do not believe so. No one wishes you harm. I would not have allowed her to stay in the house if she had."

He couldn't drag his gaze away from hers. Only the return of Nurse Eve broke the spell.

Dory smiled and took the bowl from the nurse. She held the spoon up to his mouth.

"I think I can feed myself, ladies."

Looking to Nurse Eve for assent and getting a nod, she handed the bowl and spoon to him.

The clear broth was unsatisfying but it eased the tension in his gut. By the time he'd taken half a dozen spoonsful, he was ready to sleep again. "Nurse, would you take this? I think I have had enough for now."

She focused on the bowl and shrugged. "Not bad for your first meal. Rest now. You can have more when you wake up. Several small meals for a few days will be best. You must give yourself time to adjust to eating again. When you wake, we will also try a short walk around the room."

With Eve's help, he eased back onto the mattress and closed his eyes. Skirts rustling made him force them open again.

Dory stood near the door.

"Are you leaving?"

Turning back, she smiled. "I will be here when you wake up, and if I am not Nurse Eve or Crowly will fetch me. I am just going to rest for a little while."

"Yes. You need rest. I apologize." He was a selfish cad. It was obvious she'd had little sleep, and here he was, worried he would miss her.

"None necessary. I will be back soon."

He hadn't heard her return to the bed. Perhaps he'd dozed.

She pressed her lips to his cheek. Soft and cool, like the break of day, her kiss eased his tension. "I am delighted you are healing."

~

Five days immobile, losing all that blood, having two holes in his side, plus the infection had left its mark. Every step was a force of will. Walking brought on more pain but it also eased as his muscles stretched out and the pain in his side lessened with every try. He made it all the way down the hall without Crowly's assistance, though the butler followed close behind. The hall was perfect because the dark wood walls were always close by should he need to steady himself. There was no

Desperate Bride

rug to trip over, and he had a cane just in case every other precaution failed. Crowly would never let him fall, and there was comfort in knowing that. It made him braver with his stepping, and the healing process moved faster every day.

Turning around and making it back to his bedroom filled Tom with elation. It was a small feat, but Tom was proud of it.

"Should you be up?" Michael stood at the top of the steps leaning on the railing.

Tom gripped the wall. It took all his concentration to stand and walk. Any distraction might fell him. "I am under the strictest orders to get some exercise every few hours."

"You look about to drop." Michael stepped forward and offered his shoulder to lean on.

It was no time to be too proud. He gripped Michael's shoulder and they stepped into his room.

Nurse Eve was tucking the blanket back in place. She bundled up the old sheets in her arms and bustled out the door.

Crowly waited in the threshold a hulking presence. It was amazing the loyalty he enjoyed from his staff and friends. He too often took it for granted. Never again.

"You can go, Crowly. Thank you for your help. His grace will assist me to the chair. I am not ready to get back in bed just yet. I will ring if I need anything."

Crowly bowed out of sight.

With Michael by his side, Tom made it to the chair, now returned to its space near the hearth.

"It's good to see you in trousers, Tom." Michael sat across from him.

Tom tugged the material away from his wound and leaned back against the cushion. The top of his trousers scratched against his tender, healing flesh. "I insisted on clothes if they were going to parade me up and down the hall. It was quite a conflict with Nurse Eve, but as you see, I was victorious."

Michael slapped the arm of the chair laughing. "I suppose it is the small things."

"Nurse Eve is formidable. I felt like I had defeated Napoleon single-handedly." He joined the jest.

"How are you really? You gave us quite a scare." Michael leaned his elbows on his knees. "I have corresponded with Markus. His response was difficult to decipher. He's been drinking and his mother has arrived at Rosefield. Fearing she will corrupt the child, he cannot bring himself to leave, even though he hates the place since Emma's death."

"You can tell him I am better every day and I will see him when he is free. He has enough on his plate without worrying about me."

"I shall write him this afternoon. Perhaps you might send a short note too, if you're up to it."

"It may have to wait until morning, but I will write him. I am too tired now to craft a letter." Like a child avoiding his bedtime, Tom defied his body's desire to climb back in the bed.

"He will appreciate it. You look like you might tumble to the carpet at any moment." Michael stared, the way he did when trying to read a person who was hiding something. As a spy for the crown, he'd cultivated the skill.

It was good to have friends who cared. "I believe I will live. Doctor Revel has been here a few times since I regained my wits. He said I will be myself again in a few weeks. The wound is healing."

"I am glad to hear it."

"You know, you did not need come all the way from Scotland to see me. A letter would have sufficed."

"No, it would not have." Michael leaned back. His gaze bore into Tom's. "How are things with your wife? Has the tension eased since your duel?"

Tom's heart broke at the mention of his wife. "It is hard to say. She is here and she certainly has cared for me more than most women of her station would have. Sometimes I feel very close to her, and then other times she seems so distant I cannot reach her."

"I wish it were a better marriage for you, Tom. I know it started as a marriage of convenience, but I hoped the two of you would learn to love each other."

Staring at the rug, he traced the green pattern with his gaze. "I had hoped so too."

"Is there nothing that can fix things between you?"

"I have not given up. We still have the music and my feelings for her are unchanged. Maybe she needs more time." Thomas wished he could make the rest of the world disappear and just have Dory and a room filled with music for the rest of his life. It was not reality, but it was a pretty picture.

Chapter Seventeen

Dory brought a bowl of soup from the kitchens. This one had meat and vegetables in it and she was thrilled at presenting something other than clear broth to Thomas.

Kerburghe stepped from the room into the hall as she exited her rooms. He bowed. "How are you, Dorothea?"

"Fine, Michael. How is Elinor?"

A maid hummed as she walked down the hall.

"Gertie, can you bring this tray in to Mr. Wheel for me?

Gertie's chestnut curls bounced as she curtsied. "Yes, madam."

Dory handed the tray over. Michael waited until Gertie was inside the bedroom and the door closed. He grinned. "I had a letter from her today. She is well and the children are driving her mad."

No one would ever smile at just the mention of her name. She squashed the surge of jealousy. "Will she come to London anytime soon?"

He shook his head. "I do not expect so. I intend to return to Scotland as soon as Tom is well. We much prefer the quiet of the lowlands to the hustle of London and wagging tongues of the ton."

"Indeed." There was little doubt the gossips were getting their fill from her life now. "Michael, may I asked you something?"

"Of course."

"Has marrying me damaged Tom's prospects?"

Michael lowered his gaze to the floor. "To be honest, it has not helped, Dorothea."

Even though she'd knew it was true, hearing it from one of Tom's friends hurt. "I see. Will he recover?"

"Maybe. It will depend on how he goes forward and if his larger business associates stay with him. Many of his plans may have to be put on hold."

"And if I were out of the mix?" It took all her will to keep her tears at bay.

Michael put his hand on her shoulder. "Leaving Tom would hurt him far more than his business failing. He needs you."

"Can you answer my question, please?" She had to hear the truth.

Shuffling his feet was the only sign that Michael was uncomfortable. He met her gaze. "It stands to reason that his life returning to before your marriage would help him in business circles. However, I must restate that Tom needs you, Dorothea."

He did need her while he was ill, but after that, he would do better without her. "Thank you for your honesty, Michael."

"I have an appointment with my solicitor this afternoon, so I must say good day. If you would like to discuss this further, I am at your service." He bowed again.

She curtsied. "Thank you, but I think I understand. Good day to you."

Once he had bounded down the steps and she heard the front door close, she entered Tom's room.

"There you are. When you did not bring my lunch, I worried." He put his soup on the table.

"Did you enjoy it?" She stayed near the door, looking for a way to escape.

"Real meat! I am overjoyed, and bread, glorious bread."

She hated that he could make her smile even when she wanted to be cross. "I thought that would please you."

"Why are you holding up the door? Come and sit with me. I wonder if tomorrow you might take your meals in here, or maybe we can talk Nurse into letting me down in the dining room for my supper." He bit of a piece of bread and closed his eyes while chewing.

Never had anyone gotten so much pleasure from a slice of crusty bread as Thomas Wheel. Even if he no longer loved her, he still wanted her near. There was hope in that. She shook it away. He was only being polite. It was his way and had nothing to do with love or any other such nonsense. Stepping close, she sat across from him. "I shall see about you coming down for a meal or two, though I don't know how you will manage the stairs."

"I will hold the rail and Crowly will make sure I do not injure myself."

If he fell, it could be disastrous. "I will discuss it with Nurse Eve."

Nodding, he sat forward. A pained grimace twisted his face. "I wonder if I might ask a favor from you?"

"What is it?"

"Would you play for me? Just the harp would be sufficient. I feel as if music has left my world and the void is gaping more painfully than my wounds."

Not being able to imagine her life for weeks without

hearing a single note, she could not refuse him. "Yes. I will get it now."

He grasped her hand. "Don't leave, Dory. Send a maid for the harp."

Running from the room would be cruel. None of what had happened between them was his fault. It was all her doing and nothing could fix the damage. She rang for the maid and sent her to retrieve the lap harp from her bedroom.

"Michael came to see me today." Pulling the covers loose where they tangled under his leg produced a wince.

Dory gentled the sheet out from under him and smoothed the bedding. "Yes, I know. Did you have a nice visit?"

"He is returning to Scotland at the end of the week. It is amazing the change that has taken place in him. I have known him most of my life and yet, in the past year, he is a new man. He longs for his wife and children in a way I could never have imagined."

A stone settled in her stomach. "Is it so difficult to imagine loving one's family?"

He cocked his head. "Michael was a willful and wild youth. He channeled that energy into being a magnificent soldier and spy. I could never have imagined him as a loving and doting father and husband."

The aching in her chest could only be her heart tearing in half. "I suppose his close brush with death changed him."

"Or maybe this side of him was always there, waiting for a family to bring it out."

Crowly arrived with her harp. "I intercepted Milly with your instrument as a message arrived for you, madam."

She took the note. "Thank you. You can put it on the table."

Once Crowly had done as asked and left the room, Dory opened the note.

"Is that the Marlton seal?"

"Yes, it's from Sophia. She is inviting me to join her and Daniel at the Theater tomorrow night." She tucked the note into the waist of her skirt. "I will send my regrets this afternoon."

"You should go, Dory. You have been cooped up with me long enough. I can survive an evening. It's not as if the staff will give me a moment's peace with their doting."

Her heart lodged in her throat. If he needed her and she was out enjoying an evening of leisure, she could never forgive herself. "I don't know."

"I command you to enjoy yourself." He crossed his arms.

"That is the first time I have been commanded to have fun. I will give it some thought."

Thomas stretched, unable to lift his left arm above his shoulder. Patting the edge of the mattress, he said, "Come and play for me."

Other than a few stolen moments late at night, Dory hadn't played since the day of the duel. She retrieved the harp and sat on the bed. "I am out of practice."

"You out of practice is still better than most people after decades of work." The intensity in his eyes warmed her from the inside out.

Sweet and kinder than she deserved. How would she do what was necessary? To free her hands and find balance, she pushed farther up on the mattress and rested the harp on her lap. Eyes closed, she ran her fingers along the strings and reveled in the melodic vibrations. She picked a piece she'd written years before. It was not a technically superior composition, but it was sad and sweet and she always played it when the world closed in on her.

He touched her knee.

Still playing, she opened her eyes.

His stare echoed the mixed emotions of the music, from

delight to desperation and back again. He tapped out the melody with his fingers on her leg and every touch shot desire through her. As she strummed the last note, he wrapped his fingers around her calf. "I am not familiar with that piece. Is it one of yours?"

"I wrote it a long time ago. I know it is not good, but I have always liked it." She commanded her heart to slow its pounding.

"It is a lovely composition and full of emotion. Thank you for sharing it with me." Slipping his hand beneath her skirt, he caressed her leg.

"What are you doing, Thomas?" It took all her will to keep from closing the space between them. Intimacy would only complicate an already horrible situation.

He caressed the sensitive skin behind her knee, while his gaze never left hers. "I am touching my wife and hoping she will stay with me a while tonight. Perhaps sleep with me and let me give her comfort."

Passion flooded her, warming her from her cheeks to her toes and super-heating her middle. "You are not well enough for such thoughts."

He gripped her inner thigh, branding her with desire. "I am well enough for far more torrid thoughts, sweetheart. Unfortunately, I am not well enough to follow through on them. Still, it would please me if you would sleep with me."

Every fiber of her soul wanted to stay with him, take comfort from him. She longed to be in his arms and caressed until she writhed beneath him. More wanton thoughts fought to the surface, but she pushed them away. "I could roll over in my sleep and injure you further. I think it best if I go to my own room."

Disappointment shone in his eyes and his shoulders

slumped. With a sigh, he said, "Then at least play me one more song."

"Why don't you try to play?" She eased the harp toward him, got up and put another pillow behind his back, and sat in the chair where it was safe.

The awkward half-recline and his legs being straight out made it difficult for him to find a suitable position for the harp. He rested it on his thigh and strummed a perfect chord. Unable to lift one arm sufficiently to make the strings, he only plucked out a few simple melodies before giving up. "Damn."

"That was a very good effort. You cannot expect to do everything at once." She took the harp from him and stood. "I will see you in the morning."

"I wish you would stay."

Wishing the same, but knowing it was wrong, she shook her head. "It's best if I go. Good night, Tom." She leaned down to kiss his forehead.

He tipped his head up and captured her lips with his. Warmth and joy spread from the kiss and filled her as fast as the sea at high tide.

All she had to do is take a step back and she would be out of reach for him, but she stayed glued to the spot and let the kiss take life.

He wrapped his weak arm around her waist and threaded the fingers of his other hand through her hair, making love to her mouth as if he'd been as starved for her as he'd been for meat and music, but it was an illusion. Their life together, all of it, was a farce that she had fashioned. She needed to put distance between them. She needed to do what was right. He had saved her and it was time for her to return the favor.

Pulling away was the best option, but she cupped his cheek and opened her mouth for more of him. His groan shot pleasure to her core. It was a mistake, and she pulled away. It took a long beat to find her voice. "I must go."

Passion transformed to disappointment and he fisted his covers. "If you must, then you should."

Clutching the harp, she ran from the room and down the hall and locked herself inside her own chamber. She'd lost her mind. Her behavior was of a madwoman. Wanting her had ruined him, yet he kissed her. She had almost cost his life, but there was plenty of vigor in his kiss. Forcing the thoughts away, she plopped in a chair and played the harp until everything disappeared but the music.

∾

Because Dory was unwilling to argue with Thomas and for lack of a good excuse to decline, she accepted the theater invitation from Sophia and Daniel. The Marlton box was one of the best but it was a long way from the main entrance to its safety. After weeks of being indoors and much of the time in a dim sickroom, the crystal chandelier hurt her eyes. Bouncing from shoulder to shoulder against the crush of the crowd had her nerves jumbled in her gut. She should have said no and stayed in her room.

Keeping her head down meant the rich red carpet and eveningwear filled the space.

"It's a crime what she did to the Wheel reputation."

Dory followed the cut to the pursed lips of Lady Pemberhamble. Her notorious gossiping knew no boundaries. In pale lavender and white lace, she dressed more like a debutante than a dowager.

Lady Pemberhamble narrowed her eyes, crossed her arms, and stared at Dory as if daring her to contradict the statement.

Wishing the carpet would swallow her up, Dory skirted

around an obese man and woman but only got a few feet from the clutch of gossips.

The stout woman in a navy-blue gown nodded. "He was such a fine gentleman, without a bit of scandal. Now, he has fallen from grace. He will never recover his status even as a mere gentleman. I heard he will be left crippled from his wounds and his creditors are calling in their loans."

"I have it on good authority that he was about to offer for that sweet Serena Dowder before the Flammel girl stole him away. Who knows what she used to lure him," Pemberhamble said.

"I had no idea."

Pemberhamble kept her gaze on her friends, but her voice was loud enough for many people in the crowd to overhear. "We all know it was about the money. She and that father of hers schemed to get Mr. Wheel's vast fortune. They must have been very disappointed when he lived. He will put her aside for certain, and she deserves it."

Lady Roth patted her blue hair into place. Thin-faced, with diamonds dripping from her neck, wrists, and ears, she said, "It's always about the money with their kind."

"I do feel for her mother. She does not deserve the association with such base actions." Lady Pemberhamble tugged on her lace sleeve and hoisted her nose in the air.

Daniel pushed them through a gap in the fray.

Even the stairs pulsed with people visiting before the play, and everyone stared at Dory. Some women hid behind their fans as she passed, no doubt spreading half-truths and lies about her marriage.

"I should never have come out tonight. This will only make things worse for Thomas." Grabbing her skirts, she trudged up the steps, careful to keep her eyes focused only on the landing.

A footman pulled back the curtain leading to the Marlton box.

Sophia flounced into a chair. "I cannot bear that Pemberhamble woman. She is like a viper waiting to strike."

Dory stayed near the curtain and closed her eyes while she attempted to gain control of her topsy-turvy nerves. "I should have stayed at home."

"That would not stop the gossips." Daniel took the seat next to his wife.

Below, the crowd filed into the seats while the boxes around them also filled.

Forcing a mild expression, Dory pulled her shoulders back and stuck out her chin before she sat. "Daniel, what that woman said about Tom's creditors, was that true?"

The muscle in his jaw ticked and he ran his hand through his blond hair. "I don't know, but it is possible."

Another log thrown on the inferno of her life. Shame washed over her. "He would be better off without me."

"He would not." Sophia took Dory's hand.

Meeting her gaze, she searched for some crumb of truth. "Since I forced myself on him, he has been ostracized by society, embarrassed at his club, shot by my father, and now he will lose his fortune. I am a pariah. He would be better off if I went away."

"You are exaggerating the situation." Daniel propped his elbows on his knees.

"Am I? Will Tom's finances recover after all the things that have happened since eloping with me?"

He leaned back and met her gaze. "There will be a price, but Thomas knew the risks at every turn. He would not have taken this course if it was not what he wanted. You are not to blame, and he is wealthy enough to survive until the scandal passes."

Some scandals held on for years. A juicy one like this could ruin a man, even a rich one. She had done enough harm due to her selfishness. It was time to do the right thing.

The lights dimmed as the production was about to begin. As the theater darkened, the stage illuminated. Swords clashed as two men fought. One was young and handsome and the other older and heavily mustached.

A woman screamed for them to stop.

The older duelist impaled the other, but when he rushed to claim his prize, she refused him.

The stage went dark and the next scene was a cemetery. A young woman lay crying next to a grave and lamenting she will never love another. She begged the dead man for forgiveness. Her vanity had led to his demise.

Time passed and the woman's father brought man after man to wed her, but she would have none. With each man, she explained that she had no right to happiness. She deserved to be alone. Her beauty had brought her to destroy the only man she had ever loved and she would not benefit from it.

Frustrated with her stubborn nature, her father sent her to a convent.

The stage went dark and the theater lights rose.

Dory's heart lodged in her throat. "Sophia, when do you leave for the country?"

"At the end of the week."

"If you do not mind, I would like to go with you." Finally, she would do the right thing. Thomas was too kind to put her aside and she didn't know if she could survive it if he did. This way she could spare him the pain of doing what he needed to continue.

Daniel said, "You should stay in London until Tom can travel, and then you can both come for a visit."

Why he should want his friend to suffer any longer with

her, she didn't know. "His health is returning now. Since he is out of danger, I think it best if I leave. He will recover, and then he can repair the damage I have done to his reputation." Her heart clenched. Doing the right thing hurt more than she'd expected. She stood.

Sophia took Dory's arm and stood. "You are welcome to come with us, but are you sure that is what you want? Tom will miss you and I think you will miss him too."

A wave of nausea washed over her. Music was so much simpler than real life. Why couldn't she stay lost in her passion and leave these emotions behind? "I am sure. If you don't mind, I would like to leave now. I think I have had enough of this performance."

Daniel pressed his lips into a thin line and ushered them out of the theater. When the carriage door closed, he asked, "You will explain to Tom that you are leaving?"

"I will tell him." It was all she could do to keep her tears at bay. "I am sure he will be relieved to be done with all of this."

"I wish I was as certain as you of that." Daniel took Sophia's hand in both of his but stared out the window.

The city rolled by. It was early to be going home for the night. Though her departure was for the best, she dreaded telling Tom. Always so kind and considerate, he would never show her his true feelings when she eased his burden.

Screams filled the street. A cart overturned at the intersection and people ran toward the accident.

"Stay in the carriage," Daniel ordered before jumping out and running to help.

∿

I t was late by the time she arrived back at Tom's house. She always thought of it as his home rather than theirs. Hands shaking, she handed Crowly her gloves and pelisse. "Thank you. Did Mr. Wheel have a good night, Crowly? Were there any problems?"

"Madam may ask him herself. He is in the study." He backed away with the garments.

Spinning toward the study door, she didn't know whether to be angry or excited. He shouldn't be up so late. He would overexert himself. How wonderful that he was out of bed. She pushed open the door.

Wrapped in his robe, Tom sat studying a chess game in midplay. He turned as she entered. His face lit up with the most glorious smile. "You're home. How was the play?"

"Terrible. We left at intermission."

He gazed at the clock on the mantle then moved a chess piece. "That's a shame. Where have you been?"

"There was an accident near Piccadilly. It took additional time to get through and Daniel stopped to assist." All the energy sapped out of her, she sat across from him. He'd lost weight, but his shoulders were still broad and his eyes magnetic. None of his charm was lost, only his pride. She would see he had that back as well.

Pointing to the chessboard, he asked, "Do you play?"

"Only very poorly."

"I could teach you." Hope bloomed in his eyes. It made no sense.

The pain that started in her chest spread to her head. Her ears rang with the blood rushing through them. "I am going to the country with Sophia and Daniel at the end of the week."

Lifting his chin, he narrowed his eyes. "Why?"

"You are well and my presence here serves only as fodder

for the gossips. Your life can go back to normal as soon as I am gone and that will be for the best." She plucked at the seam on her reticule. Putting the bag aside, she settled her nerves, and then folded her hands in her lap.

"Fodder for gossips? Did something happen at the theater?" He leaned back and crossed his arms.

"Nothing out of the ordinary. We had always planned to let each other live our own lives. It seems clear that the time has come to begin that process. I will go to the country and you will have your life back. If you require me for some event, you need only send a note and I will be happy to oblige you. I feel I should tell you how grateful I am for all you have done and how very sorry I am for the trouble I have caused you." There, she'd said what she wanted and managed it without rancor or tears. They could both move on without regret.

"This is what you want, Dory, to live separate lives?"

She nodded. "I have been a burden on you long enough."

"I have never considered you a burden. You are my wife." He adjusted his position and winced.

"A wife who got you shot and caused you more pain than you deserve. I will spend a few weeks with Sophia, and then perhaps go up to Scotland and see Elinor. My mother has a small cottage in Surry, which she inherited from her mother. Perhaps I will go there as well. If you like, I can keep you informed of my whereabouts."

All expression leached from his face. "I see no point. If you wish to go, then go."

It was no surprise he wanted her to go. So why did it feel like her heart was being torn out of her chest? "It is for the best." She left the study without looking back.

Chapter Eighteen

Dory's announcement shouldn't have surprised Tom. They had married out of her need and nothing more. From the beginning, she had been honest about what she wanted and it had nothing to do with love. Losing his temper was not a luxury he often allowed. Watching her hips sway as she left the room he clutched the arms of his chair until his fingers screamed for release.

Footsteps receded as she climbed the steps.

He overturned the chessboard, sending pieces flying in every direction. Pain shot through his side and up his chest. His head pounded and there was no more outlet for his fury. His body couldn't take it.

Crowly rushed into the room. "Sir?"

No longer able to hold himself upright, he bit his cheek against his sorrow. "Help me back to bed."

With Crowly's strong arm holding him up, he staggered up the stairs. He bathed in the agony of his wounds, both literal and those inflicted by falling in love with Dorothea Flammel. That was his biggest mistake. She would never let herself love him or anyone. Her parents had ruined her for love and none of his foolish hopes and dreams would change her.

He sat on the edge of his bed waiting for the pain to ease enough to lie down. "You can go, Crowly. I can manage from here."

"Are you certain, sir?"

"Yes. I need to start doing things for myself."

Once he was alone, he put his hands on his knees and let the weight of her abandonment relax. Only the discomfort in his side forced him onto the mattress where he stared at the ceiling. He could still convince her to stay. Tell her he was too sick to be left alone. There could be more moments like the one with her playing the harp in his bed.

"You are a fool, Wheel." He closed his eyes and prayed for oblivion.

∽

Thomas's arm ached and his back hurt, but there was determination mixed with his rage for the first time in a long time. Three parries in a row had kept Daniel from scoring. Sweat ran down his back and dripped from his chin into his mask. Every muscle hurt far beyond the exertion of one match.

Steel clashed against steel one last time as Daniel held up a hand to end the sparring. "Well done."

The raised platform at Jaffers Club had garnered a small crowd of onlookers. As the match concluded, the audience filed away.

"Why did you stop?" It was the first decent exercise Tom had in months and he longed to keep going despite the protests from his body.

Daniel removed his face protection and handed it and his

foil to a servant standing nearby. Taking the offered towel, he sat on the top step. "I am tired."

"Liar." Tom collapsed next to him. "But you're right, it is enough for one day."

Nodding, Daniel wiped his brow. "It's the first time you've dueled since being shot. You do not want to cripple yourself for a week. Besides, I need to talk to you."

Dread replaced the small joy he'd taken from the exertion. Talk of Dory was inevitable, but Tom wanted none of it. "Must we speak of her? I was having a good day."

"She is your wife, Tom, not some distant issue you can ignore."

The chest protector suffocated him and he tugged at the buckles until it pulled free. His claustrophobia didn't abate. "Can we at least get out of here?"

With a nod, Daniel stood. As soon as they were back in appropriate clothes for a morning on the London streets, they walked to Daniel's waiting carriage. "She is very sad, Tom."

Only a slight twinge of discomfort accompanied Tom's climb into the carriage. "I did not ask her to leave. She insisted on going. I cannot imagine why she should be unhappy."

"Can you not?" Dan knocked on the roof to alert the driver they were ready to leave.

The driver snapped the reins and they rolled through London's rainy street at a snail's pace with carts and traffic halting their progress.

"As far as I know, this is the life she wants. I offered her a life with me and she chose one on her own flitting from friend to friend. I assume she is back at Marlton?"

"Dory arrived three weeks ago from Scotland, even more depressed than when she left us."

The familiar pang of jealousy stirred in his gut. Hating the emotion did not make him less susceptible. "Is your brother-in-law visiting Marlton as well?"

Cocking his head, Dan raised an eyebrow. "Anthony has been staying with us for over a month. Why do you ask?"

He would have to trust that Dory's character was intact. She would never betray him so soon. Though as things stood, one day she would take a lover. He couldn't expect her to live like a nun for the rest of her life, but that didn't keep the pain from crippling him. "Never mind. What were you saying about depression?"

"I am tempted to toss the pianoforte from the house."

"Why?" Tom longed to hear her play. He missed it almost as much as he missed her.

Daniel pointed at him. "Your wife plays all day but where the sound of her play used to ring with joy now there is only despair. Sophia and the staff are in tears all day long. I have begged her to play something more cheerful and I believe she tries. For the first few moments, a light riff will come across, and then it turns back to some piteous dirge."

Nothing was more important to Dory than her music. There had to be a reason for it to suffer, but he was sure it had nothing to do with him. "I don't know what you want me to do about it. You may toss her and the instrument from the house for all I care."

"Does she write to you? Do you even know where your wife is from day to day?" Daniel crossed his arms and glared.

Assuming the same pose, Tom said, "My wife did me the courtesy of informing me when she left Marlton to visit Kerburghe, but she has not written since."

"Did you respond to her letter?"

"I saw no point as there was nothing of a personal nature in her letter and it was only informative. What should I have written back, have a nice time?" It had been almost a month since his rage had gotten the best of him. Becoming used to her abandonment was his only option. His health had improved in her absence, but progress was slow and had required a lot of bed rest. The pain had made it hard to think of anything else. Once he was up and busy putting his businesses in order, he eased her out of his mind moment by moment. Daniel brought her back as if it had been yesterday she'd said she would leave him.

"The two of you are impossible. How can two people so much in love be so determined to stay apart?" He pounded on the side of the carriage.

Traffic eased and they rolled past Hyde Park. When they first married and things started so well, he'd dreamed they would walk together in the park daily or at least a few times a week. They would talk of music and silly things happening in the ton. None of that had ever happened nor would it ever. "You are mistaken, Dan. There has never been a marriage with less to recommend it than mine. Dorothea most certainly does not love me."

"I disagree about her feelings. However, you love her, don't you?"

"My feelings are irrelevant. It takes two to make a marriage."

They neared Tom's townhouse and were not the first to arrive. Daniel leaned forward. "That is Markus's carriage."

"I have not seen him since the funeral. I did not think he was out and about." When Tom imagined what Markus going through, he was thankful that Dory had only left him. At least she lived. Was that hope? He brushed the thought aside as the carriage pulled behind the other.

Daniel shook his head and stepped to the street. "No one has seen him. I have written dozens of unanswered letters and even went to his house expecting to find him, but found only the staff and the baby. Markus had gone weeks before and not returned. A maid and the housekeeper were caring for the child. I understand your mother-in-law is there now."

"I had no idea." He should have known one of his best friends was suffering.

The front door flew open before they'd reached the landing. Crowly scowled. "Lord Markus Flammel is here to see you, sir."

Gut in a twist, Tom climbed the last steps and handed his hat and gloves to Crowly. "Where is he?"

"I tried to put him in the parlor, but he is in your study. I did not know what to do." If Crowly's frustration was an example of Markus's demeanor, it was going to be a tense visit with Dory's brother.

"Dan, if you want to run now, I will not blame you."

Slapping his back, Daniel said, "I will decide after we see him."

Markus lay stretched out on the dark leather sofa with a glass of brandy perched in his hand. Asleep, but skillfully not spilling his drink. He opened his eyes then narrowed them at Tom. "You. You. I." He took a long breath. "I have a complaint."

"A bit early for a drink, Markus." Tom rounded his desk and sat. Perhaps if he acted as if nothing was wrong, Markus would be civil.

Looking at the brandy like a lost lover, Markus sighed. He swung his legs over the side and yanked himself to sitting. There was a slow wobble while he steadied his torso, which kept swaying for a while. "I was thirsty and you were out. I helped myself."

"As it is Monday, Dan and I were at Jaffers." He pushed the stack of contracts to the side of his desk. The time for dealing with the mountain of work left while incapacitated would have to wait.

Markus lost focus, staring at the ceiling. Cravat hanging loose and morning coat wrinkled beyond repair, he looked more like a vagabond than a viscount. "Monday? Is it really? Well, no matter. I am angry and I will have satisfaction."

"Oh, for God's sake, not another duel." Daniel fell into a chair near the desk.

Groaning, Tom echoed Daniel's sentiment. "I am in no shape to meet you at dawn. I have only just recovered from my last bout of stupidity with your father. If you want to shoot me, you will just have to do it now and without all the fanfare."

Confusion twisted Markus's face and puckered his lips as he stood and wobbled forward. Collapsing into the other chair, he pointed at Tom. "I have no idea what you are talking about. I want to know why my sister writes me sad letters. Why do those letters come from Kerburghe and the Marlton country estate? I had just come to understand you had married her and now it seems you have put her aside?"

It took every ounce of Tom's will not to strangle Markus. "I have not put her aside. Your sister left me. Your father shot me in a duel and as soon as it was clear I would live, Dorothea left this house and has not returned. As for sad letters, I am sure you are mistaken. This is what she wanted. We do not suit and should go on with our lives."

Markus's eyes were slits, and he reeked of alcohol. "My father shot you?"

"Really, Markus, you must spend a moment's time outside your own misery." Daniel thumped his fist on the arm of the chair.

Hair pushed up on one side and in a tangle at the top, Markus tried to run his fingers through the mess, but he only succeeded in further mussing himself. "You said you do not suit." It was like the meaning was just filtering back through his mind as if a fuse was lit. "So you are putting her aside."

"I am complying with the lady's wishes."

Head in his hands, Markus swayed in his seat. "I am tired. Maybe we can discuss this at a later time."

Tom rang for Crowly, who appeared in the doorway an instant later. "Please, show the viscount to a guest room, Crowly."

"Yes, sir."

At the door, Markus turned back. "I shall have satisfaction on this matter, Tom."

"As you wish." Yet another person to worry over. Would it never end? When the thumping on the steps silenced, Tom turned to Daniel. "Did you know his drinking had taken such a turn?"

"No. I would have thought there would be some healing by now. He loved Emma, but this has gone too far."

There were not enough hours in the day to deal with the mounting issues in Tom's life. "Go home, Dan. I will take care of Markus when he wakes up."

"Are you sure?" Standing, Daniel tugged his jacket into place.

"I am well enough to deal with a foggy-headed friend. We will be fine." Tom stood and walked Daniel to the front door.

Maybe he should ask for help or run to Marlton and try to win his wife back, but he was tired of being in love alone. He'd told her how he felt, shown her in a dozen ways, including getting shot, and still she left him at the first opportunity. No. It was enough. He would live his life and she hers. That was what she wanted.

F inally, peace descended on the house as Tom tucked Markus into his carriage with instructions to the driver to take him home without stopping at a pub or anywhere else. Settling into his study, he pulled out the contracts for the West-grove property and a new ship he'd been considering buying. His duel and disastrous marriage had strained a few business relationships, but not enough to keep him from expanding.

He wrote a note to his man of business and one to his solic-itor about arranging inspections of the ship. The farm he had mixed feelings about. He'd hoped to move with Dory out to his country home for the winter. Then he could oversee the spring planting once the new land transferred. The music room in Middlesex was not as fine as the one in London, but that could be fixed. Without Dory, the prospect of wintering in the country was unappealing. He put the documents aside. The plans needed to go through. More was at stake than his heart, but he would think about it later.

A firm knock sounded on the door, followed by Crowly pushing through. "Sir, a letter has arrived by special messenger."

Tom took the envelope from the silver tray and a knot formed in the pit of his stomach. These types of letters rarely brought good news. "Thank you."

Michael's strong but messy hand scrawled the direction across the front.

Tom,

Elinor has tossed me from my own damn castle. I am sorry to bother you, but I am at my wit's end. I have gone to Faber Manor on the west side of my country estate.

Mother is at the main house and I loathe speaking to her about my troubles. Please come. I could use a friend at this time.

Michael.

Would there ever be peace for five minutes? Tom finished writing his business letters and rang for Crowly.

"Sir?"

"I must leave for Somerset immediately. Have Porter pack a small trunk. Post these letters for me. I should not be gone long."

Taking the envelopes, Crowly gave a curt bow. "Yes, sir."

Michael and Elinor had been through so much to get together; surely their marriage was unflappable. It was impossible they couldn't make a marriage work. What could have happened?

In less than an hour, he'd washed and dressed and was on the road west out of London. The dry roads made for easy travel. He stopped at dark, rose early, and finished the journey.

Faber Manor was a sturdy little house southwest of Bath at the edge of Rollins family lands. With gray stone and small windows the place had a quaintness.

A boy appeared from behind the house to manage the carriage and luggage. "There is no butler, sir. Please let yourself in the house."

Tom pushed open the creaking door. "Mike? Hello?"

The wood banister gleamed. He walked into a parlor on the left. The curtains were open, letting in light and showing off the exquisite mantle and dark wainscoting. It did not strike him as an unused cottage.

Quick footfalls drew closer.

Tom turned to greet Michael, but it was Dory who appeared in the doorway. He was dreaming. "What are you doing here?"

She looked down the hall and toward the front door then stared at him. Even frowning, her raspberry lips called for kisses. "I arrived five minutes ago. Where is Elinor?"

Why did she have to be so beautiful? Her gold ringlets called out for his fingers. Keeping his head was imperative. "How should I know? Is Braighton here?" The idea he had interrupted a tryst between his wife and Anthony Braighton was enough to triple his heartbeat. He bit the inside of his cheek to keep from letting his temper fly.

Breathing hard, she placed her hand on her chest. "No. Why would he be? He is at Marlton. Elinor wrote and said she would be here. She said she needed me."

Relief and panic flooded his chest. He pushed past her and rushed to the front door as his carriage rolled down the lane.

Dory stood beside him in the drive. "What is going on?"

Knowing at some point he would have to be in her presence again did nothing to steady his breath or desire. "I received a message from Michael stating that Elinor had tossed him from the house and he was here needing my help."

"Oh no. I received a similar note from Elinor." She crumbled and sat on the front steps. "They've tricked us."

He sat. Her lavender scent enticed him to take a deep breath. It was another thing he had missed about his wife but wished he could erase from his heart. "It would seem so."

"Now what do we do?"

"Unless you would care to walk fifteen miles to the nearest village, we have few alternatives."

A long sigh pushed from her succulent lips and she lowered her head to her knees. "I doubt very much that I am capable of walking that far. You may go. I assume they at least left us a cook or maid. I will be fine here until they send someone to retrieve me."

He could make the walk and perhaps hire a horse. The village he'd passed through on the way was without many resources. There might not be a means of transportation and no hotel in which to stay. It might be days before he arrived at Michael's house and that would mean leaving Dory unprotected. "I cannot leave you here alone."

Chapter Nineteen

D ory's heart beat so fast and hard she thought her corset might kill her. Autumn was pushing away the warmth of summer and the chill of the stone steps seeped through her skirts. "I do not see how we can stay here."

"Is the prospect so horrific?" The hollow despair ringing in his tone shot a dagger to her heart.

Standing, she brushed out her dress. "I am not afraid of you, Tom."

He rose and pulled his shoulders back. "I should hope not."

Such progress in his strength and mobility since last she'd seen him thrilled her more than she cared to admit. "My concern is being thrust together like this will be quite awkward and uncomfortable. My errors have been enough burden on you. The last thing I want is to cause you more pain." She hated the nervous shudder in her voice.

He glared at her through narrowed eyes. "I will endeavor to stay out of your way, Dory. Our friends do not intend to leave us here indefinitely. We shall return to our normal lives in a day or two."

What did that even mean? Nothing had been normal for months, not since Scotland. The rest of her married life had skewed normal for overwhelming misery. She had been a fool to think marriage could give either of them contentment. "I am very sorry that my presence is so abhorrent to you, Tom. Perhaps we might pretend we are friends as we were before I ruined everything. Then you might tolerate the next few days."

He gaped at her. "Is that what you think?"

He couldn't even imagine spending a day or two in her presence. Heartbroken, she shivered. She'd left her pelisse in the house and it grew colder by the moment. "I have taken the room on the left as you reach the top of the stairs. There are several other options for you. I will check if they left us any staff at all."

Without a word, he followed her inside and then took the lead into the parlor where she'd first found him. He pulled a cord near the door and waited with his arms crossed.

Dory hated feeling awkward and out of sorts. She sat on the overstuffed couch and fiddled with the brown piping along the trim. "You are looking well. Have you fully recovered?"

With a heavy sigh, he sat across from her. "I am well. My staff was vigilant in following your instructions. My life has returned to what it was before."

Before she'd ruined his life. Her chest ached with all she had cost him. Searching the simple furnishings did not give her an idea of what to say to continue the conversation. "Crowly did not come with you? I am surprised he would let you out of his sight."

"Crowly is my butler, and while he is not what the ton would consider traditional in the role, he does not follow me around like a valet. I left my valet at home because I was in a hurry and thought I would only see Michael. Had I known you were here..." He spread his arms out wide.

"I am your wife, Tom. You need not fuss because I am here." He thought of her as he did any woman of society. Perhaps he hadn't noticed she'd been gone, and all the while she'd pined for him. What a fool she was.

The muscles in his neck pulsed and he pulled his lips into a thin line. "There is no need to remind me of our relationship. I am well aware."

She wished the unattractive expression made her less desirous of his kisses, but she longed for him as she had the day she left London. "No, I suppose not." Desperate to keep some civil conversation going, she asked, "Have you been in the cottage before?"

He cocked his head. "When we were quite young, Michael ran away from home. His father was a lot like yours, though even more violent. After a long search, I found Mike here and took him home with me."

"So you rescued him much like you rescued me." It was his nature to save people. His letter had said he loved her, but perhaps it was just part of who he was that made him agree to the marriage.

"I would not have put it that way."

A young woman in a gray service dress and white cap stumbled into the room. "I had a bread about to pop and couldn't leave it, sir." She curtsied and wiped sweat from her brow with her sleeve, leaving a smudge of flour across her face.

"You are the cook? What is your name?"

"Jane O'Mally. I am the second assistant to the cook at Marlton, sir." She shifted her gaze to Dory.

Dory smiled and made the motion of wiping the flour off her own face.

Jane took the hint, pulled a kitchen towel from her waistband, and brushed the white streak from her skin. "I am to be your cook while you're here."

Standing, Dory stepped closer. "Did they send you here alone, Jane?"

Her eyes grew wide. "No, ma'am. Sam is here. He helps with the kitchen and any heavy work that needs doing. He's a good boy, if a bit daft."

They were good and stuck. One cook and a child for the heavy work. That would not get them out of there or her away from Tom. "Thank you, Jane. You may go back to the kitchen. We will call you if we need anything."

Darting from the room, Jane left a smudge of flour from her shoe on the wood floor.

"That is it, then." Tom stretched out his legs and crossed his ankles. "We shall have to stay here until one of our friends sees fit to collect us."

How could Sophia and Elinor have done this to her? It must have been Michael or Daniel who had arranged this mess. Still, the note she received was in Elinor's hand. Such things could be faked. Michael was a spy, skilled in many things, and would know how to imitate his wife's letters. "Your friends must have done this. Elinor would never have consented to such deception."

The muscles in his thighs flexed and as hard as she tried, she could not stop looking. "The same Elinor who conspired to use Middleton to lure Michael back and notoriously kissed Michael in public, thereby securing his proposal."

"You are twisting things around and you know it. I will not have you speak a bad word about poor Elinor. Clearly, she married a bully who forced her into this scheme."

"Poor Elinor? I have never known her to be as you describe. She could well have orchestrated this entire thing, and you sound like a petulant child." Tom stood, towering over her, and pointed his finger at her nose. "You know full well it was your friends who arranged all of this. Never have I met a more scheming gaggle of women." Glaring at her, he propped his fists on his slim hips.

Her gut twisted. At once she wanted to slap him and kiss him. Why did he have to be so, so Tom? "I will not hear another word of this." Needing to put distance between herself and him, she stormed from the parlor and up to her room.

~

Dory had paced the bedroom for an hour with the argument running through her head. She punched the bed pillow and tossed it across the room. It might have been she who had instigated the disagreement, but for the life of her, she couldn't understand why she'd done it. Embarrassed and ashamed of her behavior, she had slipped down to the kitchen and asked to have her dinner sent to her room.

She added loneliness to her complaints as she poked at her quail. The sun had long set, her corset was biting into her flesh, and she wanted the day to be over. Pushing the plate aside, she couldn't bear another bite with her stays strangling her. She stood and tugged at the ties at the back of her gown. Shoulders twisted, she pulled the bow at the bottom and it knotted. "Damnation."

Crossing to the bell-cord, she prayed Jane knew something of women's clothes. While she waited, she took off her sturdy travel boots and rolled down her stockings. The faster she could go to bed, the better. Maybe the morning would be better, though she couldn't imagine how. She waited, but no one came to assist her. Perhaps Jane was already in bed, or the bell was not working. In any case, she was trapped in her gown and corset.

It would be a long night, but she lay on the bed. The corset cut into her ribs and dug into her waist. "This is unbearable."

She got up and padded downstairs looking for Jane. The kitchens were dark and the servant's level unnerving with no one bustling about. The downstairs creaked and wind whistled above like a ghost in the grate. Dory gripped her skirts and ran up to the main level. Resigned to spend an uncomfortable night, she gave a final look in a door at the back of the house beneath the stairs. Inside, the moon illuminated a small pianoforte tucked under the window facing the gardens. With a dainty desk and tufted chair at one end, it must have been a ladies' parlor. Seating for three crowded the space.

She picked up the letter opener from the desk and brushed her thumb against the edge to test it for sharpness. Once back in her room, she would cut her stays. Great relief came with the notion of removing the torturous contraption. Still, the instrument beckoned her, and placing the knife on top, she sat on the stool. She placed her fingers along the keys and felt out a light tune.

The last note trickled from her fingertips only to be replaced by Beethoven's Piano Sonata No. 12. The pianoforte had the most delicate and resonant tone. Pachelbel's Canon in D followed. At the final coda, she sighed and closed the cover on the keys.

"I wish you would play one more," Thomas said from the threshold.

Heart leaping in her throat, Dory spun on the stool. "I thought I was alone."

"That is a lovely instrument. Perfectly tuned and suited to Pachelbel." He stepped closer and picked up the knife before raising his eyebrows.

Face on fire, there was no avoiding her purpose for the blade. "I could not find Jane and I am unable to get out of my dress. I found that and thought to cut myself free before I suffocate."

Tom smiled more with his eyes than those kissable lips. "Shall I help you?"

Before she could plan a response, he knelt behind her. "You have a knot."

It took two full breaths for her to find her voice. "My attempts to pull the bow ended badly."

"Why did you not come and ask me for help?" His fingers at the base of her spine sent a thrill through her.

Unbearable. She jerked away, but he wrapped a hand around her waist, keeping her seated. "I am no ladies' maid, Dory. You must give me a moment to work the knot out. It is unfortunate you would rather cut your gown than ask me for help."

"You were angry with me."

"Never so angry that I will not help you." Fabric slipped through with a whoosh and he unlaced the back of her dress.

Every inch of her skin burned with desire as she gripped the front of the gown to her breast lest it puddle on the ground. How was she going to get back to her room without making a fool of herself? The air in the parlor was heavy and fueled by longing and sorrow. Unable to move, she stared at the full moon.

"Shall I untie your corset?"

She should have told him no. She should have run from the room and suffered the night, but her voice betrayed her. "Please."

Warmth seeped from his deft fingers to her skin as he relieved the pressure of her undergarment. She sighed.

He ran a finger along the skin at her hip. "You have rubbed your flesh raw. This corset was tied much too tight, sweetheart."

Had he meant to use the endearment? It must have just been habit. "I had not planned on traveling. Normally, I would have changed to a light corset, but Elinor's letter sounded desperate, so I rushed from Marlton."

His lips pressed to her scratches sent her thoughts into a frenzy. He turned the stool so she faced him and stared up from his knees. "Are you in love with Anthony Braighton?"

Having heard his question did not make it translate into anything sensible. "What are you talking about?"

"He is a good man. I can understand that you might have fallen in love with him."

If he hadn't been so close she might have raged at him, but he was inches away and her heart pounded, her flesh burned, and she longed for more of his touch. "I think you have gone mad. Why would you ask me such a thing?"

"You have been much in his company. He is young, good looking, rich, and we have been estranged." In contrast to his words, he rested his head in her lap. "I have missed you, Dory. I have missed the music and I have missed talking with you."

"Just talking and music?" Her heart screamed at her that danger lay in her current path, but she ignored the warning. If she could have a night with Tom, she would treasure it, even if it was only one night. She ran her fingers through his soft hair.

"I missed the sound of your soft slippers walking down the hall toward me." Under her skirts, he ran his hand along her naked calf.

Wanton and no longer caring about the outside world, she ran her foot along his thigh. "An odd thing to miss."

"You have no slippers on now, nor stockings."

"I was getting ready for bed."

"You should have brought Emily with you." Kissing her stomach, he caressed the back of her knee.

It was as if he were touching her everywhere at once. She pressed her hips forward, welcoming his attention. "I returned her to my mother because I could not pay her and did not wish to spend your money. I have already cost you enough, Tom."

He stilled.

She wished she had kept her mouth shut. Expecting his anger to flare and another argument to ensue, she stiffened her back and gripped the front of her gown higher.

Lifting his head from her lap, Tom sat back on his heels. "I think it is time we had a talk, Dory."

"I did not think talking was what you had in mind a few moments ago." How she longed to have the warmth of his touch on her skin again and to hear the sultry tone of his voice.

Tucking a stray hair behind her ear, his fingers shot desire down to her toes and everywhere in between. "Our desire for one another can wait. I think we have both made errors. Perhaps if we talk, we can sort out what it is we want from this marriage. You injured me when you left London and I never wish to feel that way again. From what you just said, I glean that your feelings are different than what I believed. Can we sit and talk?"

That she'd hurt him broke her heart. She slid from the stool, crossed her legs, and sat on the rug in front of him. "I never meant to hurt you. I left so those things might heal."

"What things?" Tom took her hand and toyed with her fingers. Even that slight touch unlocked desires she'd buried months before.

"The damage my father and Hartly did. I know it was all my fault, but I had hoped you could recover your business losses and my going away would ease the social effects of my selfish acts. I am very sorry, Tom. I should have said so a long time ago. The last thing I ever wanted was to hurt you by asking you to marry me. It was selfish, but I only wanted to escape a terrible life and thought we might do well together as friends. I thought it would be amicable to be married and you might be happy. It is clear now I was only thinking of myself."

Dropping her hand, he shook his head. "Do you know why your plan did not work, Dory?"

"Because it was a foolish idea." She would never forgive herself for what she had done to him. So good and kind, he'd tried to save her and she could have killed him.

Taking her chin with his fingers, he tipped her head up to look at him. "No. It didn't work because you wanted to live like friends."

"Are we not friends, Tom? Please do not say I have ruined things so severely we cannot be friends. It is bad enough we live apart, but to lose your friendship, I could not bear it." How would she go on knowing what she had done? Everything she touched outside of music was doomed.

"Shh, Dory." He pulled her into his lap and brushed her hair from her face. "We are friends, but we cannot live as such because I am in love with you and have been for many years. Even though you do not return the sentiment, I had hoped love would grow between us. Then when I heard what you told Elinor on our honeymoon, I let the truth poison everything pleasant we had made. I am sorry."

"I was a fool, Tom. I was afraid that if I loved you, you would leave me or hurt me the way my father always tortures my mother. That is why I told Elinor I could never fall in love."

"I would never treat you that way." He hugged her tighter and kissed the top of her head.

The thing that had gone from her heart poked back in and hope spread through her. Hope that something good might come of all the pain she had created. "I was afraid and stupid. I am so sorry."

Easing her off his lap, his expression stern, he sighed. "Why did you leave London? Crowly told me he had shown you the letter I wrote. While I was embarrassed you had read a letter meant for after my death, I had hoped the rapport we shared during my recuperation was a good sign."

Cheeks on fire, she considered running from the room. Her heart pounded and her stomach knotted. No. Running away and keeping secrets was how they had come to this point. If he planned to leave her, hate her, or rail at her, it would be because of the truth and not an assumption. "I spoke to Michael. While he discouraged me from leaving, it was clear that your finances would make a quicker recovery if I was not under your roof. I should have stayed until you were out of bed for good, but I could not bear it and your life was no longer in danger. I saw the best thing to do to help you was to leave. That way my family and my mistakes would no longer harm you or your business."

Silently, he turned away from her. "It is getting chilly in here." Standing, he offered his hand to help her up.

Confused at the change of subject, she stared back.

"I thought I might light the fire and we can warm up. I have a few things I would like to say to you. It may take a little while and I do not want you to catch a chill."

She took his hand and stood. Her dress and corset puddled at her feet and he swept her into his arms in only her chemise before placing her on the thick rug near the fire. Lighting the fire in the grate sent flickers of white and gold across the room. Once the tinder caught, he tugged off his jacket and cravat and sat next to her.

Chapter Twenty

How had they gotten so far from the truth? Tom didn't know how it had happened but he wanted to pull them back to reality before it was too late. The last few moments had made it clear his belief in her indifference was untrue. Maybe she was lonely and wanted attention, but if that was the case she could have found comfort with Anthony Braighton. He liked Sophia's brother, but killing him was not out of the question. "Can you answer my original question before this goes any further?"

Wide-eyed, she searched the fire as if she might find the question there. She gasped. "I am not in love with Anthony Braighton. It is an absurd question."

"Is it?"

"Yes, Tom, it is." She crossed her arms, pushing her breasts up until they almost breached the lace trim of her chemise. Her hair hung around her shoulders, picking up the flicker of firelight.

His mouth watered at the sight of her. Still, he had to know. "Why? Why is it absurd?"

Rolling her eyes, she harrumphed. "Because I am in love with you."

The air evacuated the room. Perhaps the world was coming to an end. It could be he was dying. If that was the case, he would die contented. Tom's lungs ached and his hands shook so hard he fisted them to keep control. "Are you?"

"Yes," she whispered. Lovely in every way, she blushed the most charming pink from the part in her hair down to where her golden skin dipped beneath the cream fabric. "I love you."

"You are certain of this?" Maybe none of the rest mattered. They could begin from this night in the music parlor of an unused cottage and forget everything that had come before.

Leaning forward, she took his hand and kissed his fingers. "I have never been more certain of anything. Leaving you was the most difficult thing, but being apart from you broke my heart. I have never felt anything like it in my life. Every day I thought, this will pass, but it grew worse by the day and night. I longed to hear your thoughts. Teach you to play the harp. Learn how to be a wife to you. Discover new music together. I missed your input when I play and all I could write were dirges, which sent the house into tears, and me as well."

He should pull her into his lap and kiss every inch of her flesh until they were both sated and exhausted. Let Jane find them in the morning naked in front of the hearth. He wouldn't care. However, the misinformation standing between them gave him pause. They couldn't pretend the past had not happened. Too many things drove them apart. "May I set the records straight, Dory?"

She nodded and brushed her cheek along the back of his hand.

Skin as soft as a rose petal. Lord, it was painful not to touch her. "I have loved you for years. First, I loved you because you played like an angel sent from heaven and I could not resist your talent. When I knew you better, my love spread beyond the music room. You were above me in station, so I had resigned myself to never having you. When you came with your proposal, my heart reeled at the idea."

"You said no, if I recall." Letting go of his hand left a gaping hole between them.

"You were still above me, and more than that, you only wanted to marry me to escape Hartly. I knew a relationship would suffer because I was the only one who had any emotion invested. I was afraid loving you would destroy me."

She opened her mouth to speak, but he held up his hand.

"If I may."

She frowned, but nodded as she frayed the bottom of her chemise.

"With all my doubts, I could not allow Hartly to have you. It was too horrible a thought. Things were good at first and I let my hope outstep my good sense. Then I heard what you said to Elinor and it scared me to have left myself so open to the pain you could inflict with so little effort. I closed myself off and for that, I apologize. If I had made my presence known immediately, we could have talked the matter over."

She tugged the fabric, causing a tear. "Why did you accept the duel with my father?"

Rescuing her garment, he pulled her into his lap and took her hands in his. In part the position kept his hands from wandering all over her luscious body. "He challenged me in public. There was little I could do without becoming a joke among the ton. Still, killing him was not an option. I could not kill your father. Despite your strained relationship with him, I knew you would never forgive the man who killed him. My plan was sound. You would inherit my estate and never have to rely on your family to survive again."

"I am glad you survived."

"As am I. If he had been sober, it might have been a different outcome." He plucked at the lace along her shoulder and kissed her warm skin.

Resting her head on his shoulder, he was intoxicated by the scent of lavender. "So you would have died all because of me." Her tears dripped on his hand.

"I would die for you but it would not have been because of you, love. You are not responsible for the acts of your father or that ass Hartly. You are innocent of blame and I never thought otherwise."

"But what Michael said?" Her grip on his hands tightened.

"Michael told you the truth, but that does not mean I put a higher value on my finances than our marriage. I would lose a hundred fortunes to keep you in my life." He pressed his lips to her temple.

"But what about your farming plans and the country estate? You must be upset about that. I heard a land deal fell through. I know you had hopes for a new farming process."

Taking her by the shoulders, he turned her to face him, which landed them both on their knees. "If I lost a few pounds over the duel, so be it. Still, it was not your doing. I am very wealthy, Dory. Deals fall through all the time. Another piece of property will avail itself when the time is right. None of those things matter if I lose you. When you said we would be better off living separate lives, you tore my heart out. That is the only part of this that was your doing and I see now it all came from misinformation and lack of communication."

"I was a fool." She stared at the green and brown rug and wouldn't meet his gaze.

"We were both fools. I would like to make a bargain with you, sweetheart."

Her eyes were gleaming green pools he longed to drown in.

"No more hiding the truth. No more hoping the other will

say or do something to make us believe they love us. I love you. Do you believe me?"

"I do. I love you, too." Her breath came in short bursts, lifting her breasts in the most alluring way.

"I never thought any four words could make me so happy. From here forward we can have anything we want, Dorothea Flammel."

She cocked her head. "That is not my name."

"Dorothea Wheel." If a man could die from happiness, Tom was closing in on his demise.

Leaning forward, she kissed his jaw. "Would you be shocked if I suggested we make love right here on the rug, Tom?"

Already aroused, he came to full attention. "I am shocked." He pulled her close and kissed her. "But since I'd never make it up the steps in my current condition, I am also relieved."

She giggled. Her lips softened under his and she opened for him, welcoming his tongue inside and sighing against his mouth. "No more hiding and no more running away."

He quivered from the kiss. A million nightmares of a life without Dory washed away with the touch of lips. Her breath mingling with his was the elixir bringing him back life. Surviving the last few months had all been worth it to kiss her again. He knew he could never let her go. No more separations. "I cannot be without you," he mumbled against her neck.

"You shall never have to be." She released his blouse from his trousers and caressed his back.

On fire, he pressed her to the rug, intent on making up for months of separation.

She trembled beneath him.

"Are you cold?"

"No."

"Afraid?" He hated that she might be afraid of him or lovemaking.

"Not in the way you think."

"Why are you shaking?" Soft as satin, her skin shuddered beneath his fingers as he tried to caress away whatever caused the shudders.

Reaching up, she brushed the hair out of his eyes. "I have never wanted anything as I want you right now. Not company, not love, not music, nothing has ever been more urgent than the way I need you. That is both terrifying and wonderful."

The passion in her voice struck to the heart of him. "I understand."

"You will not make me wait, will you, Tom?"

In his head, he wanted to go slow and savor this moment. Other parts of him couldn't be as patient. He released her, stood, and stripped out of his clothes.

She scanned his body from head to toe. A warm blush bloomed over her entire body.

Wherever she gazed caught fire until he could bear it no longer. He knelt between her legs. "I will not make you wait because I am not capable of holding back."

Lying on top of her, he eased forward until his shaft pressed inside her. Pure heaven encased him as he waited for her body to stretch.

Gasping, she gripped his shoulders.

Nothing would ever be so perfect again. He eased back, intent on slowing things down and seeing to her pleasure first.

Dory wrapped legs around his hips and pulled him inside for a quick thrust. Crying out, she threw her head back and tipped her hips to bring him deeper.

Lost, nothing could stop him. He thrust deeper and faster until the world and everything in it exploded.

Her body quivered around him and she shuddered out her pleasure.

His own rapture blinded him to hers. "We shall have to do that again, my love."

Idly, she traced her fingers up and down his back. She lifted her hips. "Will we?"

Needing a few minutes, he groaned, but let the pleasure wash over him. "I forgot to open my eyes and watch as you found pleasure. I love to watch you."

Eyes closed, she smiled sweetly. "I can deny you nothing."

∼

Sweat glistened on her skin and he kissed her shoulder. For Tom, only one thing could make the night better. "Will you play for me?"

She rolled to face him. Gloriously naked, her hair a mass of tangles around her heart-shaped face, she'd never been more beautiful. Her smile lit the room. "It will be dawn soon."

"We only have two servants here. No one will look for us, and I will lock the door if you will play for me as you are." The notion had him fully aroused.

"Are we exchanging wishes?" A serious tone fell over her question.

Propping himself up on one elbow. "What do you wish, love? If it is in my power, you can have anything."

"I want to go to Kent and meet your mother."

Nothing could have brought him more joy or surprised him more. She did not want a house or a new harp. She wanted to be part of his family. "As soon as we are free to leave, we will go see my mother. She will love you as much as I do."

Catlike she stretched along the rug. Golden and delicious, she pulled herself up in a languid motion.

His mouth watered and his body burned for more of what he should have already satisfied. Did she know what she did to him? Watching her cross to the instrument, he banked the fire. The room had become stuffy. In part to open the window and in part to be close to her, he followed her.

The morning air lifted the room even though he kept the curtains closed.

Full breasts exposed and her nipples tight from the breeze, she placed her hands on the keys.

Tom forced his breath out as he leaned against the pianoforte and let the first strains of Handel flow through him. He hoped he lived to be an ancient man and woke every morning to the sights and sounds before him. They would be old and wrinkled, but he would adore watching her play and making love to her until they left the earth.

Her body, the music, the quiet of dawn. Perfection.

She played the last note, her eyes full with passion as the tone resounded off the walls. "Thank you," she said.

"What can you possibly be thanking me for?" His heart had lodged in his throat. In spite of the large music room in his London home, he was considering putting an exact replica of that one in the back parlor.

"For agreeing to let me meet your mother, and loving my music and understanding it. Mostly, for loving me despite my mistakes."

He wiped the tear that escaped her eye and kissed the moisture from his thumb. He longed to be a part of her happiness. "If you knew how happy I am that you want to meet her, you would not say it. Your music is a gift from God and I would be a fool not to understand and love it. We have both made mistakes, Dory. I dare say we will make more before long, but we shall make them together from now on." The stool was too small for two. Tom brought a chair over and sat next to her.

"I love this room." She trilled out a few randomly beautiful notes and then a chord.

He placed his hands alongside hers and played a third creating harmony. "I was thinking we should put a parlor just like this in the London house."

"We already have a very nice music room in London." She began the Sonata for Piano for four hands.

Elation shot through him as if he'd been set on fire by the idea she wished to play a duet with him. He joined her in the music. "Can we put a pianoforte in the bedroom?"

"It would have to be a small one." She emphasized the next stanza more than it was written in the score.

Loving someone so much would be more wonderful than he expected. She could tear him apart with a word. He trusted she never would. "I shall see if Michael would like to sell this fine instrument. I quite love the tone."

Her smile was worth the fleecing Michael would give him for the sale. She gentled her play. "Until I married you, I had never written a piece for four hands."

"It shall be a fun endeavor for us to take on."

～

Two days later, Tom and Dory were walking the property when three carriages paraded down the drive. Tom gripped her hand tighter and she returned the squeeze. Regretting the end of their short holiday would not keep the carriages at bay. "It would seem our rescue is at hand."

She sighed and kicked the gravel path. "A shame."

Lifting her hand to his lips, he gave a squeeze then kissed her fingers. "I agree, yet it will not keep me from giving our friends a sound talking to. They had no right to trap us here."

"If they had not, we might never have spoken and worked out our differences."

He stepped in front and faced her. "It might have taken longer, love, but I believe you and I would have found our way back to each other."

She closed the gap between them and brushed dust off his jacket. "I am glad we did not waste any more time."

Dreams of growing old with Dory warmed him as much as she had warmed his bed. They had started writing a promising duet for pianoforte and put the music room to good use in other ways as well. "I would not trade a moment of the last two days."

The carriages stopped near the front door. Daniel and Sophia hopped down from the first and Michael and Elinor from the second. The third carriage was his own, and he narrowed his eyes at Mally atop the driver's seat.

Mally did not make eye contact.

Daniel grinned like an idiot. "Do not blame poor Mally, Tom. He had his orders and I made serious threats to get him to comply."

Swept away into the house by Sophia and Elinor, he missed Dory next to him more than was healthy. She had become as important as air to him. He forced a deep breath. "Fine, then I shall take up my complaint with you two. How dare you trap me here with no means of getting away."

A cool breeze rustled through the trees. Autumn had arrived and winter would not be far behind. Tom dreamed of warm fires and fur throws with Dory wrapped in his arms. It was difficult to remain angry with his friends while entertaining such thoughts.

Michael slapped him on the back. "You could have walked to town."

"Dorothea could not have traversed that distance and you know it."

Walking toward the front steps of the cottage, Daniel said, "You could have left her here and gone about making your way home."

"It isn't as if you had no options." Michael followed Daniel. "Your health has returned. You had the means to leave."

It had been a beautiful day for a walk when he'd asked Dory to join him. Dark clouds blew in on the cool wind. "You know full well I could not leave my wife here with no protection. An assistant cook of perhaps sixteen years and a kitchen boy are not ample staff for a lady. But you both knew that and know me well enough to recognize I would not leave her. This was all carefully planned and I will have my say about it."

Daniel turned at the top step and fisted his hands on his hips. "Have your say, then. I regret nothing. You were both acting like children and someone had to put a stop to the stupidity. So, your friends conspired to trap you with the one woman who can make you happy. Oh, and she happens to be your wife."

"You had no right to interfere." It was a weak argument. Tom had never been happier in his life, making it difficult to drum up any real wrath.

Michael climbed the steps. "You gave us little choice, Tom. Someone had to get the two of you in the same room. Besides, from the way you were looking at Dory when we rolled up, I'd say things have worked out for the best."

"The outcome does not justify the means. Do not interfere with my life again."

Daniel raised an eyebrow. "As long as you do not act the ass, we will mind our own business. Beyond that, I make you no promises."

It was too funny not to laugh. He and Dory had behaved like idiots. They'd made assumptions and avoided subjects, which undid any good between them. It was their inability to communicate that had landed them in trouble. "Fair enough. Since I have no intention of ever allowing my wife to journey more than one hundred feet away from me, I should be safe from your trickery."

A wide grin spread across Daniel's face. "I am happy to hear it."

The first drops of rain tapped his jacket.

Michael said, "I think we had better get inside. We need to speak on a subject less pleasant than the state of your marriage, Tom."

Tom's gut tightened. "What now?"

The ladies were in the music room so they settled into chairs in the parlor. Daniel paced as he often did when struggling with a problem.

Not much out of short pants, Sam ran in. Awkward arms and legs, he took their hats and gloves before tripping out of the room.

Sitting and stretching his legs in front of him, Michael said, "Hartly is looking for you. They have that Sanford Wormfield asking around town about your whereabouts. It seems they took the opportunity of your absence to spread rumors about your shipping line being in trouble and near collapse. Our plan had been to leave the two of you here a fortnight, but this new scheme brought us back earlier. The word is that Hartly contacted the Westgrove heirs and they will pull out of your arrangement before the deed is signed."

"Damn him. It took me months to get them to agree and I have offered them more than the property is worth." Tom shook his head. "Gordon Westgrove and I were in short pants together. He will not believe anything without checking with me first. I am certain I can smooth it over. The shipping line rumor will take a bit of work to fix. We must go to London immediately."

Dory would think this was her fault. "Is Castlereagh still involved? I paid his debt to that old codger."

Stopping his pacing, Daniel ran his fingers through his blond hair. "The word at White's is that as soon as you had paid his old debts, the earl set about creating more. His gambling and bad business dealings are getting worse. In the past, Markus has kept him in check, but since Emma's death he has not been watching his father."

"I suppose Lord Hartly will have to be dealt with. Perhaps we can get my father-in-law out of this and save Markus's inheritance as well."

Dory opened the parlor door and all three women joined them. Her smile fell as soon as she saw his face. "Is something wrong?"

There was no debating what he would tell her as there had been in the past. It was a new relationship and promises had been made. "Unfortunately, we will have to delay our trip to Kent."

"I see. What has happened?" As she sat on the couch, her lavender skirts fluffed out around her and she stared at him.

He hated to say it. How could he? She would blame herself. "I am hesitant to tell you."

It was as if all the air went out of her at once. Her shoulders slumped, her head bowed, and she sighed. "It's Father again, isn't it?"

"Hartly and his man, Wormfield, are making trouble. They have gotten the rumor mills churning, and your father is running up debt again." He put his hand on her shoulder.

Shaking her head, she gripped his hand. "Then we must go to London and put a stop to this insanity. I for one have had enough."

Pride swelled in his heart. If she blamed herself, she did not give in to it. "We can start back as soon as this rain eases."

Chapter Twenty-One

The rain continued unhindered past the dinner hour. Young Sam ran in during the meal and informed them that the bridge had washed out. Dory sighed, but she liked having another night in the cottage even if it was small for six people.

Sitting down for cards in the parlor, it was nice to think she would host her friends in her own home as Mrs. Wheel of Middlesex.

"Will this rain ever stop?" Elinor fussed with her cards.

Dory laughed. "It is justice for you stranding us here. Now you see what it is like to be trapped and unable to leave at one's leisure."

Cuddled on the couch Sophia and Daniel looked the perfect match. Sophia said, "I love this little cottage. I have a mind to use it as a holiday spot. Look at the miracle it worked with you two."

Cheeks heated, Dory found Tom smiling at her from across the table. "I would not mind returning from time to time."

Michael said, "You are welcome to it whenever you like.

Though keep in mind, you will need to send staff ahead. Most of the time, I keep this old place closed. I only sent Jane and Sam with a cart full of supplies so you wouldn't starve."

"It is a good thing you sent enough for a fortnight, or there would be scarce enough to feed the six of us overnight." Dory's cards were terrible. She doubted they could make a pass.

It was unusual to see Michael so animated. Tossing his cards in the middle of the table, he stood. "I have a crazy idea."

Dory put her cards down, glad the hand was over.

Tom asked, "What idea?"

"To do with your problem, Tom. I think I know how you can stop any further damage by Hartly and perhaps mend what he's already done." Michael crossed to the window. The constant spray of rain against the glass droned on.

"As long as your plan does not include separating from my wife, I am listening."

Michael turned and looked from Dory to Tom and back again. "It's a bit dangerous. It would be better if Dorothea stayed with Elinor or Sophia until this was over."

"I know Father has been impossible and I think he should be taught a lesson. However, we must keep in mind any financial damage we do to Father, we do to Markus, Mother, and Adam." Dory had been a part of Michael's schemes before and while it started out exciting, in the end, it had been frightening.

Michael added a log to the dwindling fire. "I am well aware. You will pardon me, Dory, but your father is a fool and easily handled. Hartly's jealousy was likely behind the duel. He hoped to keep himself out of the fray and still get his way. Hartly is not a fool and he employs a dangerous man. He had his money and would have been wise to walk away, but instead he continues in his attempts to harm Tom. If we set the stage, he will make his move."

"What is the danger?" Dory asked.

Michael, Daniel and Tom exchanged glances. Michael said, "We do not know how far he will go. He may intend to finish where your father failed."

"You think he will try to kill Tom?" She had to catch her breath.

Tom took her hand and rubbed the tension out of her fingers. "Relax. We are ready this time. Nothing will happen to me."

"Michael said Mr. Wormfield is dangerous, Tom. Maybe it would be best if we went to the authorities. Surely someone from Bow Street would be able to offer us protection."

"Do not let Michael bully you into doing anything you do not wish."

"Thank you, wife." Michael leveled his gaze on Elinor but his eyes danced with laughter.

"I have been Dory's friend far longer than your wife, and you can be a bully about these schemes of yours."

Shrugging, Michael said, "It is entirely up to the two of you. I have no objection to contacting James Hardwig. He has proven very helpful in the past."

"What am I to tell James? There has been no threat made. Spreading rumors is Hartly's only crime and the inspector has better things to do than chase those." Tom tugged on the bottom of his jacket as he stood.

Daniel stopped his pacing. "He's a good friend. Tell him you are laying a trap."

So much of what the men were planning was unspoken, Dory had trouble keeping up. "I am not privy to your silent communication. Can you tell me what it is you plan to do?"

Michael laughed. "Sorry, old habit. My idea is to leak information that Tom is back in London. I will see that Hartly or Wormfield is informed about his whereabouts. Then we wait and see if he does anything."

"Tom is bait? No. It's too dangerous."

"I am not without skills, Dory." Tom leaned against the mantle.

"My father shot you and you nearly died." Her voice had taken on a shrill that was too reminiscent of her mother in one of her states.

Tom shook his head. "That was a matter of honor and I let your father shoot. It is not the same."

"You said yourself that Wormfield is dangerous."

Michael said, "He is, but we are more dangerous and with better resources. Send James a note, Tom. Tell him what has happened and what we plan. If I know him, he already knows all the gossip."

Shaking his head, Tom met her gaze. "Please, Tom."

"I can deny you nothing, Dory. I will write him as soon as we return to London."

~

London was emptying as the colder weather came in. Dory was glad Mother had gone to see Markus. Father would not leave until there was no one left to drink with. She spent the morning trying to convince Father to stay away from Hartly and go to the country, but he just ranted about her marriage until she was forced to leave the house.

Tom opened the carriage door as soon as it stopped in front of their townhouse. "Are you all right?"

Here was her family. Her brothers would visit. She would make Tom's mother love her, and perhaps even Mother would stay close. Whatever Father's objectives, they soon wouldn't matter. "I am fine. He reacted exactly as expected despite his inebriated state."

Lifting her down from the carriage, he kissed the top of her head. "Was it terrible?"

"Nothing I did not expect, but I admit I had hoped for a different reaction." If only she could stay in Tom's arms forever, she could lose herself and think of nothing else. His spicy, warm scent made everything better.

"Michael has already made certain Hartly is aware of my itinerary for the evening. James is in the study." Embracing in the middle of the street, they were a spectacle.

A carriage rolled down the street. She pulled away. "You left a guest alone in the study?"

Hand in hand he led her up the steps. "James understands such things. He is a very old friend."

"From when you served the crown?"

"Yes."

"And he protected you?"

Crowly opened the door and took her coat and gloves.

"We protected each other when we were in France. James saved my life a few times. He is a good man."

"Then I like him already." She preceded Tom into the study.

James Hardwig stood looking out into the garden. He wore a rumpled gray coat and his belly protruded over his breeches. His thinning blond hair was combed back across a bald spot and he ran his hand over it. Rocking from toe to heel, he turned as the door closed behind them.

Tom stepped forward. "James, this is my wife, Dorothea Wheel."

James bowed. "A pleasure to meet you, Mrs. Wheel."

Reaching out, she took his hand and held it in both of hers. "The pleasure is mine, Inspector Hardwig. I cannot thank you enough for assisting us."

Blushing bright, James stuttered, "I—it is my honor,

madam. However, I hope there will be nothing to assist with. For tonight, Mr. Wheel will go to White's and then a gaming hell. His Grace is making sure Hartly knows where and when. We will keep watch and make sure if anything happens Wheel is out of danger."

"I have to tell you, Inspector, I am not at all comfortable with this plan. White's may be respectable and easy to control, but a gaming hell? How will you keep Tom safe?" She gripped the edge of the chair and forced her voice to remain steady. Inside she was screaming.

Tom's steady hand on her shoulder helped. "Dory, sit down. I will be fine. I know you think I am some soft gentleman, but I do know how to defend myself."

"I think nothing of the sort." She sat. "It is only that placing yourself in harm's way is foolish."

A chuckle from James reminded her they were not alone. "Don't worry yourself, Mrs. Wheel. I will keep a close eye on him."

"And what if nothing happens at White's or the gaming hell?" She leaned back and closed her eyes. Taking deep breaths, she tried to slow her heart.

Tom sat behind his desk. "Michael insists on staying with us here until this is resolved. If you want to go and stay with Marlton or Elinor, you will be safer."

He was trying to get rid of her. Even though it was a ridiculous thought she couldn't help it. "I will not leave my home or you."

"It may all amount to nothing," James said. "In a few days, it will all blow over and life will be back to normal. Do not fret, madam."

"He's right, Dory. Relax. I am not sending you away. I only suggest it as an option if you are insecure about staying here."

"I am not." She stared him in the eye.

"Very well, then." Smiling, Tom met her gaze before turning to James. "You had best get in place, James. I will make my way over in a little while."

Taking a step toward the door, James nodded then stopped. He turned toward Dory and bowed. "It is an honor to meet you, Mrs. Wheel. I am extremely happy my friend has found such a fine lady to share his life with. I hope you do not think me too bold for saying so."

There was something charming about the inspector. He was rough and unkempt and without means or title, yet he managed to endear himself. "Thank you, Inspector. You are too kind."

James closed the door behind him.

Tom pulled her from the chair into his arms.

Settling her head on his chest, she sighed with the comfort of it. "Should you not go to White's?"

He closed his arms around her and kissed the top of her head. "I do not wish to leave you alone. I will go soon enough."

Being tucked in next to him was delicious. "Do not be silly. Crowly is here, as is the rest of the staff. I am hardly alone. You should go."

People chattered in the foyer.

"We are here," Sophia yelled from behind the door.

The door opened, admitting Sophia and Elinor in a shuffle of skirts. Crowly stood behind them and shook his head before he shrugged and walked out.

Dory pulled herself upright. "What are you two doing here?"

"We could not possibly let you wait all alone." Sophia flounced into one of two club chairs.

Tom stood and bowed. "Thank you, ladies. I had better go. As soon as this is finished, I will return with a full report."

Watching him leave, Dory wished she'd had another

private moment to tell him she loved him and to be careful. She stared at the door long after he was out of sight. Left behind was a hole, which no other person had ever filled. She was being childish. "Elinor, please sit. I will call for tea."

"Tea would be lovely." Elinor sat in the other club chair. "It seems odd for us to be having tea in such a masculine room rather than a lady's sitting room or parlor."

Sophia ran her hand along the worn leather chair. "I like it. All that lace and damask gets on my nerves. This is cozy."

Leave it to an American to see through all the frills. Dory loved this study because it was where Tom worked throughout most of the day, but she also liked the warm aesthetic.

A scratch at the door sounded, and the under-maid dragged in a bucket of wood and fed the fire. Once the blaze was going well, she stood and wiped her hands on her apron.

"Fiona, please tell Cook to bring tea."

Half grabbing her bucket and half curtsying, Fiona said, "Yes, madam."

Elinor leaned back in her chair. It was not her normal lady-like, straight-backed pose. "I hate waiting for news. If we were men, we could stomp into White's and watch what happens firsthand."

Sophia rubbed her stomach. "Speaking of firsthand accounts, how did it go with your father?"

"As expected."

"Fathers." Elinor harrumphed. "I am sorry, Dory. It must have been terrible for you."

Elinor's anger was clear while Sophia's gaze dropped to the burgundy rug and she repeated the rubbing of her stomach.

It was a telling move and the three were close enough that Dory asked, "I do not mean to be indelicate, Sophia, but are you with child?"

Her golden eyes lost their sorrow and filled with joy. She nodded. "I suspect a few months."

Squealing with delight, Elinor bounded from her chair and threw herself at Sophia. "Why did you not tell us?"

"So much has been going on that I thought I would wait until we got back to normal."

Dory laughed. "I am afraid this may be our normal."

"You may be right."

They talked of babies and other craziness long after the tea arrived.

~

Tom left the gaming hell when an argument broke out. He never saw Hartly, Wormfield, or Hardwig for that matter. Eyes blurry from cigar smoke and bad drink, he knew why he'd stopped going to such places. He made his way around the crush of men who had filed down the hallway when the commotion began.

Daniel and Michael had left after White's to see to the safety of the women. Michael would make it look like he went home with Elinor, but he would make sure Dory was safe. Between him and Crowly, no one would get inside the townhouse. Dawn was only an hour away and Tom's bed was calling to him. Maybe they had overreacted. If Hartly wanted him dead, he'd had ample opportunities tonight. He climbed into his carriage. "Mally, take me home."

The dodgy neighborhood had no streetlamps and the road was badly rutted. The carriage jerked from side to side. Tom grabbed hold of the seat to keep steady as they turned a corner. The carriage was moving too fast. Mally knew better than to run these streets recklessly.

Banging on the roof, he yelled to Mally to slow down. His

heart raced and the hair on the back of his neck prickled. This was all wrong.

They turned another corner. Outside, Parliament, the river, and the scent of doom all filtered through the blur of a quickening pace.

The cab shifted sharply, its weight forcing it to balance on one wheel.

Tom leaned to the other side, trying to create counterbalance. As if he were in some strange dream, the carriage slowly toppled to its side. His shoulder smashed against the wall as it hit the ground.

Horses cried and tugged the carriage on its side for several feet.

People yelled and barked orders.

Tom's head spun and he had to blink to clear his vision. Head aching and shoulder screaming with pain, he righted himself ready to climb out of the door, which was now the top of the carriage.

The barrel of a pistol poked through the window with the scarred face of Sanford Wormfield. "You didn't think a fine gentleman like Lord Hartly would let a nobody like you walk away with his prize, did you?"

Fury roiled in Tom's gut. If he hadn't had Dory to go home to, he would have rushed the man and his pistol with no regard for his own life. Threats only served to sharpen his senses and feed his resolve. "Dorothea is my wife and killing me will not change anything. I have made arrangements for her to be a wealthy widow."

"It don't make no difference to his lordship. He will have her even if he must use her father as leverage to get her. You don't think that sweet thing will let her father die, do you?" Grinning, Wormfield exposed rotting teeth. Even at a distance, his fetid breath soured the air.

Dory would not be able to withstand threats to her father even after all he'd done. If Tom died, she would end up with Hartly and this monster. "Shoot me, then, and you will go to jail for a crooked old man."

"I'm well compensated, and once the carriage goes in the river, the evidence will be washed away. This time of day, no one of note will have seen a thing." He pulled back the hammer on the pistol.

"That will be enough of that." James called from somewhere in the street. "Now you just ease that gun out of Mr. Wheel's carriage and step down. We have your men in custody and I have heard more than enough to get you sent down to Australia and might even do some damage to that lord you work for, too."

The click of several pistols being readied sounded from the street as Wormfield turned away from the window.

"I'm innocent. Lord Hartly made me come after Mr. Wheel. It's all his doing."

"I am sure of that. Now put the pistol down and climb off that carriage," James said.

The carriage shook and Wormfield moved out of Tom's view.

Tom climbed up the seat and threw open the carriage door. It slammed against the carriage.

"All right there, Tom?" James asked.

"Just a few bruises, James. It took you long enough."

"You're lucky we managed to follow at all as fast as the maniac was driving. We nearly lost you round the first bend. Then I needed to hear the evidence before I stepped in, didn't I?"

"I am relieved you arrived in time," Tom admitted.

Mally sprinted up the street toward them with a distinct

limp in his left leg. "Sir. They grabbed me and tossed me from the carriage. I tried to follow."

Tom jumped down to the street. "You are hurt. James, call a doctor."

"I'm all right, sir. It's nothing. Do you think the horse will go home?" Mally stared at where the bridle had ripped away from the wreck.

Tom helped Malley into a Scotland Yard carriage. "James, can you see if your men can find my horse and bring her home?"

"It was the Earl of Hartly. I'm innocent." Wormfield struggled against two of Hardwig's men before they locked him in a wagon bound for jail."

Shaking his head, James approached Tom. "What do you want to do about his lordship?"

"I suggest we pay him a call, Inspector. I may get something good out of that pig after all. I think he owes me now, and there are some children in Middlesex who need a school. Perhaps Lord Hartly will think it a good idea to pay for renovations rather than go to prison or at the very least be left socially dead."

"Just tell me when, Tom. You know, whenever I see you, it is great fun." James pounded Tom's back and walked away.

Tom told the driver to take he and Malley home.

~

It wasn't very ladylike, but Dory was waiting outside at the top of the steps when his carriage pulled up. It was daylight and she gleamed like an angel. She rushed down the steps as soon as he stepped out. "Are you hurt? Your face is bruised. What happened? Why are you in this carriage? Is Mally limping?"

Unable to stop himself, he wrapped her in his arms and kissed her until his head spun.

Her gasp gave him opportunity to deepen the kiss. Wrapping her arms around his neck, she pressed against him.

Giggles sounded from the doorway.

Daniel cleared his throat. "You are giving your neighbors quite a show. Perhaps you might take all that inside the house."

Laughing, Michael said, "We may need to call the fire brigade."

Inside the house, she held him near the door while the others went to the study.

"Crowly, Mally needs a doctor. Can you see to it?"

"Yes, sir."

Keeping her hand in his, Dory waited for Crowly and Mally to disappear through the door to the servant's stairs. "What happened? Are you all right?"

"I am fine. The carriage is destroyed, but we have what we need to keep Hartly from ever bothering us again."

Lavender filled his senses and shot waves of desire through his body. "I think we should rush through visiting, go to the music room, and play until we cannot help but rip each other's clothes off."

The most stunning pink filled her cheeks. "I could do that without playing a note."

He pulled her into his arms and took the steps two at a time.

"Tom, we have guests who stayed all night waiting for news of you." Despite the urgency of her tone, she threaded her fingers through his hair.

Fighting taking her on the steps, he made it to their bedroom door. "They will figure it out in a few minutes and go home. We can make it up to them later. I love you, Dory. I do not wish to share you with anyone right now or maybe ever again."

"We cannot stay locked in the bedroom indefinitely." She pulled him down as he rested her on the bed.

Nibbling her soft shoulder and up along her neck to the back of her ear pushed little gasps and sighs from her delicious lips. "Just for a while, then. I will share you in a few days when we go to visit Mother."

"Mm, yes, a few days. Until then you are all mine."

Tom's heart was full to overflowing. "I thought you were all mine."

"We must agree to disagree on that point, my love." She kissed along his jaw.

"Perfect."

Epilogue

One Year Later

Dory let the music take her where love and light met and euphoria blanketed her from head to toe. It was the last piece she would play for the evening and she lost herself in the sorrow and joy. Notes rolled into phrases and trilled from her fingertips in an emotional story, which pulsed through the cavernous music hall. She sat up straight for the Crescendo, heart pounding. Then, breathing as she reached the Delicato of the final notes, she relaxed.

The last note vibrated against the strings inside the pianoforte and faded to silence. Resting her fingers on the ivory keys, Dory breathed in the silence.

A clap shattered the quiet. A second set of hands joined the first in a tentative staccato.

The hall erupted into a hail of cheers, bravos, and applause. Somewhere between horror and relief, Dory's heart found its normal rhythm. She indulged in two long breaths before sliding to the edge of the bench. Once standing, she took a moment to steady her shaking legs and curtsied to the large audience at the royal hall.

In the center of the front row, the Prince of Wales stared at her, his flop of curly brown hair as unruly as ever and his royal robes a rich burgundy. He stood with eyes so intense she wondered if she had dirt on her face.

The hall fell silent. Never had a woman performed such as Dory had tonight. Some things, no matter how beautiful, were still aberrant to the ton. If Prince George cut her, she was finished as a musician and in society. With one word, this man could ruin her.

With tears in his eyes, Prince George gave Mrs. Dorothea Wheel a nod.

Heart in her throat, she curtsied, dropping until her head was inches from the floor. When she rose, His Royal Highness's lips twitched in a half-smile.

The audience resumed their vigorous clapping, stopping only long enough to bow to Prince George as he left with his entourage. He shone as bright as the gilded walls and the ton moved in a wave of colors like spring flowers. It was a rainbow of indulgence and he was the center of it.

Thomas, dressed in elegant black with a crisp white cravat, rushed up the three steps to the stage and took her hand. "Magnificent, my love. You were the best I have ever heard you. I could not be more proud."

His pride sent a surge of warmth through her. "Thank you, Tom. I have to admit, while it feels good to have done it, I am quite glad it is over."

A smile spread across his handsome face as he threaded her hand through the crook of his elbow and accompanied her down to the crowd waiting to give her their approval. "You have done it, and if you choose to never do it again, this night will be remembered as the greatest musical event for years to come."

"And would you be satisfied if I never perform in public again?" The question had haunted her for months as she prepared for her debut concert.

He stopped short of the main floor and leaned close to her ear. "This night is about you, my love. I am only a grateful spectator. I have the supreme honor of hearing you play daily. Doing this, accomplishing what you did tonight, was for you and you alone. Enjoy it. If you never play in public again, I will love you as much as I do today and feel just as lucky to call you my wife."

The tension eased around her gut and she took a breath before scanning the crowd for their friends. Markus had not come, but Elinor, Michael, Sophia, and Daniel were there.

Even her young brother Adam was in attendance. He ran over, all legs and arms, to give his congratulations. "You really were good, Dory. I cannot wait to tell my mates at school that my sister played for the Prince. No one will believe it."

Dory hugged him. "Thank you, Adam."

At the back of the room, Margaret Flammel watched.

Dory met Mother's gaze over Adam's shoulder.

With a nod, Margaret smiled and left the hall.

Tears filled Dory's eyes and she dashed them away, pushing down the brick of emotion lodged in her throat. It shouldn't have matter what Mother thought, but seeing the pride in her eyes washed away a lifetime of censure. The irony was if Margret had given her approval years before, Dory might have felt no need to have the heir to the crown of England validate her skill.

Sophia pushed through the crowd and grabbed Dory in a hug.

Elinor had cried a river, making her eyes red and her nose

swollen. "You played as if no one was watching, Dory. You broke my heart and mended it a dozen times tonight. I wish I could bottle up the perfection you created and take it home with me."

Always her greatest musical admirer, Elinor's praise brought Dory to tears, which she pushed down by biting the inside of her cheek. "I am glad you enjoyed it, and you know I will play for you anytime you like."

Friends and acquaintances paid their respects to Dory. Some congratulated Thomas, though he brushed those off, saying it was not he who played.

* * * *

It was hours before they could leave the Royal Music Hall and go home. In the privacy of their bedroom, Tom poured them each a brandy before sitting by the fire.

He had spent most of his life wishing to have the gifts he so admired in Dory. Watching her play to the most prestigious crowd in London had been a singular moment in his life. Even a year later, he was in shock every time he considered his good fortune. Why she would want him when she could have had anyone was still a mystery to him, but he thanked God every day for his luck. "Now that you have done what you thought only a man could do, what will you attempt next?"

Wearing her nightshift and wrap, she shivered and pulled the wool blanket from the hassock. Snuggling in, she sipped the brandy. "I do have a project in mind, but I shall need your approval, Tom."

"Since when do you require my permission to do anything?" Tom put down his drink and pulled the lap harp close before he strummed a C chord. One of his favorite parts of the day was how they finished each day with music. Some nights they indulged in a session in the music room and more than once the downstairs maid had discovered them after dawn. Usually, she found them asleep on the chaise, but more than once she found them nude and sprawled on the rug by the hearth.

Tom suspected his staff enjoyed a good giggle over some of the antics Dory and he engaged in while sharing their love for each other and music.

She put the brandy down. "For this, it is necessary that you and I work together."

Intrigued, he played a G chord. "Have you been working on a duet for us?"

Her cheeks turned the loveliest shade of pink. "No, but that's not a bad idea. What I had in mind is more permanent."

Heart racing, he put aside the harp. "You are not leaving." Part of him meant it to be a question, but desperation forced out a command.

Eyes wide, she shot forward and knelt before him grabbing his hands. "Never again, Tom. I will never leave you. You must toss me from this house if you wish to get rid of me."

The knife, which had stabbed him in the heart, eased back and he breathed. Lifting her from the carpet, he pulled her into his lap. "What then, Dory? What could you want that you are so hesitant to speak about?"

Still on his lap, she pulled the harp close and strummed the most beautiful few notes. Her bottom fitted against him with perfect symmetry and his body responded to both her form and the gentle glide of her hands on the strings. He may have imagined the vibration from the harp shooting to his groin, but all the same, he wanted her to continue.

A few more phrases plucked from her fingers then she pressed both palms to the strings, stopping the music. "I would like to start a family, Tom."

All the air rushed out of his lungs. "I did not think you wanted children. You have not mentioned it."

She rested her head on his shoulder and pulled one finger across the full set of strings. "I have thought of it on the occasions when enjoying my friends' children. However, of late it has been more and more on my mind. I would like to be a mother. I pray I will be better at the task than my parents were, though I fear I will fall into the same category."

If a heart could burst from joy, his was at the brink of eruption. "You are nothing like either of your parents, my love. Our children will be loved openly just as we love each other. It is honesty that pulled our hearts together and that is how we will always go forward."

"Does that mean you would like to have a child?" This shyness from Dory intrigued him.

Thomas pulled the hassock forward with his foot and moved them so that Dory sat between his legs with the harp in front of her. He put his hands on the strings above hers. "It means I can think of nothing I would love more than to have a child with you. I know you will be a wonderful mother."

"I am not as certain, but you will make up for what I lack." She strummed several chords.

Moving his hands to the deeper notes, he attempted a counterpoint. It was surprisingly successful. "Perhaps we might write a duet for the harp."

Her laugh was full and round and made his heart sing. "I think perhaps we should attempt that on two harps, Tom."

Pulling her bottom tighter into his groin, he nuzzled her neck. Her soft blond waves tickled his face and her scent intoxicated him. "You do not wish to play a duet as we are now?"

Leaning her head gave him better access to her soft skin. She played the melody from the Sonata in G. "I do not mind, but for whom would we play such a duet?"

He fumbled the harmony, hitting the same string as her on two occasions, but then he found the balance and the sound filled the room. "Do you think our friends would be shocked by a duet on the harp?"

She kissed his jaw and let her hand trail along his thigh. "I do not know of a society function where our sitting like this would be acceptable. Not even amongst our closest friends."

With her right hand, she played at a speed he had no hope of keeping up with. Still, he plucked out the harmony as best he could. "Perhaps then, we shall need to purchase a second harp and save the duet on one harp for the bedroom."

Craning her neck, she met his gaze. "You would play harp in public, wouldn't you?"

Lord, how he loved the way she looked when he surprised her. Her eyes filled with a wonder only he inspired. He would spend his life finding ways to keep her so inspired if only for his own selfish reasons. "I find no shame in making beautiful music with you regardless of the instrument."

"Shall we play it at the Royal Music Hall then?" Dory raised an eyebrow.

It was one thing to play the harp for his friends, but he doubted his skill level was paramount to playing for the Prince of Wales. "Perhaps not right away."

The music of her laughter filled his life in ways Thomas had never imagined possible. The harp strings sang in perfect accompaniment to his happiness. He captured her lips with his and her fingers faltered.

Moving the harp aside, he deepened the kiss and enwrapped her in his arms. "Dory, do you know how happy you have made me?"

She brushed the hair from his forehead in a gesture that had become intimate over the last year. "Only half as happy as you make me, Tom."

"Not possible."

"Why not?" Her lips pursed, distracting him.

Desperate Bride

Thomas brushed his thumb over her bottom lip and she sucked the digit into her warmth before smiling a wicked grin.

"If you were twice as happy as me, you would grin all day and get nothing done. Do you know how often I find myself staring at a contract for half an hour before I give up and come and play in the music room with you?"

"Do you know how often I tinker in the music room, praying you will join me so I can stop wondering what you are doing and when I will see you again?"

His heart pounded like the first time he saw her after she made her debut. That night, he realized his friend Markus's little sister was all grown up and he was in trouble. Six years later, he was still doomed. "Is that true?"

"Of course. I love you, Tom. Far more than I thought I could love another person. I love you more than music."

Thomas Wheel could not catch his breath. "More than music." He swallowed down a lump of emotion.

Sitting up, she turned and took his face between her hands. Those green eyes were like Cupid's arrow to his heart. "You did not know. How can that be? Nothing matters more than you, Tom. Nothing."

He turned his head and kissed her palm. "I do not know what to say, Dory. I never dreamed you would care for me this way. I knew you loved me but always assumed I would continue to be second to the music."

She kissed his cheek, his chin, and then captured his lips. "More than the music, Tom. You are my music."

The universe tilted and righted itself. "And you are mine, my love."

Thank you for reading Desperate Bride. I hope you enjoyed Dory and Thomas's story. It's ever so helpful if you leave a review. Here are some great places to review Desperate Bride:

Amazon – BookBub – Goodreads

Looking for more from A.S. Fenichel? How about a little magic in Regency England. Check out Magic Touch next.

MAGIC TOUCH

ESME

I never dreamed my small curatives shop in Windsor, England would attract the attention of war hero Sir William Meriwether. My feminine heart is aflutter when he enters. But I'm a witch and a healer, and he's a man in pain, so I heal him. Desperate to do him a good service, I stretch my powers to the limit—or perhaps beyond. Somehow, in curing his ailing leg, I unleash powers inside William. At a loss to stop what's begun, I'm forced to seek assistance from the coven I've sworn never to join. I dread the encounter, but for William's sake, I put my family's hatred aside. Getting to spend more time with William is an added enticement.

WILLIAM

I'm mesmerized by Esme O'Dwyer from the moment I lay eyes on her. Despite our different stations in society, I want something more personal than any restorative tea she might offer. As a gentleman, I contain those baser needs and accept her assistance to ease the pain in my leg. When the alluring witch's touch bestows me with magic of my own, I want no part of it. But the coven's leaders insist magic never makes mistakes, and for this to have happened, I must be needed. I've never been one to shy away from duty, and being secluded for training with Esme is magical in more ways than one.

ESME

Trouble is coming to Windsor. The signs are all there. The race is on to train William as a witch before his power is needed, but our growing attraction is as undeniable as the battle that lies ahead.

Read Magic Touch

Forever Brides Series

FOREVER BRIDES

Tainted Bride

Foolish Bride

Desperate Bride

Also by A.S. Fenichel

HISTORICAL ROMANCE

The Wallflowers of West Lane Series

The Earl Not Taken

Misleading A Duke

Capturing the Earl

Not Even For A Duke

The Everton Domestic Society Series

A Lady's Honor

A Lady's Escape

A Lady's Virtue

A Lady's Doubt

A Lady's Past

The Forever Brides Series

Tainted Bride

Foolish Bride

Desperate Bride

Single Title Books

Wishing Game

Christmas Bliss

～

HISTORICAL PARANORMAL ROMANCE

Witches of Windsor Series

Magic Touch

Magic Word

Pure Magic

The Demon Hunters Series

Ascension

Deception

Betrayal

Defiance

Vengeance

Visit A.S. Fenichel's website to view her full library.

www.asfenichel.com

∽

Writing contemporary romance as Andie Fenichel

Christmas Lane

Dad Bod Handyman

Carnival Lane

Changing Lanes

Lane to Fame

Heavy Petting

Hero's Lane

Summer Lane

Icing It

Mountain Lane

~

Writing contemporary romance as A.S. Fenichel

CONTEMPORARY EROTIC ROMANCE

Alaskan Exposure

Revving Up the Holidays

CONTEMPORARY PARANORMAL EROTIC ROMANCE

The Psychic Mates Series

Kane's Bounty

Joshua's Mistake

Training Rain

The End of Days Series

Mayan Afterglow

Mayan Craving

Mayan Inferno

End of Days Trilogy

About the Author

A.S. Fenichel also writes as contemporary romance author Andie Fenichel. After leaving a successful IT career in New York City, Andie followed her lifelong dream of becoming a professional writer. She's never looked back.

Originally from New York, Andie grew up in New Jersey, and now lives in Missouri with her real-life hero, her wonderful husband. When not buried in a book, she enjoys cooking, travel, history, and puttering in her garden. On the side she a master cat wrangler, and her fur babies keep her very busy.

Connect with Andie
www.asfenichel.com
www.andiefenichel.com

Printed in the USA
CPSIA information can be obtained
at www.ICGtesting.com
LVHW021225181024
794099LV00004B/977

9 781088 058138